The Wolf's Bane Saga

Wolf's Bane

M. KATHERINE CLARK

Editing by Ashton Clark

This is a work of fiction. Names, characters, places and incidents are the product of the author's imagination or are used fictitiously, and any resemblance to any actual persons, living or dead, events, or locals is entirely coincidental.

Book cover photo *Lupines in the Fog* by Derek Dammann ddphotos.com.

ISBN-13: 978-0-9909915-3-3

Other works by M. Katherine Clark

The Greene and Shields Files:

- Blood is Thicker Than Water
- Once Upon a Midnight Dreary
- Old Sins Cast Long Shadows – Coming 2017

Soundless Silence a Sherlock Holmes Novel

Love Among the Shamrocks Collection:

- Under the Irish Sky
- Across the Irish Sea – Coming Soon
- In Dublin Fair City – Coming Soon

The Wolf's Bane Saga:

- Wolf's Bane
- Lonely Moon
- Midnight Sky
- Star Crossed – Coming 2017
- Moon Rise – Coming 2018

Silent Whispers a Scottish Ghost Story

For the woman who instilled the love of Scotland in me; my amazing, beautiful and loving Mother.

Legend has it, that before the Romans invaded Britannia in 55 B.C. the people of that land roamed wild and free. Once the Roman legionnaires pushed back the wild and untamed Celts, they built a wall; Antonine's Wall. It was once magnificent, once imposing... trust me, I was there, I saw it.

But was it the humans they feared... or us?

There are so few of us left. But under the Hunter's Moon, we lived and we died and this is the story of both.

Chapter One

Aberlyall north of Aberdeen, Scotland – 650 A.D.

Alexina's trained ears heard it before the rest of her family. Piercing the silence of the wintery night, was a long, low wolf howl in the woods behind their house.

"The wolves are coming closer," her father said gruffly, stoking the fire and touching the long knife tied to his leg.

"Afton was saying that the Hunter's Moon is supposed to shine within the week. He said the wolves come down to the village and kill *everyone* that night. Is it true they can rip your heart out with one strike?" Alexina's ten-year-old brother, Niels asked.

"Och nay," their twelve-year-old brother, Harailt, said. "They are much stronger than that. They can take your *head* off in a single blow."

Niels leaned over and clutched their mother's leg, frightened.

"Harailt, donnae scare your brother like that," their

mother said as she sat knitting beside her husband.

"We have nothing to worry about," their father said. "This town is well protected by the wolf's bane that grows in every garden," he indicated the purple flower that hung above the door like a garland. "Never leave the house without it," he tapped near to where a flower was pinned to his tunic. "And *never* go into the woods," their father warned just as another howl rippled from the wolf outside.

"What about real wolves?" Niels whispered almost afraid the wolf would hear him. "Afton's father says 'tis easy to tell them apart."

"According to legend," their father began, "you can tell those born naturally from the yellowed-eyed demons due to their size. If you see a smaller wolf, you should never engage with it, but you are safer than you would be if you met one of *them*. But, the wolf-men have killed practically all of them anyway. They are nothing but animals," he spat.

Alexina looked down and breathed deeply. Normally their times before the fire were filled with tales and legends but with the Hunter's Moon approaching, the only things she heard in the village were the tales of the yellow-eyed demons and their perverse ways. Even her much younger siblings had heard of them. Nearing her eighteenth year, Alexina had heard all of the stories and half of them were too fanciful to be believed.

"You are rather quiet, Alexi," her mother said eyeing her over her knitting. Alexina looked up sharply afraid her secret was known. "Are you all right?"

"Actually, Mother, my head aches. May I go to my room?" Alexina asked.

"Of course, dear," she replied as her daughter stood from the floor. "I have feverfew if you require it."

"Och nay," Alexina said rubbing her temples. Her light brown hair was pulled away from her face in a braid around her head. "Thank you, 'tis nothing a rest will nae cure. Goodnight," she called.

She walked slowly to her room and closed the door. The second the door was closed, she hurried to her bed and placed the pillows under the furs to show her outline. Then she rushed to her chest and took out her brown cape. Pulling it on, she raced to the window and threw open the shutters. She eased out of the house and pulled her hood over her head. Running toward the edge of the woods, the sound of the dead leaves that had fallen earlier that month, crunched beneath her soft leather clad feet. Every step and sound made her flinch, thinking it would give her away to her family.

The snow blanketed the ground and made the Highlands glow white under the moon. She hardly felt the chill as she walked. Reaching the edge of the woods, Alexina looked back to the cottage. The smoke from the peat fire still billowed out of the chimney. There was no movement inside, her family did not know she had left.

She ducked into the forest just as another wolf howl ripped through the silence of the night.

Weylyn's yellow wolf eyes flew open when he heard the door to his hut creak and close softly. He stayed exactly how he was, resting on his side, his back to the door. Sniffing the room, the familiar scent of his pupil filled his nostrils.

"Where have you been?" Weylyn asked softly, not moving.

"Gods above, Weylyn, you startled me," Tristan breathed. "I thought you were asleep."

Turning over, Weylyn sat up and looked at him, his eyes back to the brown color of his human form.

"I ask you again, where have you been?" Weylyn asked.

"Out in the forest," Tristan answered simply, not meeting his mentor's eyes.

"You were with that human lass again," Weylyn said standing.

"Nay, I was no'," he replied shuffling towards his own bed.

Weylyn took a deep breath, smelling the scents that surrounded his student.

"Donnae lie to me, Tristan," he replied gently.

"So what if I was," Tristan turned to his cot and pulled off his cloak.

"She is nae of our kind. She will nae understand," Weylyn said.

"She does. She does understand," Tristan replied finally looking up at him.

"A relationship with a human is nae a good idea, trust me," Weylyn stressed. "When your father finds out—"

"You are nae going to tell him!" Tristan stepped towards him, panicked.

"Nay," Weylyn replied calming him. "No' as long as I have your promise that you will never see her again."

Tristan stared at him for a long moment, searching his face for something. Finally, he lowered his head and nodded once.

"I promise," he swore.

"You are lying," Weylyn replied simply.

Tristan locked eyes with his mentor. "I love her," he breathed.

Weylyn closed his eyes for a moment, an unpleasant memory coming back to him. When he opened his eyes, he looked at his young student. Tristan, his dark blonde hair was not quite long enough to be tied back, his deep brown eyes were pleading with him. The man looked twenty-five, but was actually seventy years old in wolf years and was still a boy in so many ways. In human years, he would have only been nineteen.

Weylyn breathed deeply. *Dear gods, is this what my father felt?* He wondered. Hating that he had to advise Tristan away from a love Weylyn knew first hand was stronger than any other bond; he could not let Tristan go through the pain that he had felt all those years ago... Weylyn shook his head clearing it. *Donnae think on it,* he thought to himself. *It is in the past... there is nothing you can do but save him from the absolute heart wrenching ache that you felt.*

"Does she ken what you are?" Weylyn asked treading lightly.

"Aye and she does nae care," he answered.

"Have you mated with her?" Weylyn asked.

Tristan looked at him, sharply.

"Nay," he breathed truthfully. "We have no'."

Weylyn breathed a sigh of relief.

"All is no' lost then," he whispered.

"But we plan on getting married," Tristan replied. "Human married, no' wolf, with her family's blessing and with witnesses. She thinks she can convince her parents to meet me and rid their cottage of wolf's bane."

"If you do this, you will be cast out of the pack, or killed. You ken what that means?" Weylyn asked. "Is she really worth it?"

"You tell me," Tristan replied heatedly. "I ken you loved

a human once. Was she worth it? You left her!"

"You donnae ken of what you speak," Weylyn said feeling an old wound reopening in his chest.

"Do I no'?" Tristan asked harshly. "I am no' a child, Weylyn! I ken what I want and I am more of a man than you are! I willnae let anything stand in the way of my love! You left yours out in the cold and she died carrying another man's child. Can you honestly tell me that your course is better than mine? Alexina and I will be married. We will mate. And we will live together forever! She will be mine! She is mine! And I love her, which is more than you can say!"

Weylyn's hand swiped across Tristan's face in a hard slap. Tristan turned back to his mentor; his eyes yellowed, his hair falling in his face, his teeth barred, his body growing taller and his muscles tightening ready to pounce in a half-phase. Tristan's upper lip was pulled back as he growled and snapped at him.

"Calm down," Weylyn ordered still in his full human form.

Tristan's lip lifted on one side as he snarled.

"You cannae stop me," he said his voice rough, the sound vibrating in his chest in a half-phased growl. "Face me."

"I willnae," Weylyn replied calmly.

"Coward," Tristan roared and pounced on him.

Even though Weylyn had not phased, he was still able to throw Tristan off of him. Tristan attacked in anger and even though Weylyn's heart was breaking again after so many years, he still was able to remain calm.

The boy stood back up from the corner where Weylyn had thrown him and Weylyn's body convulsed into a half-phase. The wolf men faced each other, their teeth barred and their eyes staring into each other's. Their chests heaved as they panted. Their bodies ached anticipating a fight.

Finally, almost as if Tristan realized what he was doing, he backed down and phased to his full human form. Weylyn did the same.

"I am sorry," Tristan said. "I did nae mean to fight you." Weylyn nodded once, accepting his apology.

"I am sorry for striking you," Weylyn replied.

"I deserved it," Tristan answered. "I did nae mean to hurt you with my words. You are right. I donnae ken anything about what happened between you and your mate, I only ken what you told me. And I am truly sorry for it. But I love Alexina."

"I understand that," Weylyn started gently. "And I am glad you were able to experience that sort of love, but for your own sake, you must think of your father and your position. You are to be Alpha. You must understand the ramifications of what you are doing. Trust me; I ken how strong the pull is. But you have to understand that even if you do marry this human girl, you ken your father," he stressed, stepping towards him and placing his hands on Tristan's shoulders. "Marrock will hunt you both down and the gods only ken what he will do to you, no' to mention her family, when he finds you. If you love her, the best thing for her would be for you to let her go."

They were both quiet for a long time, Tristan staring at his mentor hearing the truth and the weight of his words. Eventually, Tristan nodded.

"You are right," he said. "I cannae do that to her. I will tell her in the morning."

Weylyn saw something flash in his pupil's eyes, but decided to ignore it, hoping Tristan's history with his father would prove incentive enough.

"Get some sleep, everything will be all right in the morning," Weylyn finally said.

"You are right," Tristan mumbled turning to his cot. "Things will be different in the morning."

Weylyn awoke to an annoying bird chirping right outside the window that was just above his bed. He growled and it flew off. Stretching, he breathed in the early morning air and smelled the threatening snow. It had been a harsh winter for the villages near them and Weylyn knew they could not handle another snowstorm. If the repairs he had helped with were any indication, Weylyn was certain another large snow fall would be detrimental.

Pulling his tunic over his head, he tightened the strings of the *leine* just at his neck. Slowly he stood and stretched again. Looking over at Tristan's cot, he saw the outline of his student still there under the blankets. Not wishing to disturb him after the emotional encounter late that last night, Weylyn took a deep breath.

Tristan's scent was faint.

Concerned, Weylyn went over to his cot.

"Tristan?" He called softly. There was no movement. Weylyn touched the place where his student's shoulder should have been. Confused, he pulled down the blanket slowly. He yanked it back when he saw what was beneath. Several pillows were placed strategically to show the outline of a body, but Tristan was not there.

Weylyn convulsed into a half-phase and sniffed the air. Tristan's scent was very faint. He had been gone a few hours. Weylyn growled.

How could I have been so blind? He thought, angry with

himself. He knew Tristan was going to leave and he did nothing to stop him. *Where is he?* Weylyn saw a folded note resting on the pillow. His name was scripted across it in Tristan's hand. He phased back into his human form and picked it up.

Weylyn,

I am sorry. I love her too much to live without her. Please understand. I would rather spend what little time I have with her than a hundred years alone. Please wait to tell my father until the sun is at its peak; it will give us enough time to get away. I ken I have no right to ask this, but I have always felt that you loved me as a son. Please, I beg of you, donnae raise the alarm. We are going far enough away, somewhere he will no' find us.

Forgive me, my dear friend, but I have seen what it has done to you no' being with your mate and I cannae let that happen to me. I was wrong last night; I am no' more of a man than you. I realize that now. You have had to live without her for over forty years. You have survived. Whereas I am very selfish and I refuse to live without her at all. Forgive what I said last night, it was from anger and I did nae understand. I pray you donnae suffer for my selfishness and I hope we will meet again. This is no' on you. This is my choice.

Goodbye, my friend. You have been more of a father to me than my own blood. Thank you and be at peace.

Tristan

"Fool," Weylyn breathed rubbing his eyes with his fingers and pinching the bridge of his nose.

There was a sharp knock at his door and Weylyn looked up suddenly. He folded the note and threw it into the fire before him. Turning back to Tristan's cot, he removed the pillows. Straightening it as best he could to look like Tristan had awakened earlier and made his bed, Weylyn glanced back into the fire and saw that the note was completely charred then went to answer the door.

"My king," he bowed low when he saw Marrock, his Alpha and Tristan's father, standing in front of him. "Please come in. Forgive me for keeping you waiting. I slept poorly last night and was still recovering."

"Weylyn," Marrock nodded, lowering his head as he stepped through the low threshold. "Leave us," he said to his guards. They bowed and walked away. The small hut was dwarfed by Marrock's mighty frame. He was the biggest of them all. Marrock's black hair was longer than Weylyn's and unbound. His light eyes scanned the room and landed on his son's empty cot.

"To what do I owe this great honor, Sire?" Weylyn asked after shutting the door behind his Alpha.

"I wanted to see how things were progressing," Marrock said. "I wanted to come and speak with you without my son here. I suppose he has gone out early?" Weylyn nodded not knowing what to say. Remembering that Marrock hardly visited his son after the death of his first wife and Tristan's mother, Weylyn knew Marrock wished to speak with him alone. "Good, now tell me, have you been able to get these ridiculous notions out of my son's head?"

"The notion that all men are created equal, sire?" Weylyn clarified holding back his scorn for his Alpha's request. Weylyn believed in that *ridiculous notion* as well. "Unfortunately your son still holds to his convictions on that."

"What about his inane notion that we should live at peace with the humans?" Marrock asked chuckling as he spoke.

"That one, sire, I *have* been able to discuss with him," Weylyn replied but, knowing where Tristan was at that moment, it seemed like a fruitless discussion.

"Good," Marrock replied. "I wasnae too sure if you were the correct choice to instruct my son regarding that considering your history with the human race. But I kenned you could nae refuse me."

"Nay, sire," he answered lowering his eyes. "I believe I have made that perfectly clear in the past."

"Aye" he replied smirking. "Good..." he turned to the empty cot. "Well, where is he?"

"Tristan?" He said.

"I was nae asking after the servants," Marrock replied smoothly.

"He... um... went out early," Weylyn said.

"Tell me the truth," Marrock's alpha order made Weylyn quake. He could not prevent his answer; he could however give him only part of the truth.

"He left early, sire," he said. "He woke and went for a walk."

"A walk?" Marrock asked enjoying seeing Weylyn quake at his command. "Where?"

"I donnae ken, sire," he said. "Tristan likes to be alone with his thoughts."

"Hmm," Marrock answered walking around and smelling for his scent. "He has been gone for a while now."

"I donnae ken, sire, as I said I had a difficult night and was no' awake when he left," Weylyn explained.

"I see," Marrock went on. "Well, when he returns tell him I want to see him."

"Uh – of – of course," he replied bowing. Marrock never asked to see his son. Nodding once, Marrock left without another word. Weylyn waited until he saw Marrock outside through the window near his bed. He was walking back towards the keep with his guards. "Oh, Tristan, you fool." Weylyn sighed softly looking back at the cot and closing his eyes for a moment.

Chapter Two

Ten Months later

Marrock and his two lieutenants, Faolán and Conchor stood in the great room of the keep, the largest building of in village and Marrock's home with his two mistresses. The sun shone through the window cutouts as he and his lieutenants stood around the table with a map of the nearby area.

"This village kenned nothing about Tristan, sire," Faolán said.

"Burn it," Marrock replied. "They are of no use."

"We think he may have taken this route," Conchor said pointing to a location on the map. "We are trying to find something or someone who saw him."

"His scent would be gone after all this time," Marrock said. "If you do come across anything, come tell me immediately before you do anything."

"We donnae have anywhere else to look, sire," Faolán said. "No one kens anything. We have already destroyed all the villages within a half days run."

"I want to ken where he is!" Marrock yelled. In one mighty movement, he swept his broad arms over the wooden table clearing it in an angry outburst. Everything clattered to the wooden floor with a loud noise. "Find him!" His alpha order caused the other two wolves to cower low as they could not refuse him. "And bring me Weylyn," Marrock's voice was low and menacing again. They both bowed and left the room quickly.

When his lieutenants left, Marrock fell into the chair beside the table and shielded his eyes with his hand. It was not long before he caught the scent of one of his mistresses. She entered the room and called to him softly.

"May I approach?" Heledd asked. He looked over at her and gestured her to come forward. She walked to him, her dark eyes not raised to his blue ones.

"What is it?" He asked looking up at her.

"I have come to ask you a question, my Alpha," she said.

"Then look at me!" He roared. She flinched and instinctively backed up two steps. "I am sorry," he said gently and took her arm. She looked into his eyes as she felt his lips on her forearm. "What answer would you have of me, Heledd?"

"I beg you for mercy for Tristan," she said hesitantly. "Please, donnae punish the boy for following his heart."

"He is nae even yours, why do you care about him?" Marrock asked.

"I love that pup as if he were mine," she started. "When I took your queen's place beside you after she died, I saw a young boy who needed a mother, just as our children do. I beg you, Marrock, show mercy."

"He disobeyed a direct order from me, you ken what that means. I cannae allow him back into my pack," he said.

"Mercy, please, let him go. You have other sons who can take your place," she said.

"I will have no other but the child of my queen sitting on my throne," he growled.

She felt a sharp pain in her chest at his words. They had several children together and it was clear he did not care about them.

"You care nothing for our children?" She breathed.

"Of course I do," he said. "But none of them are worthy enough to sit on my throne. None but the child of my queen, my mate will be allowed. My throne will die with me. Tristan has proven himself unworthy."

"But then why take us?" She asked. "If you wanted no other children, why take two other mates when Mabh died?"

"You ken what it is I desire, children are merely a byproduct of it," he said as he kissed the crook of her arm. Heledd stopped the shudder that ran down her spine when she felt his hand on her cheek.

Years ago, Mabh, Marrock's true mate and Alpha Queen, died at the hands of human trappers.

"Why do you hate Tristan so?" Heledd asked. Marrock turned hard eyes up to her. She looked down not wanting to see the hatred in them. "Please, I love him," she went on, her voice barely a whisper. "Donnae hurt the pup. Show him, the child of your queen, mercy. 'Tis what Mabh would have wanted."

"Enough," he snapped. "You donnae speak of her! You ken nothing about it! She is dead because of that lad's stupidity."

"He was a pup," she said. "He never meant for it to happen. Please, Marrock, donnae destroy your own house."

"He does nae deserve my mercy," Marrock replied.

"Please," she whispered.

"I said enough!" his voice rose as he shouted his alpha order. Heledd flinched, stepped back from him and lowered her head in recognition of his command.

"I am sorry," he said a little softer. "Come here, come to me," he reached out to her. She hesitated but took his hand. He pulled her down onto his lap, nuzzled her neck and kissed her shoulder. She tried not to flinch at his advances. Trailing kisses up her throat, he reached into her hair and pulled her lips up to his with a strong yank. She did not cry out, used to the tears that stung her eyes. He pressed his lips hard onto hers.

"I did nae mean to command you," he panted. "You ken how I feel. Ever since I first saw you, I wanted you as mine."

She nodded, returning his kiss without choice. She was his and there was nothing she could do about it. A wave of relief came over her when one of his lieutenants knocked on the main hall door and walked in. But when she looked up to see who it was, she came face to face with Faolán. As always when she saw him, she longed for the time of her youth before Marrock took her as his own. Faolán froze when he saw Heledd in Marrock's lap and for a moment, they locked eyes, remembering a love that was stolen from them.

Heledd attempted to get up from Marrock's lap but Marrock held her tightly, enjoying the look of pain on both of their faces. Knowing she was his, Marrock enjoyed seeing their unrequited love.

"Sire, we have Weylyn," Faolán finally said, his eyes did not rise to his Alpha.

"Excellent," Marrock replied. "I am on my way."

Faolán bowed and once he was gone, Heledd looked back at Marrock.

"No' Weylyn as well," she said.

"He lied to me," Marrock replied. "How… I donnae ken."

"Please donnae do this," she begged. "Weylyn is a good member of your pack. He is loyal to you. He has proven that on many occasions."

"You have always had a soft spot for him," Marrock said.

"He is my cousin," she answered. "You ken our mothers were sisters."

"Aye, I do," he replied. "But he must be held accountable for what he did and for what he allowed Tristan to do."

"Please," she said. He sighed exasperated and pushed her away from him.

"This conversation is over," he said. "I have a judgment to give." He started towards the door then turned. "You will be at my side," he said. She looked up at him.

"Please donnae make me," she said.

His eyes burned yellow and a deep growl resounded deep in his chest, even though he had not changed from his human form. She cringed knowing full well what she would endure that evening for daring to question him. And as usual, she wished was dead.

"You will be by my side," he ordered. She lowered her head hearing his command and headed towards the door. They walked out together.

Weylyn stood from his desk and half-phased when the front door of his cottage caved in. Faolán and Conchor appeared in the doorway.

"Marrock wants to see you," Conchor growled half-phased.

Weylyn looked at them. He raised his head high, phased back into human form and walked out with them. They both grabbed his arms. Faolán's grip was not nearly as tight as Conchor's and Weylyn locked eyes with his best friend. Faolán told him all he needed to know with that one look. They walked him through the village and to Marrock's throne. The entire pack came out of their huts to watch Weylyn, one of the most esteemed members of the pack, being treated like a common criminal. Conchor threw him down in front of the platform. Weylyn fell onto his stomach, raised himself up and sat back on his heels. Marrock stared at him for a long moment. Finally, he spoke.

"Tis very simple, Weylyn. I ken you have something that you are not telling me. So, I will make my question very plain... Where is my son?" Marrock asked enunciating every word as he sat twirling his sword on its tip. Heledd stood beside him, his other mistress on the other side of him.

"I donnae ken, sire," Weylyn answered.

"Donnae lie to me!" Marrock's order made Weylyn shake.

"I am no', sire," Weylyn replied. "I donnae ken where Tristan is. All I ken is that he left."

"You ken more," Marrock's voice was harsh. "Tell me! What was my son doing out in the woods? Was he meeting someone? None of the females have been missing so I ask you... what was he doing?"

Weylyn swallowed attempting to delay his answer as long as he could.

"He was in love with someone, Sire. They would meet in the woods. He kenned you would no' approve," Weylyn explained.

"Why?" Marrock demanded.

"Please, sire," he begged.

"Your loyalty is to me, Dog," Marrock yelled. "Tristan has been gone for ten moon cycles! Where is he?" He bellowed.

"He was in love with a human, Sire," Weylyn's voice was quiet when he answered.

Silence blew through the entire pack like an icy wind in winter. Tristan had broken his father's most absolute law. They all knew, the only way he could do that was to embrace his alpha blood and become who he was born to be… An Alpha Wolf.

"A human?" Marrock's voice was low, his tone dripping with condescension. Marrock stood and walked to the edge of the platform. Raising the sword, he pointed it at Weylyn. "I kenned there would be an issue having *you* as his tutor. What nonsense have you been filling his head with?"

"Nay, Sire," Weylyn looked up sharply. "I tried to dissuade him from his course kenning it to be a crime."

"One punishable by death," Marrock replied. "I showed *you* mercy."

Weylyn wanted to scream that he had not and he carried the physical and emotional scars to prove it but he remained silent.

"Please, Sire, he is merely a lad," Weylyn finally said, begging as his own father had begged when Weylyn was on trial.

"I ken he is," Marrock answered. He turned and walked back to his throne. Sitting down with a flourish, he looked at Weylyn and finally said, "But you are no'."

Weylyn's eyes grew large in shock.

"I had nothing to do with this," Weylyn breathed.

"Take him to the dungeon," Marrock ordered quietly. "Give him to the wolves." Weylyn's breathing increased as he panicked. The wolves were humans that the wolf men had bitten. After they were bitten, the next moonrise they turned into wolves and were no longer humans. They lost all sense of humanity and forgot that they were once humans. Normally Marrock had them kill each other for sport but he kept five of the strongest in the dungeon as his pets.

Weylyn's eyes trailed up to Heledd as she stood on one side of Marrock's throne. Quickly averting her eyes, she looked over at the Alpha.

"Marrock, please," she whispered. Marrock looked over at her, his eyes yellowed with a look that silenced her. She looked down at her hands clasped in front of her and Marrock looked back at the guards.

"To the dungeon," he ordered again. Faolán and Conchor reached down and pulled Weylyn to his feet. Weylyn half-phased and tried to get out of their hold, but the guards were just as strong as he was and they held fast to his arms. The guards started to drag Weylyn to the door that led through the great hall and into the dungeons. Weylyn fought them as they went.

Marrock turned to Heledd. "I will deal with you later." She looked down, tears filling her eyes.

"Sire!" a warrior came running up. Marrock stopped Faolán and Conchor from dragging Weylyn away just as the wolf guard reached the platform where Marrock's throne sat and knelt in a bow. "I have news; one of the villagers in Aberdeen said they saw Tristan just a moment ago. He is heading to the village of Aberlyall."

"After all this time?" Marrock smirked.

"Aye, sire," he answered. "We were able to make it to the village before him and we caught his scent from several months ago. 'Tis faint but it is there. We followed it to a cottage. What his scent is doing there, I donnae ken. It is a human cottage, Sire, a man and woman with two lads. There is something else as well, sire, there is no wolf's bane around the house."

"Excellent," Marrock grinned. "Take your best and raid the village. They are all at fault for hiding my son. If this is the house of the human whore my son is infatuated with, we must ken it. Wait in the woods and see if he does return. If those Aberdeen villagers were lying to you, show them the true strength of the wolf… destroy their village as well."

"Aye, sire," the guard bowed and stood. He called for five other warriors to join him.

"Wait!" Weylyn yelled struggling in the guards' grasp. "I beg you, Marrock let me talk with these humans. Donnae kill them!"

Marrock's smirk made Weylyn sick. He enjoyed killing innocent people.

"You always did have a soft spot for humans, Weylyn… What that fool of a son of mine does no' understand is that *I* will pay a visit to this house myself," Marrock said rubbing his hands together and grinning. "This will be an enjoyable afternoon. Wait to feed him to the wolves until I get back." Marrock said to Conchor and Faolán. "I will want to watch."

"Sire," they bowed. Marrock headed towards the steps of his platform.

"Marrock, please," Heledd begged once more. The entire pack held their breath hearing her plea. Marrock froze on the bottom step and turned slowly back to her. "Donnae do this." She pleaded. "'Tis no' what Mabh would want! Remember your true queen! She loved all creatures. She would rejoice that your son followed his heart as you followed yours with her. Donnae sully her memory by more slaying of innocent blood. She never forgot her true origin as one of us and she would be appalled at how bitter your heart has grown! If you cared for her at all, you would remember her words."

Without another word, Marrock raised his sword in anger and afterwards wiped the spray of her blood off his face.

"Nay!" Weylyn and Faolán both yelled as they watched in horror as Heledd fell to her knees. Weylyn struggled against his captures feeling Faolán's grip loosen on his arm.

"Let him go," Marrock called to Conchor. "I have no use for either of them anymore."

Marrock stepped down off the platform and signaled to several of his guards, leading the group of wolves out of the village. The second Marrock was out of sight, Faolán and Weylyn rushed to Heledd. Faolán cradled her in his arms as she struggled to breathe. Her eyes fixed on him.

"Faolán," she breathed. "You are here."

"Of course, I am here," he replied. "Did I nae swear to be here with you always?"

"I was worried you hated me," she gasped.

"Hate you?" Faolán breathed. "Never, my love. I have loved you since I first saw you."

"I never loved him, Faolán," her words were staccato. "I always loved you."

"And I you, my darling," he clutched her to him.

"Forgive me for causing you pain," she said.

"The pain of losing you was the only pain I feel," he replied. "I had such dreams for us."

"As did I, my love," she said. "Whenever he touched me… I thought of you. Oh how I wished it was you. To ken your touch, to bare *your* children. That was all I ever wanted in life. But that was stolen from us because I was such a child and did nae understand. Forgive me."

"The fault of lust lies with Marrock, Heledd," Faolán said. "No' you. And I have had you in my arms every night in my dreams."

"But you have never kenned love," she said.

"I have," he replied. "When I held you and kissed you that was all the love I needed. I could never love another."

"I have never kenned love, either," she said. "I only ever have kenned lust. Forgive me, my love, please."

"Shh, Heledd" he said soothing her. "You have raised wonderful children. I would have been honored to have been their father."

"You were more of a father to them than he ever could have been," she said. "I will be waiting for you, my love, come to me when it is your time."

"We will be together soon," his tears fell to the ground.

"Kiss me?" she asked. "I want the last thing I feel to be your touch. The touch of love."

Faolán leaned down and gently kissed her lips.

"I love you," she said.

"And I love you, my mate," he replied.

"Weylyn?" she called.

"I am here, Heledd," Weylyn said softly stroking her hair.

"I am sorry," her voice was low and raspy as she tried to breathe, her eyes turned to him. "I tried to help you and Tristan. Forgive me, I couldnae do anything."

"Nay, nay, Heledd you did everything," Weylyn said soothingly.

Faolán held her close. She turned to look at her love.

"I am scared," she whispered.

"Donnae be," Faolán replied softly stroking her face. "I am here. I will look after you. Be at peace, my darling. You have done your family proud and I will follow soon."

He leaned down and kissed her once more. When he pulled back, she kept her eyes on his. Slowly they closed. She went limp in his arms as her body gave up her life. Faolán shook and his breathing came in short gasps. Tears ran down his cheeks faster than before and landed on Heledd's face. He finally looked over at Weylyn who put a hand on his friend's shoulder. Half-phasing together they howled. One of their own had died.

Weylyn stroked her hair and kissed her forehead as Faolán still held her close. Her children came up to her and wept. Weylyn watched as the man who should have married his cousin laid her out gently and crossed her arms over her chest. Faolán comforted her children as if they were his own, but once Heledd was surrounded by her own kin, Faolán's gaze turned murderous. His hand clenched into a fist as he started towards the gate. Weylyn stepped partway in front of him bumping his shoulder with his own, stopping him with a hand on his chest.

"Let me go," Faolán said not looking at him.

"You have to think of what she would want," Weylyn said softly. "And you dead at his feet is not it."

"He did nae think of her when he took her as his own," Faolán rebuttaled. "Or when he raised his sword against her!"

"Nay, he did nae," Weylyn said. "But you must think about what you are doing. You are angry, I understand, trust me. You want nothing more than revenge. But think of what he could do to you. You would be dead before you could avenge her. Is that what you want?"

Faolán closed his eyes for a moment and shook his head.

"At this moment, her children need you," Weylyn said. "You have been more of a father to them than he ever could. Faolán, trust me it would no' be worth it. The best way to honor her would be to care for her children and - Oh, gods, Tristan," Weylyn breathed.

"You could be too late already," Faolán said.

"Where is he?" Weylyn demanded.

"Go," Faolán replied. "Aberlyall."

"My thanks," Weylyn said as he ran out of the village and rushed through the woods as fast as he could, praying he was not too late to save him.

Chapter Three

"Do you think it is all right to return?" Alexina asked Tristan as they walked towards her parents' cottage in the village.

"I am sure they will want to see us," Tristan smiled at her. "It has been too long already and the Harvest Moon festival at Samhain is the perfect time. Besides, they have a right to ken of their grandchild," he caressed her stomach gently.

"What about your father?" She asked.

"It has been nearly a year since I left," he answered. "He must have stopped looking for me by now."

"I am nae so sure," she replied.

"Are you all right? Are you tired? I could carry you for a bit," Tristan offered.

"You carried me far too much already," she stroked his face. "It feels good to stretch my legs."

"Just wanting to ease the strain for you, love," he leaned into her hand.

"Your child is no strain," she kissed him softly.

"It is hard to believe," he said as his hands gently and lovingly stroked her stomach. "I never thought I would feel this way."

"In a few short days we will hold our child," she replied.

"It cannae come swiftly enough," he answered. "I cannae wait to hold our pup."

She smiled at him and covered his hands with hers. Looking up into her eyes, he kissed her softly once more. Pulling back, Alexina's cheeks tinged with blood as she blushed.

"Where is everyone?" she whispered.

"I am no' sure," Tristan replied. "But no one saw us, my love," he stroked her cheek. "Their scents are still very strong. Perhaps they have already started for the town square."

Tristan reached for the door of her parents' cottage and knocked. The door fell in. Half-phasing, he sniffed the air.

"Nay," he breathed when he phased back to his human form.

"What is it?" Alexina asked. It was too dark for her to see anything.

"Nay, my love, come away," Tristan tried to pull her to him.

"What is it, Tristan?" She asked breaking free of him. Stepping inside and holding up the lantern, she screamed. "Mother?!" She raced to the body on the floor. The sickening odor of blood filled her senses. Touching her mother's light brown graying hair, she saw the gaping wounds on her chest revealed her bones. Alexina's body revolted when she saw the crimson blood that pooled around the body of the woman who gave her life and she retched onto the floor. Her mother was still slightly warm to the touch and Alexina let her tears fall as she cried out, releasing some of the pain housed deep within her chest.

Scanning the room, she could not believe what she saw. "Father?!" She cried seeing her father's body resting near her mother's, his knife still in his hand. His dark hair was matted and tangled, his body was cold, clammy and stiff. Sliding over to him, her palm touching a pool of blood. Frantically she wiped her hand on her outer gown. She grasped her father's tunic and shook him, trying, in vain, to wake him.

Suddenly she looked up. Through her tears, she frantically searched the cottage for her brothers, screaming their names.

"Alexina," Tristan's voice was soft. Finding him in the darkness, she followed his gaze to a darkened alcove beside the fireplace.

"Harailt? Niels!" She screamed when she saw her little brothers' bodies holding each other huddled in a corner. "Nay!" She screamed. Falling to her knees, she clutched them to her bosom. "Gods above, nay, please!" She cried. Harailt and Niels were still warm and Alexina would have sworn they were still alive if it had not been for the gaping wounds in both their chests and their life's blood in a pool around them.

Tristan could smell his father's scent in the house. The bodies had been ripped apart by wolf claws and teeth. Feeling tears on his own cheeks, Tristan swallowed them away and went to his wife as she wailed over her little brothers' bodies. Kneeling beside her, he wrapped his arms around her.

"Why?" Was all she could say when she turned to him.

"I donnae ken," he answered gently. "I am so sorry."

"They were just children," she said looking back at her brothers. "They had no' even reached manhood yet."

"I am so sorry," Tristan held his wife close to him. She

cried into his shoulder.

"Who did this?" she asked.

"It was my father," he answered.

"Why?" she breathed as she stared into his eyes.

Tristan shrugged. "I broke his laws by loving you." She cried into him again. "I would have given my life to protect them, Alex," he said. She pulled away sharply and stared at him.

"And leave me and our child?" She demanded.

"*Before* this," he stressed. "I love you and our pup, but nothing would have been worth the precious lives of your family. If I could have spoken to my father, given myself up to him in place of them… I would have."

She turned to him and lifted his chin with her fingers.

"I love you, Tristan," she said. "Never doubt that."

"Even though this was my fault?" he asked.

"This was your father's doing, no' yours," she said. "You cannae blame yourself for this."

"Tristan," a rough, half-phased voice came from the doorway behind them. Tristan turned, his eyes yellow, ready to pounce until he realized who it was.

Weylyn phased back into his human form and Tristan let his eyes change back.

"Weylyn," Tristan breathed standing from Alexina. Both men crossed the room in two strides and embraced, holding each other tightly.

"I thought I lost you, lad," Weylyn said.

"I thought you would have been killed because of my selfishness," Tristan replied.

"Nay," Weylyn answered. "No' yet anyway." They pulled back and stared into each other's eyes. "Your father has been terrorizing the villages around here trying to find you," Weylyn explained. "This entire village has been slain."

"What?" Tristan exclaimed.

"I tried to stop him but you ken what his alpha order does to us," Weylyn said.

"I am so sorry for what happened here and to my wife's family," Tristan replied.

"Your wife?" Weylyn asked.

"Aye," he answered. Walking back to Alexina, he bent down to help her up. "Come away, my love," Tristan said. "Please, this grief is nae good for the child."

Pulling her away from her brothers' bodies, he tucked her into his side and they turned back to Weylyn. Weylyn's eyes immediately went down to her stomach, heavily swollen with an unborn child.

"Oh gods above, Tristan what did you do?" He breathed.

"We must go," Tristan coaxed not answering his mentor's question.

"I have to bury them," Alexina cried.

"All in time, my dearest," Tristan said turning her to him and framing her face. "I promise you. Right now we must go. My father will return."

"He has yet to return to the village. Marrock ordered his men to stay in the woods to see if you came back. I only just got away to warn you," Weylyn said. "You must go now. Both of you. He will stop at nothing, Tristan, and Heledd paid a price for that."

Tristan's eyes flashed with pain.

"Come away, my love, we must get you to safety," Tristan replied. Alexina leaned into her husband emotionally and physically weak. "Where would be safe?" he asked Weylyn as they walked out of the house.

"I am no' sure," Weylyn answered. "But you cannae stay here."

Just then, there was a howl in the distance. Instinctually, Tristan and Weylyn half-phased. Out of the corner of his eye, Weylyn saw Alexina shrink back away from them and tremble.

"They ken I am here," Tristan growled. "We have to go."

"It is too late," Weylyn replied, his yellow eyes seeing that the wolves were running as fast as they could towards them. "They are mere moments away. They will catch up with you." He looked at Alexina and his eyes trailed to her unborn child.

Reading his thoughts, Tristan phased back to his human shape.

"Take her, Weylyn, please," Tristan begged.

"What?" Weylyn asked confused phasing back as well.

"You must take her," Tristan said. "It is me they want. I will give you time, go please. Get her to safety." He pushed his wife towards his mentor. Weylyn took her arm before she stumbled.

"Tristan," Alexina screamed realizing what he was saying. "Donnae leave me!"

Tristan took her face in his hands and kissed her hard.

"Forgive me, my love," he whispered. "We will meet again. I swear it. Until then, be strong for me, and tell my child I love them," after a moment and a second kiss, he pushed her away. "Weylyn, take her. Go!" Tristan shouted his first Alpha order. Weylyn bowed having no choice but to obey.

"Tristan!" Alexina screamed when Weylyn grabbed her up in his arms. Carrying her as a child, he started to run. "Nay! Please, Tristan! Put me down!" She hit Weylyn's chest, back and arms trying to get him to put her down, as she kept screaming

Tristan's name.

As soon as they were far enough away, Weylyn turned to look back. He saw the wolves burst through the woods. Tristan fought with animal ferocity, Weylyn had never seen him, or anyone, fight like that before.

"Tristan!" Alexina screamed when she saw a wolf slash at him and he fell to the ground. Almost immediately, the wolves were on top of him. Tristan fought with all the strength he had left. "Put me down, I have to go to him! I want to stay with him! Tristan!"

"He told me to keep you safe," Weylyn said. "And that means getting you as far away from them as possible." One wolf looked up, saw them and howled. Weylyn took off running before it was too late. She struck at him demanding that he put her down. Watching over Weylyn's shoulder, she screamed when she saw the wolves grab Tristan and tie him up. Still, Tristan struggled against his restraints. She watched in horror as one of the wolves stood over him and struck him hard. He fell unconscious and stopped fighting.

"Nay!" she shrieked and screamed again when the wolf who saw them chased after them.

Weylyn closed his eyes when Alexina screamed but he could not turn around, if he did, his body would betray him and he would be forced to return to help Tristan.

"Put me down! He needs me!" She cried. Weylyn ignored her and kept running. When she realized he was not going to put her down and the wolf disappeared behind them as Weylyn outran it, her emotions finally took over and she wept. Burying her head into his chest, she cried until she did not think she could cry anymore. She held on to Weylyn's neck for dear life. Her entire life had been ripped from her. As if arguing with her,

her child moved within her protesting that he or she was still there. Alexina sacrificed one hand from around Weylyn's neck and caressed her stomach.

You are right, wee one, I still have you. I donnae ken what will happen to us, but I swear I will protect you. Your father and I love you so very much. He will fight for us. Alexina thought. As if the child agreed, but wanted Weylyn too, the child kicked.

Weylyn felt the jolt against his chest and almost smiled. He gazed down at Alexina and then her protruding stomach.

That is right, little one. I am here. I will protect you, have no doubt of that. Your father means everything to me and you are destined to be the alpha whether you are male or female. I will protect you. You have my oath. And a wolf oath can never *be broken.*

The baby kicked again and Alexina flinched. Weylyn felt her eyes on him, scrutinizing him.

"Who are you?" She finally asked.

"My name is Weylyn," he answered simply.

She leaned away from him for a moment to have a better look.

"*You* are Weylyn?" She asked surprised.

"You ken of me?" He asked raising an eyebrow.

"Tristan speaks of you fondly," she replied. "I did nae expect you to look so... young. Tristan said you were his teacher. I ken how old he is... but you..."

"I am much older than he is," Weylyn answered. "Wolves donnae age like humans."

"I have heard so much about you. I feel I ken you," she said.

"Then you ken I will do anything for him," Weylyn said. She nodded. "I am taking you somewhere safe. I donnae ken exactly where yet, but I will find a place. If you can, rest. You are safe. I will no' harm you."

"I ken," she answered holding on to his neck tightly. "Tristan has told me that you are more of a father to him than his own." Weylyn stiffened but did nothing, only spoke softly.

"Sleep now," he replied. Slowly, he felt her body relax.

As soon as she was asleep, he half-phased and ran as fast as he could to put some distance between them and the wolves that held Tristan captive.

Chapter Four

Every fiber of Weylyn's being wanted to turn around and go save Tristan, but Alexina moved slightly in his arms and he knew he would not be able to go back, even if he tried. An Alpha's order could never be broken and Tristan had issued his first. Feeling the child kick again, he looked down.

I have you, little one, he thought.

Alexina woke slowly and Weylyn phased back to his human form before she opened her eyes. Immediately his pace slowed. Her eyes turned up to him and recognition crossed her face.

"Weylyn," she said his name. He nodded once. "Where are we?" She asked.

"West of Aberlyall," he answered. "Within the boundary of the forest but only for a short amount of time."

"How long have I been asleep?" She asked confused.

"The sun slipped behind the horizon but a few moments ago," he answered.

"How have we crossed this much land is so little time?"

She asked.

"Wolf speed," he replied.

"Could we stop?" She asked looking down. "I need a moment and would like to walk around."

He nodded and chose a spot deep in the woods. Setting her down, he held her arms so she did not fall.

"There are some bushes over there that should serve your needs," he said.

"I thank you, with the child it can be difficult to wait," she tried to explain.

"No need to explain, Alexina," he replied. "I have been a healer within the pack for a number of years and have attended women at their whelping. I will stand guard, take your time," he watched her duck behind the bushes. Turning his back, he changed his eyes to yellow even though he was still in his human form. After a moment, he heard her approach. "How are you feeling?" He asked.

"Still very tired," she answered. He turned then, his eyes back to the brown of his human form. "'Tis hard to believe what has happened; Mother and Father, my brothers... Tristan."

"I ken, I am truly sorry for it," he said.

"Do you ken... did they suffer?" She asked.

He bit back his initial response. The wounds he had seen had told him all he needed to know.

"I was nae there. I did nae see what happened," he treaded lightly. "I would have tried to stop it if I had."

"I am sure you would have," she smiled slightly back up at him. "Tristan has told me that you always loved the human race. I ken you would have tried to save my family if you could have. I thank you for it. You have my gratitude for saving my child's life."

"And yours," Weylyn stated. "You are my Queen now. Tristan is my Alpha."

"But," she looked up at him confused. "Tristan told me that your alpha is his father. How could he…?"

"Tristan is my Alpha now, no' Marrock. He is my pack," he explained.

"Tristan told me that wolves can hear each other's thoughts," she began softly. "Can you hear his?"

"I donnae ken. When Tristan broke from the pack, we stopped hearing him," Weylyn replied.

"Could you attempt it?" She asked. "I need to ken he is all right and he needs to ken that I am safe."

"I cannae in this form. I have to phase," he said. "Will you be all right with that?"

"I have only seen Tristan half-phase a few times, his yellow eyes scared me," she looked down.

"Then close your eyes," he told her gently.

His soft human breathing changed into the ragged growl of a half-phased wolf, it resonated deep in his chest and throat.

"'Tis all right. You can open your eyes now," Weylyn said his voice human again. Looking up at him, she questioned what he had heard. "He is alive and he is back at the village, though he is being forced to participate in combat with another wolf."

"Is he hurt?" her voice was small.

"They are no' treating him like the prince he is," he dodged.

"I would rather ken the truth than any form of a lie, Weylyn," she replied. "What is happening to my husband?"

Weylyn paused briefly looking deeply into her eyes before he answered.

"He is no' winning nor does he have any hope of winning

against his opponent," he said. "He in strong. He can handle it."

Closing her eyes slowly, she began, her voice hoarse, "I ken he is strong, but if he thinks I did nae make it out of there safely..."

"Nay, he could see you for himself. He kens you are safe," he said. "You and the pup." Her hand went instinctively to her stomach.

"Thank you," she replied. "If he is phased can others hear him as well?"

"I am the only one who has pledged my loyalty to him. It is only those within the pack who can hear one another. Come. You need your rest," Weylyn said indicating a spot near a large tree. "We should be all right here for a time. Sleep. Regain your strength. The child is coming soon."

"How can you tell?" She asked her eyes wide.

"I can sense it," he answered. "Rest, it is dry here." She wrapped herself in the warmth of her cloak and lay on the cold ground. Weylyn sat on a log near to her and watched her fall into a deep sleep.

As Weylyn kept watch over Alexina as she slept, memories over took him, and he remembered the feeling of waking up with his mate by his side. The pain in his chest grew, and as he took a deep breath, he stopped his thoughts before they made him weep.

Alexina shivered in her sleep. Without another thought, Weylyn stood, gathered her cloak that had slipped from her hands, and pulled her into his arms. She immediately stilled and sighed. Burning at a warmer temperature than humans and immune to the cold, Weylyn grasped her to him merely to warm her.

"Tristan," she sighed.

"Nay, but I will get him back for you," he said.

"You are so warm," still asleep, she spoke softly.

"Aye," Weylyn answered. "Sleep, Alexina, you are safe."

They were silent, the only sounds filling the night air was Alexina's soft breathing and the insects that called the woods home. Smelling snow mixed with rain in the air, he looked up when he felt the first freezing drops on his arms. She needed shelter.

"Alexina," Weylyn gently shook her awake. Waking slightly she looked up, gasped and pushed away from him. "'Tis all right, you were cold." After she nodded, he continued. "We should move on. We have been here for too long. 'Tis beginning to rain."

"'Tis difficult for me to stand," she revealed.

"Allow me," he stood and took her up in his arms. She gasped but immediately stilled.

"I must be heavy for you, what with the child," she looked down and lovingly stroked her stomach.

"Och, nay," he replied. "You are but a wee thing and no burden at all."

"I thank you for your kindness," she said.

"May I ask what age you are?" Weylyn asked.

"I have reached eighteen summers," she replied. Weylyn said nothing as he carried her. "May I ask you a question?"

"Aye," he answered.

"This child that I carry," she began. "It is Tristan's child, but he refers to it as a pup."

"You are asking what form of a child you will be delivered of?" Weylyn finished her thought.

"Aye," she breathed.

"The child was conceived in Tristan's human form, was it no'?" Weylyn pried gently but with the flash of color staining her cheeks, he was not sure if he asked gently enough.

"Aye," her voice was quiet.

"Then there is nothing to worry on," he said. "As long as the wolf father was in his human form, the child will be human."

"Do wolves do... that... in their non-human forms?" she asked surprised.

"Aye," he replied. "To us it is a sacred rite to mate as humans and wolves alike. But that is only done if the mates are both wolves. It is our way of claiming our mates fully. We can make love in human form but it is not until we mate as wolves that our union is truly unbreakable."

She was silent for a moment, her eyes staring blankly out before them watching the trees pass as Weylyn ran. It was a long time before she spoke again.

"Tristan has never done that," she said softly. Her eyes turned up to his, tears rimming her lashes. "Does that mean our bond is nae secure?"

"Nay," Weylyn was quick to put her mind as ease. "That is only for wolf-mates."

"Has there been no other wolf and human mating in the past?" she asked.

Weylyn looked down at her and for a moment was not sure if he was going to answer. He did not know her, but he did want her to be comfortable with him and that meant answering her questions and sharing a little about himself in the process.

"Aye," he replied. "But it did nae end well."

"What happened?" she asked.

"'Tis a tale better left for another time," he said. "Rest. I can cover more ground phased."

"I donnae want to sleep right now," she replied, her gaze pulled back before them. "Phase, I will be all right."

"Are you sure?" He asked. She nodded but said nothing. "I am sorry for scaring you, but just ken that it is still me."

Alexina said nothing and did not look at him. Steeling himself against the fear he thought he would sense in her, he half-phased and began running through the woods at an impossible speed. Taking in her scent, he did not smell the fear he was sure she would have but he did feel the wet tears she shed on his arm. Her little body shook even though she tried not to show it. His heart broke feeling her pain as assuredly as if it was his own. A face flashed before his eyes and his heart nearly gave out. That face was one he had seen every night in his dreams the face of he held on to and the one he would never see again. The pain in his chest grew and the strain was too much for him.

If he were alone, he would have left his hut in the village and wandered to the edge of the loch. He would phase fully into his wolf form and let out a howl, releasing his pain. He would shed some tears for the life lost, the future stolen and he would not return to his hut until the pain was bearable again. He did not have that option so after a little while, he slowed and phased back to his human form. Alexina looked up at him. Her gaze unnerved him as if she was seeing right through him. Setting her down for a moment, he held on to her arms.

"Forgive me," he said his voice strained. "I need a moment."

She nodded but still held his arms.

"Does it ever go away?" she asked.

"What?" he replied.

"The pain of loss?"

He stared at her, his face devoid of expression.

"Nay," he replied. "But it does ease over time." A single tear slid down her cheek. Weylyn reached forward and wiped it away.

"It was you," she stated. At his questioning gaze, she continued. "You were the wolf who mated with a human."

Weylyn took a deep breath, wincing at the sharp pain.

"Aye," he replied.

"What happened?" She asked.

His gaze never faltered when he replied simply.

"She died."

Chapter Five

Alexina processed Weylyn's words slowly but he did not give her a chance to respond. He turned his back, walked a little farther away and looked up at the moon. He did not speak but he told her everything. His back rose and fell with his breath. She knew the struggle he was having breathing, she was having it too. But he fascinated her.

"Her name was Brietta," he began. "She was human, she was beautiful, but, gods, she was strong. You remind me so very much of her. We met when Tristan's father Marrock, my alpha at the time, sent a few of us on a scouting party to her village and the lands surrounding it. She was picking heather with other women of her clan when she caught sight of my yellowed eyes. I was the fastest you see, I was sent on ahead to make sure there were no Druids nearby and that the way was safe. We met, we courted, we mated, I was forced to leave her, and she died. But I hold her in my heart with me every moment of every day. Every thought in my head is a thought of her, her smile, her laugh, the way my name sounded on her lips. She was stolen from me. Our love was stolen from us and then... she was no more." He finally turned toward her.

"But no' a day goes by where I donnae thank the gods for the pain I feel, because of it I ken she was real and our love was real and our time was real. So no, lass, the pain does nae go away but it becomes something far greater than mere pain, it becomes memory and life. The same will be of your family. One day you may forget the smell of your father's peat smoked tunic as he carried you, or the way your mother stroked your hair to help you sleep, but when your pup is born and you watch Tristan carry him or her to bed and you see your own hand stroking your child's hair, you will remember them. The pain may intensify for that moment but revel in it, donnae shun it. It is proof that they *lived*. And that is all any of us can ask for; to be remembered."

Alexina wiped the tears from her face and nodded.

"I am sorry for your loss," she said. "But I thank the gods that you are here with me. I donnae believe I would have been able to face this without Tristan. You made it possible. So I thank you."

"You never need to hide your tears from me, lassie," he went on. "Shed them, mourn for the dead, then get on with living again."

"How far have we come?" Alexina asked when Weylyn came to a stop and let her down.

"We are about a half day's journey from the edge of the forest," he explained as he sat on a log to give his body a rest.

"Are we out of danger?" She asked looking southward.

"Hardly," Weylyn answered untying the leather that bound his feet and removing a small pebble from inside.

"Marrock's land is this entire wood. It stretches on for many days."

"Are there any wolves following us?" she asked.

"Nay, I made sure to backtrack our scents. They will be confused and unable to find us," he replied standing again. "And I am the fastest in the pack," he said with some pride. "I have outrun them all even carrying a wee lass such as yourself."

"So I am no' the first wee lass you have carried through these woods?" she tried for a tease to lighten the mood around them.

"Aye lass, you are my first lass I have carried like this," he replied laughing lightly.

"'Tis good to ken you donnae make it a habit of picking up young women and carrying them through the woods," she suggested.

"No' as often as I would like," he winked. She giggled feeling some of the stress melt around them.

"May I ask something?" she said.

"Aye, of course," he answered.

"Why did you no' find another mate when you lost Brietta?" she asked. "Could you no' have another wolf from your pack? Could you no' have a family? You are young still and a very handsome man."

"Nay, I could nae, lass," he replied. "You see... wolves mate for life."

Walking on, they stopped every so often for Alexina to stretch her legs. Tristan's torture had begun and, half phased, Weylyn felt every slice, every puncture and every broken bone.

She is fine, Weylyn's mind let Tristan know as he watched Alexina walk away from him. *But I am sorry; I have to block it out. I will be of no use to her if I am feeling the same things you are.*

Protect her please, that is all that I need, Tristan's half choked plea resonated in Weylyn's head.

She is safe. You stay strong, Weylyn told him.

It is all right Weylyn, I will be fine. Tristan replied. *You have trained me well. I am strong thanks to you.*

I will come back for you, Weylyn said.

If it is a choice between my life or that of my wife and child, you ken which one I want you to choose.

You are my Alpha. How could I nae come for you? Weylyn asked.

Tristan's surprise when he heard and understood his meaning, resounded in Weylyn's mind.

Please, all I care about is Alexina. Will you tell me when my child is born? Tristan choked out.

Of course, Weylyn promised. *You are strong, Tristan, you will survive this. Remember when Faolán, you and I used to train? You were quick to learn. I was so proud of you. I never thought I could be more proud. But now, you have shown me the measure of the man you are and I am honored to be your friend and a member of your pack.*

Thank you, Tristan replied. *And ken that you are the only man I would be honored to call Father.*

Weylyn's voice choked as a swell of emotion rose in his heart. *I never had a son, Tristan,* he began. *But if I did, I would hope he is half the man you are.*

Tristan screamed when a bone cracked in his arm. Weylyn shook as he felt the pain radiate through him; his stomach twisted and heaved. Recovering before Alexina turned to look at him, he apologized to Tristan and blocked out the pain.

Alexina walked slowly back towards him and he phased back into his human form. She gazed up at him when she approached.

"It is fascinating," she began looking up at him. Only then did he realize his eyes were still the yellow of his wolf form. He shook his head and when he opened his eyes they were back to brown.

"Forgive me," he said. "I did nae realize. It happens at night."

"'Tis all right," she replied. "I used to be afraid of them, until Tristan showed me there was nothing to fear."

"Aye, lass, you have nothing to fear from me," he said.

"What is your story, Weylyn?" she asked.

"My story?" he asked.

"Aye, I find that my mind wanders to my husband's plight and I need a distraction," she stated. "Please tell me something about yourself that will take my mind off of it."

"I am a teacher," he began. "As my father before me."

"How old are you?" she asked.

"I celebrated my hundred and twentieth year last solstice," he said.

"The winter or summer?" she asked.

"Winter," he replied. "Snow covered the ground when my mother whelped."

"Winter births are kenned to be strong of character, healing and spiritual. But you are also mysterious and like to be alone. But that loneliness can burden you and cause you to shoulder your pain alone," she said.

"How do you ken this?" he asked.

She shrugged. "My mother taught me much." At the mention of her mother she lowered her head and wiped a tear.

"You were speaking to Tristan before I came up, were you no'?"

Weylyn stared at her.

"I was communicating with him, aye," he said.

"Through reading his thoughts and giving your own," she stated.

"Aye," he replied.

"The torture... it has started?" she asked looking down.

He breathed deeply but decided to answer her with confidence.

"He is strong and he will survive," he said.

"I ken," she replied stroking the child within her. "He has to."

Attempting to divert her thoughts, he looked around desperately for something else to say.

"Are you hungry at all?" He finally asked.

"I am a little," she said.

"I will get you something," he made sure she was settled near an oak before he rushed off to find something for her to eat. Once away from her line of sight, he phased and foraged the forest floor for something edible.

There would be nothing substantial without a fire but he did not want to light one afraid that Marrock's pack still followed them. Perhaps if he could find shelter for her and then light a fire, he could hunt a red deer. His own stomach growled at the thought. When was the last time he had eaten?

Just as he thought about hunting a rabbit or two to satisfy his hunger, he came across some wild berries, growing late in the season. Smelling them, his mind wandered to the human village near Marrock's keep. They were constantly checking berries for poison. Some children had died eating some of them. *Can humans eat these?* He asked himself. He would never forgive himself if he picked as many as he could and they were poisonous to Alexina or the babe.

Aye, he heard Tristan in his head. *She can have them.*

Even through his torture Tristan still found the strength to answer Weylyn's unconscious thoughts. Weylyn blocked Tristan's pain again but shuddered when he felt the wolf's claws ripping through the skin on Tristan's thigh and the heat of his blood running down his leg. Picking as many berries as his tunic could hold, he headed back to Alexina; asleep against the trunk of the oak.

"Alexina," he called softly. "Alexina." She opened her eyes slowly and looked up at him. "I was able to find some berries," he said. "I ken humans cannae eat certain kinds, but I have been told these are all right."

She thanked him as he laid them out on her cloak that rested on the ground like a blanket. She grabbed a handful but in the light of the moon, she saw what kind they were and tears welled in her eyes.

"What is it?" Weylyn asked concerned.

"Tristan told you these were all right, did he no'?" She asked.

"Are they?" He asked confused.

"Och aye," she replied. "It was berry picking that we first met. I was out in the woods behind my house picking some for a pie my mother was making. I felt something watching me. When I turned I saw a wolf, no' one of your kind, an actual wolf. It charged me. Tristan came out of nowhere, killing it. After, he rushed to me and asked if I was all right. Something about him made me feel comfortable. We talked for quite a while and he helped me pick the rest of the berries saying he did no' trust me being by myself in the woods. He said there could be other things out there and he wanted to protect me. I found out later that he had been watching me. He saw me once when you both went into the village and since then, he said he had been fascinated by me… humans in general and wanted to learn more about us.

"I asked him to come to the cottage so that I could tell my parents of the heroic deed he had done. It was only then he smelled the wolf's bane surrounding me and his eyes turned yellow. I screamed. Immediately he changed his eyes back to brown and apologized. I could nae believe it. I had always been told that wolves would kill humans on sight but he was unlike anything I had been told. Turning away from me almost ashamed, he started walking away but I called him back. Shortening the distance between us, I gave him a handful of berries and never thought I would see him again.

"It was two days later when we found a pile of berries on the stones of the well outside our cottage. I think that was as close as he could get to the house. I kenned he was telling me something, it was his way of communicating with me. I removed the wolf's bane around my window every night and would find berries on my window sill the next morning. Sometimes he would tap on my window shutters when he kenned the rest of my family was asleep. I would slip out and we would walk for hours…" she stopped and looked at Weylyn. "I donnae ken why I am telling you this… But when the berries on the well and my sill started to raise my family's suspicions, he began to howl outside in the woods just as a usual wolf would, but I could hear the difference."

"You are sharing it because you want to relive the memories and ken they were no' dreams. You believe that telling someone about him will keep him alive and alive in your mind," he explained.

"You sound as if you have experience with this," she said.

"I do," he replied. "He also told me some of this when I caught a foreign scent surrounding him. I kenned he had met you."

"You could smell my scent on him?" She could not bring herself to look him in the eyes. "We never touched."

"It does nae matter," he answered. "He was around you, that is enough. I ken he loves you very much."

"I love him too," she said.

"Och I can tell," he answered. Reaching out, asking her permission first, he touched her stomach and stroked the child inside, smiling when the babe kicked his hand.

"Can you tell what it is?" She asked.

"Nay," he replied not moving his eyes from her swollen stomach.

"I think 'tis a girl," she said. He smiled softly.

"Either would be a blessing," he replied. "I ken Tristan is very happy. Fatherhood is such a blessing. There are some who donnae believe as I do."

"Do you have any children?" She asked.

He shook his head.

"Tristan is like a son to me," he answered. "But Brietta and I were no' together long enough to conceive children."

"But you were mated," she said.

"Aye, under the moon," he replied.

"Sometimes once is all it takes," she answered.

"No' when she died shortly thereafter," he said. She was quiet for a long moment and Weylyn bit back his words. "Forgive me, I donnae mean to be callous."

"It is a pain you have lived with for years, Weylyn," she

said. "You donnae offend me with your brusqueness. I merely weep for your plight."

"I donnae remember what life felt like before this emptiness inside me," he revealed. After a moment, she reached for his hand and held it tightly in hers.

"Then we will face it together," she said. "As friends."

"Yours will be short-lived I swear to you," he answered. "I will get Tristan back for you."

"I ken you will," she said leaning into him. For a moment they held each other giving the comfort they sought. Nothing passed between them, merely likeminded pain. Soon Weylyn pulled back and indicated the berries, quite forgotten upon her cloak. "Eat," he said. "We cannae stay here long."

She nodded and began to eat, her stomach growling and the child within her moving.

"Will you no' eat?" She asked him as he turned around scanning the woods behind them.

"I have never had them," he answered turning back.

"They are very good. Tristan likes them," she offered him one. "'Tis safe."

Tentatively, he reached for what she offered. Taking the berry in his mouth, he put it between his teeth and bit down, surprised when the juice squirted out of it. Alexina giggled watching his face.

"Hmm," he said chewing.

"No' bad," she replied.

"Nay, no' at all," he answered taking another one and studying it. "What are they?"

"They are called blueberries," she replied.

"Original," he answered sarcastically looking at the color of the berries.

"I suppose we humans have a very limited imagination," she laughed.

After a time, Weylyn stood and dusted his hands on his trouser pants.

"We should move on," he said. "If we can reach a safe place I will get you something a little more substantial than berries."

With the promise of actual food, Alexina finished the last of the berries and let Weylyn help her stand.

"All right?" he asked when she wobbled on her feet. She nodded, smiled and looked into his eyes. For the first time, she noticed how handsome he was. He looked to be in his early-forties. Half of his dark brown hair, with glints of red, was tied back and it fell wavy to his shoulders. His eyes were deep brown and sad but the corners of his eyes crinkled when he smiled giving him a genuine look of amusement. He looked completely different from Tristan and yet in some aspects they were exactly the same.

"Are you all right?" He asked noticing her watching him.

"Forgive me, I suppose am a little thirsty," she said, glad he did not ask why she was looking at him.

His ears pricked up and back as if listening for something and his nose rose into the air as he sniffed.

"There is a stream close by," he said. "Let us get something to drink. Come. We need to get you out of the rain and snow."

Confused, she took in the area around her.

"'Tis no' raining or snowing any longer," she said.

"Nay, but it will be very soon," he answered.

She nodded and waited for his body to convulse in a half-phase. When his wolf-self looked at her and nodded, she took a step closer and wrapped her arms around his neck. He bent at the knees and picked her up taking off at wolf speed through the woods.

"I do feel better after having eaten," she said breaking the silence.

"Good," he replied his voice a raspy growl. She pulled back to look at him. "What is it?"

"I just have never heard a half-phased voice clearly before," she replied. "It sounds so…"

"Inhuman?" He offered.

She shrugged.

"I am *nae* human," he replied.

"I am starting to see that," she teased.

He had not laughed in his half-phased form for many years, it sounded odd to him. They were silent again for a little while until Weylyn's ears perked up again and he spoke.

"The stream is close," he said. "When we arrive, I will check the water to make sure it is all right."

She agreed and within moments, she felt him slow and phase back to his human form. Weylyn set her down, holding her arms until she balanced.

"Let me taste the water," he said walking over to the edge of the stream. Kneeling on one knee, Weylyn cupped some water to his lips. It was cool and refreshing. "'Tis good," he replied beckoning her over. Standing beside her as she drank, his eyes turned yellow and he watched for any movement in the woods.

Finally, when she had had her fill, he helped her stand.

"Let us move on," he replied. "Are you all right? Do you need a moment?"

She smiled slightly knowing he was trying to be delicate.

"Aye, I could use a moment," she answered. Motioning to a place, he turned his back and waited. After a little while, he felt a hand on his arm and turned. "I am ready now, unless, do you need a moment?"

He cleared his throat embarrassed but shook his head.

"It would be all right," she replied. Debating for a moment he finally agreed and headed deeper into the woods. When he returned, tears were rolling down her cheeks and he cursed his stupidity for leaving her alone even for a moment.

"Is something the matter?" he asked.

"Nay... Aye... Nay," she shook her head as the tears came faster.

"I may be a stubborn old wolf, but I loved a human once, I ken tears are usually spent for a reason," he said.

"You said Brietta died," Alexina said remembering their earlier conversation. "How?"

Weylyn's eyes went to her unborn child and Alexina covered her stomach with her hands understanding his silent tell.

"I am so sorry," she had tears in her eyes. "Was the child yours?"

He shook his head.

"She married another," he replied. When he finally looked up at her, she was crying again. "Are those tears for me?" He asked. When she nodded he shook his head softly. "Donnae cry, lass, donnae shed any tears for me. I had my love, some donnae even have that," Faolán's face flashed before his eyes. "Enough about me, let us go."

He lifted her gently in his arms, half-phased and started to run. She leaned her head against his shoulder, warm from his wolf temperature of one hundred and two degrees. Feeling the muscles around his shoulders defined through the fabric of the tunic, he wanted her to feel safe in his arms.

"Tristan used to hold me to him tightly as we slept," she mumbled into his chest. "I was never cold when he was there and I had never felt so loved and protected."

"You will feel that way again. I promise you, you will be in his arms again," Weylyn pledged. Slowly, she closed her eyes against the pain and he felt her relax again him. Sleep claimed her as he ran and he sent a prayer to the gods that she slept well.

Weylyn carried her until the moon was highest in the sky and shone down on Weylyn giving him comfort. Feeling Alexina slowly fall asleep in his arms, he was grateful she found rest. His body ached from carrying her. Even though he lied to her and told her that she weighed naught, after the day he had, nearly being killed, losing his cousin, losing Tristan and the comfort of his pack, and then fleeing into the woods, his mind was fatigued and his body ached. They both needed rest and he needed to hunt if he was to be of any use to her.

Passing a small village on the outskirts of the woods, he contemplated stopping and asking for help, but the smell as he passed the outer wall of the village burned his nose and churned his stomach. Wolf's bane; that wretched flower that was poisonous to all wolves, he could not take her there. They would never help if they knew what he was. Due to his exhaustion, he was not sure he could control his instincts and his eyes would change unbidden at the smell of the flower, giving them away to the Celts and possibly their Druid friends.

The freezing rain had turned into little pellets of hardened snow that struck his face as he ran. Watching his footing as he slipped a couple times on the ice beneath his feet, he was grateful when the temperature cooled slightly and the pellets turned into snowflakes giving him more traction. The snow melted the moment they touched his heated skin and by the time his shoulder length hair was dripping wet and his tunic was soaked through, the ground glowed white beneath the moon. Sending a prayer to the gods that Alexina would stay slightly dry, he looked around the woods hoping they were out of danger. The smell of that sickening poison finally left his nostrils and he took a deep cleansing breath. His arms were aching and he was weakening. Slowing, he walked for a little while.

Still there was no shelter for Alexina and when he felt her clutch to him even more in her sleep, holding on to the warmth that radiated from him, he needed to get her out of the wet and cold.

Finally, about half a league away, his eyes caught a glimpse of a barn. Hoping there would be no wolf's bane, he slowed and phased to human form just in case there were any Highlanders who had dared the storm.

The clouds parted for a moment and the warmth of the moon shown down on him. He stopped, closed his eyes and took a deep breath, the moon gave him the energy and strength he needed to keep going. It was full, brilliant and white. The comfort it gave him was brief as the clouds covered the moon yet again and the temperature warmed slightly causing the snow to change back to raining pellets.

As he walked on, his nose flared and his eyes turned yellow when he smelled something roasting on a peat fire. His stomach growled and he suppressed his animal instinct when he felt the child within Alexina kick his chest. Shuddering as it was one of the most difficult things for a wolf to do, he forced his mind on his human form and forced his body to obey him. Focusing on his Alpha's order, he promised himself that he would hunt as soon as Alexina was safely inside that barn.

The old thatched wooden barn came within human sight. He walked around to the front of the structure. The door was open and cautiously, he stepped inside, sniffing the air. Hay, horse, and peat. His eyes darted around the stalls but there were no horses. The smell was faint, perhaps there had not been any for some time. He was grateful. Horses and wolves were not a good combination and he had no desire for the owners of the barn to come out to see what had the horses in an agitated state. Although, he reasoned, horse meat did sound very appetizing to him at that moment. The cottage was across a small courtyard and a light still burned brightly though the shuttered windows. Smoke rose from the chimney and billowed out tinging the crisp night air with peat and roasting lamb. His eyes flashed yellow and he licked his lips with barely suppressed hunger.

Entering the barn fully, he found a clean pile of hay and set Alexina down. She moaned and turned away from him, still asleep. The child was coming soon, sooner than he had hoped. His head pounding from all the poisonous smells he had endured while protecting her. Taking one more look at her to ensure she was sleeping, he silently promised her he would be within hearing distance if she needed him. Half-phased, he left the barn in search of something to satisfy his hunger.

Chapter Six

Tristan's half-phased body fell to the hard ground as his father's guards threw him into one of the cells in the dungeon carved into the side of the mountain. He heard the clink of metal as the door closed and locked. He could barely open his eyes and realized he did not want to. He wanted to curl up and die. As he willed his mind to stop and his breath to end, he heard the echo of his wife's plea not to leave her. His body ached but his tears were shed for her. Sending up a silent prayer to the gods that they protect her, he slowly got to his knees and dragged himself to the small barred window.

Looking out, he felt the moon shine down warmly on him and he closed his eyes to the healing the moon gave. Just as quickly as the moon shone, it disappeared and he felt the biting pellets strike his face. Again saying a prayer for his wife and unborn child, he hoped they were safe but he had not seen some of his father's wolves return to the village. They still searched for Weylyn and *the whore*, as his father had named her. Guilt whirled in his belly.

Oh gods, gods, Alex, I love you. Please be safe and ken why I did what I did. Feeling the wet tears on his face, his mind turned to Weylyn. The man who had been like a father to him. The man who loved him and the man he had abused by ordering to do his bidding. *Why did I have to command him?* He tormented himself. He never meant for his plea to become an Alpha's order. Now that he had a chance to realize exactly what that meant, icy dread filled his heart. Was he ready to be Alpha? *Forgive me my order, my old friend.*

Och, Tristan, I do, lad, he heard Weylyn's voice in his head.

Weylyn! Thank the gods, how are you? What are you doing? Tristan asked.

I am half-phased. Hunting. Alexina is asleep. She is fine. The child is coming soon, Weylyn said.

Donnae say or show me where you are. But tell me, how is she? Tristan asked.

She misses you. She is scared. But she is strong. I have done what I can and am no' far from her but I had to eat. I am too weak to help her in this state, Weylyn replied.

Of course, I hope you *are all right,* Tristan said concerned for his mentor.

I am fine. But I removed the block, and can feel your pain. What have they done to you? Weylyn asked.

You donnae want to ken ... Tristan moaned. *Tell me, is she out of the rain? Is she all right?*

She is fine. Trust me, Tristan. I will take care of her. And aye she is out of the rain. I found an old barn. I donnae ken if it is deserted but I am nae far from her. I hope to wait out the snow and rain and then leave early in the morning, Weylyn explained.

Where will you go? No one will help you, Tristan said.

I donnae ken yet, Weylyn answered. *I am hoping to make it past your father's lands. But there is only Druid groves and human villages past that, neither of which I trust. I ken the child will be here before sunrise. I donnae ken if I should move her. I am no midwife, Tristan. I will do what I can. I promise you. I will find her someone if your child comes sooner.*

I ken you will; that is why I asked you, Tristan started. *Weylyn, you are under no bond. I release you from my Alpha order. Please forgive me, my friend. I only meant to ask you to do what you will for her of your own free will.*

You are my Alpha, Tristan and order or no, she is my Queen. She carries your child. I will take care of her. I will give my life for her, Weylyn pledged.

Thank you, Tristan felt all of his pain at once and cried out as tears for both his fears and his pain stream down his cheeks. *I am going to sleep now, I need to be ready.*

Have no concern of your family's safety, Tristan. I will protect them 'til my last breath.

My dearest friend... Tristan cried. *Thank you.*

A human woman dared the storm to get more peat for her fire. It was only a short walk to her barn, a walk she knew by heart having lived in her little cottage since her marriage forty years ago. Wrapped in her shawl, she grabbed her lantern from the wall and headed out into the gale.

The wind was blowing hard, whipping around her fiercely. The chill went straight through her thin gown and she shivered as she fought her way to the barn. Her blondish-white hair blew about her face until she finally was close enough to see the entrance through the snowstorm.

Walking in, she immediately screeched and covered her

mouth. An impossibly tall man, with rain soaked hair falling into his face turned suddenly towards her, his yellow wolf eyes burned with surprise and she watched as he immediately phased back into human form.

"I am sorry. I did nae ken anyone lived around here," his silky voice did not match the monster she had just seen.

"What are you doing in my barn?" the old woman asked pulling her shawl tighter around her.

He paused a moment, his eyes darting to and fro between her and the doorway she stood before.

"My... sister is with child, due to be delivered very soon. I was trying to get her out of the rain. We are... on our way to our parent's house in... *Baile Chloichridh*," he explained.

Raising her lantern to see the sleeping woman behind him, she heard his simple reply.

"I wanted to get her out of the cold."

"Bring her into the cottage," she finally said.

Weylyn looked at her surprised. She had just seen what no human could understand. Any normal human would have gone running back to the house for weapons and that cursed flower, wolf's bane. He discretely took a sniff of her scent by pretending his nose was running. Something about it was familiar but he could not place it.

She locked eyes with him and he watched as she gathered bricks of peat with her old, withered hands and he realized she had not asked for their names.

"I am... Kinnon, this is my sister Alexina," he answered with the only alias he could think of, his father's name. He was not about to give this woman his real name, not when it meant *wolf's son* in their language.

The woman nodded and looked into his dark eyes, her

gaze unnerved him.

"Well... Kinnon," she said. "Bring your sister into my cottage. 'Tis nae much, but 'tis warm."

"I thank you," he replied and debated. For Alexina's safety and that of the child, he agreed. Once more, he sniffed the air; there was no scent of wolf's bane around her. He turned to Alexina and lifted her in his human form. It was difficult for him to not phase in order to utilize his full strength, but he knew he could not. He had to convince this woman that he was human and that what she had seen was just a trick of the moonlight.

He followed the old woman into the house. Before he entered, he made sure he took a deep breath smelling for that poison.

Nothing.

Odd. He thought. Humans always carried the flower with them as a talisman to ward off any wolves.

Setting Alexina on the pallet she offered, he made sure she was comfortable and none of the bedding irritated her.

"She should get out of these wet clothes," the woman's voice broke into his thoughts and Weylyn looked up at her surprised. Knowing she was right, he worried that she expected him to do it. But when she went towards the cupboard in the room and removed a long *leine* shirt, Weylyn breathed a silent sigh of relief. Again, he sniffed. A different scent mixed with hers and immediately he was on alert.

"Are you alone here?" He asked seeing that it was a man's tunic she held and it was a man's scent that clung to it. Celt, peat, earth, male, human.

"Since my hus..." she began. Her voice caught unable to get the word out. Clearing her throat she continued stronger. "Since my husband died," she answered slowly walking back to him from the cupboard.

"I am sorry," he said breathing out.

She did not answer and merely stood near to him.

"Would you like me to do this? I would rather she slept. I can dress her," she offered.

He watched her. She seemed genuine and there was something about her he found oddly... comforting. He nodded and stood from the side of the bed and away from Alexina.

"There is another tunic, some trousers and my husband's plaid in the drawer if you would like to change as well," she offered.

"I am all right, thank you," he said.

"You could catch something," she replied. "You are soaked through."

He almost laughed. Wolves were immune to *catching something*. But he realized humans were not and if he was going to keep his pretense of being human and distract her from what she had seen earlier, he would need to change. Nodding, he went to the cupboard and took out the other tunic and the trousers. They were much too big around the waist for him, and their length was too short. But it was dry and clean. He eyed the plaid folded in the corner of the cupboard drawer. The material was one men would drape over their shoulders indicating to which clan they belonged. It was an honor for humans to wear their clans' colors and he respected them for it. Honor was the highest trait he valued.

The woman was watching him; he could feel her eyes on his back. He was not used to humans staring at him. However, to them, the wolves in human form were the most beautiful people, even at his age. He had reached wolf maturity nearly forty-five years ago and stopped aging then. Looking the human age of thirty-five for all those years, the only thing to indicate his age was one or two greying hairs he found in his dark brown locks.

In his culture, wolves aged slower than humans did and once they reach seventy years old, or the age of consent, they were able to mate with the wolf of their choice. Tristan would be seventy-two in a few short months once the flowers began to bloom. The age of consent was equivalent to the human age of eighteen summers when a child is deemed an adult. But, unlike humans, wolves could not physically claim their mate until they reached that age.

Ignoring the woman's eyes on him, Weylyn went to the drape that separated the bedroom from the main living space and turned.

"I will be out here," he said. Whether or not he said it to the woman or out loud for Alexina's sleeping mind to hear, he did not know. Nevertheless, he lowered the drape and began to disrobe.

Chapter Seven

Weylyn crouched low by the fireplace stoking the flames when the woman walked out of the bedroom. He stood when he sensed her approach.

"I added another peat brick to the fire, it was dying out," he said.

"Thank you," she answered moving towards him, watching him. A part of him felt like this was normal, the other – the wolf in him – stiffened and was ready to pounce.

She stood in front of him, inches away and he hoped the heat from his hundred and two degree body would be attributed to the heat of the fire. Her eyes caught a glimpse of something metallic beneath his tunic and she reached up to touch it gently.

"What is this?" she asked.

Weylyn's entire body had stiffened as she touched the medallion necklace that hung around his neck.

"It is something someone very special gave to me," he said.

"Your wife?" she guessed. He nodded. "Where is she?"

the woman asked.

Weylyn caught her hand in his and lowered it. Her sudden intake of breath surprised him but then he realized he burned hotter than the average human.

"She is dead," he replied turning away and looking into the fire.

"Dead?" She questioned, the tone of her voice startled him.

"Is that so bizarre?" he asked looking back at her. "People do die, daily."

She looked up at him, swallowed and turned away.

"Would you like something to drink?" She offered.

Her sudden change of subject unnerved him.

"That would be lovely, thank you," he said. Watching her work around the cottage getting their drinks prepared over the flame, a thought occurred to him. "Would you happen to have anything for my sister to eat? She has not had much. I would be happy to pay you for your hospitality," but she waved him off preventing him from continuing.

"Of course," she replied reaching for some bread and a left over leg of lamb. Luckily Weylyn had eaten earlier, if not, he may have licked his lips in a very un-humanlike gesture. "Have you eaten?" she asked but he did not know what to say.

Somehow, *aye, I killed a fox and two rabbits and ate them raw while I was half-phased,* did not seem like the best answer.

"I am all right," he answered. "Thank you, I am more worried for my sister's welfare."

The woman set the food down where she could see it and offered him a seat on one of the chairs beside the fire.

It did not take long for the honey liquor, mead, to warm

over the fire. After the woman pulled it off and poured it into the wooden cups beside her, she handed one to him. He smiled. It had been a while since he had tasted mead but he had rather enjoyed it, perhaps a little too much for he did not remember much from the first time he had tried it.

They had been seated with their drinks for several long moments when Weylyn started to speak.

"You have a lovely cottage," he said. It seemed like the appropriate *humanly* thing to say.

"Thank you," she answered. "My late husband built it."

"How did he die?" He asked.

She looked over at him and he bit his tongue. Wolves did not need to worry about niceties but his question could have offended her.

"I am sorry," he said.

"Nay, it is all right," she replied. "'Tis just that everyone around here kens." She waved her hand towards the door. Weylyn did not realize they were near a village. "I am a little off the main path. The village is a league away."

Then he remembered the walled area he had passed while he carried Alexina and the putrid smell of wolf's bane.

"I am sorry, I… I am nae from around here," he stuttered. "I am a stranger here."

She nodded slowly and took a drink of her mead. Without lowering her eyes from him, she replied simply; "He was killed by a wolf."

"A wolf?" He asked attempting to prevent his body from going rigid.

"I did nae ken there were any near here."

"They are much closer than anyone thinks," she said.

He blinked. Her gaze burned through him, he began to

squirm uncomfortably and to second-guess whether he should drink the mead in his hand.

"I am sorry to hear that. Did they ever catch the animal?" He asked trying to think if any of his kin had died recently in a human attack.

She shook her head.

"Nay," she answered. "It has been many years."

Be human, be human, be human, he chanted to himself. *What would they ask next?*

"Any children?" He asked.

"One son," she answered. "Aedan."

"Oh, that is excellent," he smiled.

"Do *you* have any children?" She asked him.

"Nay, but my… sister's husband is like a son to me. There is a vast age difference between us," he explained. "But none of my own and I am too old now," he chuckled. "No woman would want me."

"I doubt that very much," she laughed.

"You are very kind, but it is true. No young woman would want an old teacher as a mate," he shook his head. "No' when there are younger men."

"We were all young once," she replied.

"I donnae ken," he chuckled. "Sometimes I feel I was born this age and was never young."

"Och, Weylyn, stop it," she laughed.

He froze; his entire body felt like pins and needles. She was still laughing. The whole thing had happened in moments. She looked over at him and the look on his face stopped her cold.

"How do you ken who I am?" He asked, his voice low.

"What?" She asked him.

He stood and faced her, pulling himself up to his full

height intending to be intimidating.

"You called me Weylyn. How do you ken that is my name?" He demanded.

"I am sorry, I did nae realize I did that," she answered setting her cup down on the wooden slats that served as a table beside her.

"Who are you?" He demanded. She took a deep breath, not looking at him.

"Do you no' ken who I am?" she finally asked. Looking up at him, her gaze pierced his heart. "You swore once you always would."

He stared at her, his mind clouded with the unbelievable truth. He recognized those eyes. He would always know those eyes, even if the skin did wrinkle around them. Those great, big, beautiful, blue eyes. Eyes he never thought he would see again. How could he ever have forgotten them? Everything around him disappeared. He could not move. He could not think.

"Brietta?" He breathed.

She let out a small gasp.

"It has been so long since I have heard you say that," the woman said, tears running down her cheeks.

"Brietta?" He breathed again, his breath quickening as his voice grew stronger affirming what his heart already knew.

"Have I changed that much, Weylyn?" She asked. "You have nae. You are just the same. I recognized you the moment I saw you. Even half-phased, I couldnae believe it was you. You did no' ken who I was, so I playacted."

"I thought you were dead," he breathed falling to his knees before her.

"And I thought you were as well, my love," she answered sliding to the floor to kneel with him. "I thought that as long as I could have you here with me, I would no' need you to ken me, but I was wrong. I needed you to ken it was me."

"I did, the moment I caught your scent. I kenned there was something familiar and comforting about you," he said. "How could I have nae kenned you immediately?"

She threaded her fingers through his and held his hands.

"I hoped you would nae have forgotten me," she said. "But it has been many years and I have aged."

He lifted their hands and kissed her fingers one at a time before pulling her to him in a strong possessive kiss. It was not a gentle exploratory kiss, this was a kiss of a lover too long separated from his woman. Weylyn's lips were like fire and it was a fire she willing stepped into. His heat surrounded her, the warmth from the fire felt oppressive as she wrapped her body around his. Soon his lips turned softer and sweeter, his need for passion abated for the moment. She had dreamt of his kiss every night and the feel of his body pressed to hers. Age may have withered her body but her spirit was just as fierce as it had been forty years ago.

Her lips eagerly accepted him and her fingers ran through his long hair as they had done years ago when they pledged their lives to each other. All those years he had thought her dead and lived with the pain of losing her, and she was right there. At their meeting spot, every day. She had built her cottage where they had first made love. Still he kissed her and still she never wanted the kiss to end. She had lived without him for forty years and not a day went by that she did not ache for his touch, his love and his kiss. When he finally broke their connection and gazed into her eyes, neither said anything but they both knew what they wanted, what they needed. They needed to reaffirm their vows, reconsummate the love that flowed through them.

Without dropping her gaze, Weylyn slipped his hand up to the strings of her dress. Closing her eyes at his touch, she never wanted to wake if it was a dream. Need did not rule them any longer, but love, joy and desire were rushing through them. Afraid he would look upon her differently as he slipped her dress from her shoulders, Brietta reached for the cloth to cover her exposed flesh and averted her eyes. Gently lifting her face with his fingers, Weylyn's eyes reflected the same love she had seen forty years ago when they had become one. Inhibitions forgotten, Brietta let her dress fall away and basked in the look her husband gave her as he took in her body. When he looked back up at her, she leaned forward and began tugging at the ties that held his tunic in place.

Too far gone to think, Weylyn helped her and once they were both bared to each other, they lay back before the fire, slowly and gently becoming one once more. Husband and wife, a wolf-man and his mate. For them no time had passed for they moved together in harmony with one another. Weylyn laid claim to her again and this time as he clutched her close and relished in her response to him, he swore he would never let her go.

Brietta laid her head on her husband's shoulder tracing strips of scars on his chest that she had never seen before. Weylyn held her tightly to his side as he ran his fingers through her hair. They said nothing, merely basked in the warmth and love they had just created. Still, she stroked a particularly jagged scar that covered his left breast. Puckered and pale, it looked old but she knew he did not have it when they were first married.

She had felt the scars on his back as they made love, but she did not want to break the spell they were casting to stop and ask him about them, but now, as the peat fire crackled and snapped and the snow and winter wind beat against the cottage walls, she looked up and kissed his jaw. Waking from a doze, he slowly moved his head to look at her. Kissing her again, he reveled in the look she gave him as she stroked his stubble covered jaw.

"You have no' aged a single day," she whispered.

"Neither have you," his low voice still sent a shiver through her. Gazing at the medallion that still hung around his neck, she stroked it and followed her fingers with a kiss. The metal felt oddly cold against her over sensitized lips. "I never took it off," she felt Weylyn's voice vibrate through the metal and it made her smile. She gazed up at him and smiled softly. "It was my only memory of you," he said softly winding his fingers through her hair and grasping the back of her head.

"*My* Weylyn," she sighed feeling the pressure on the back of her neck and closing her eyes. "I have missed you so," she whispered.

He waited until she opened her eyes again. "I have mourned you, missed you and never forgotten my love for you," he spoke in earnest. Understanding dawned in his eyes, "that is why you have no wolf's bane," he said softly. She nodded.

"I hoped that one day you might come looking for me and when that day came I wanted you to be able to find me and come to me," she explained.

"I am sorry. I never did," he replied pulling her down to lay her head on his chest, which had been empty for so long.

Snuggling her head deeper into his chest, she breathed him in. His scent was the same musky scent of pine, peat, and rain mixed with sweet holly berries that she had known so well all those years ago.

"What happened to you, my love?" she asked. "Why did you nae come to me when you promised?" He sighed bitterly and when he did not answer, she leaned up and waited for him to speak. A myriad of emotions passed over his face but she continued. "I waited. I went out every night for two weeks waiting for you. What happened?" She pressed.

"The Alpha," he confessed. "Marrock ordered me nae to go and you ken I cannae disobey his orders."

She did not want to think about Marrock. Weylyn had told her everything about his pack when they first met. If Marrock had denied her acceptance into the pack as Weylyn's mate, he could not be with her. Then an awful thought occurred to her. She did not want to ask, afraid of his answer, but after seeing the medallion she had given him on their wedding night she hoped she knew the answer. Taking a deep breath filling her senses with his scent, she gathered her courage.

"Did you ever marry again? Find a mate?" Her voice was strained.

Weylyn chuckled but it lacked humor. He pulled her chin up so he could gaze into her eyes. The desire that she saw in them made her weak.

"Wolves mate for life," he said pointedly before he kissed her again.

The fire snapped and made her jump, pulling away from him. She smiled but reached for her dress, laughing as Weylyn growled when she slipped it on.

"And what if your ward wakes up and comes out to find us intertwined as lovers?" She asked.

"I donnae care," he replied simply. Giggling, she slapped his hand away as it snaked up her body, under her dress.

"Nay, we have had our fun, now 'tis time to come and sit

with me, husband," she said. Smirking, he watched her get up, rummage around inside a cupboard and pulled out a jug. "Whisky?" she offered. He looked at her confused. "You have never had it?" he shook his head. She smiled brightly and poured them both a cup. Sighing, Weylyn raised both arms and intertwined his fingers behind his head. Brietta turned back to him and her gaze raked over him.

"You had better stop staring at me like that, wife," he grinned. "You ken I will nae be able to stop myself."

Biting her lower lip, she smirked, placed the cups of whisky down on the table and picked up his tunic.

"Shall I dress you, husband?" she asked.

"Och, woman, I thought ye would never ask," he pulled himself up and stood before her. Raising his arms, Brietta pulled his tunic over his head and belted it around his waist. Grasping her to him, he kissed her again then moved his lips to her neck and sucked gently. Shaking with desire, Brietta held on to the last ounce of strength she had and placed her hands on his shoulders pushing him back.

"Nay," she replied. "There will be time for more of that later."

He released her with a sigh and a short nod. Taking his hand to her chest, she led him to the wooden pew before the fire. Weylyn pulled her down onto his lap and held her tightly to him. The turf fire sizzled and cracked with the falling rain and the sight warmed them as the smell surrounded them.

"Tell me everything, my love. What have you done for the past forty years?" She asked with a little too much emphasis on the number.

"I am still a teacher," he answered his fingers gently glided up and down her arm and back.

"You always loved being a teacher," she smiled. He tightened his arm around her, buried his face into her hair and rested his forehead against her collar.

"I do," he sighed. Kissing the hollow at the base of her neck, he looked up at her. "I trained the alpha's son, Tristan after Marrock banished him from the keep."

"Why would he do that?" she asked.

"It is a complicated story, my love, but Marrock cares nothing for his own kin," Weylyn said with more feeling than he intended. "After I lost you I needed someone I could care for, so I took Tristan in as my own son and taught him the pack's history and trained him," he explained.

"And this young woman you are protecting?" She asked.

"Tristan's mate... wife," he replied. "He is a little younger than I was when I first met you."

"But she is human," Brietta said, her eyes unconsciously drifting towards the curtain that covered the entrance to the bedroom where Alexina slept.

"Aye, she is," Weylyn answered. "Tristan sacrificed himself to give us time to get away. Marrock killed her family and the entire village when he caught Tristan's scent. Marrock sent the pack to find him and he was captured as I took Alexina away."

"What is happening to him? Can you hear him?" She asked. His heart lightened even more. She remembered. He had told her once that the wolves in a pack communicated over vast areas by reading each other's minds.

"I have been able to communicate with him, but whenever I do all I feel is pain and him begging me to keep her safe," he answered.

"Pain?" She asked concerned pulling back to look at him

more fully. Weylyn stared into her eyes.

"He disobeyed a direct order from the Alpha," Weylyn explained. "In that moment he claimed his birthright to be Alpha. An issue arises as there can only be one in each pack and Marrock never allows a new pack to form. I pledged my loyalty to Tristan that is why I can hear him but no other. Marrock is torturing him, his own son... slowly."

Brietta closed her eyes and unconsciously sank deeper into his chest feeling his arms tighten around her.

"Were you?" she asked remembering the scars on his back. "Were you tortured when we..."

He took a drink of the mead, stared into the fire but did not answer her.

"I wasnae as strong as Tristan," he murmured. She let out a small sob. "He made sure I couldnae break his order by locking me in the dungeon for several weeks." She gasped but he gazed deeply into her eyes and said the words he had always wanted to say. "It was no' nearly enough and I would proudly do it again. My time with you was worth any time I had in the dungeon or any lashes I endured."

"Lashes?" She whimpered slipping her hand down the back of his tunic to touch the puckered flesh. Resting his head on her collarbone again, he nodded.

"He would have killed me had..." his voice trailed off.

"What?" she asked.

Shaking his head, he clutched her closer.

"Nothing," he replied. "I remember the night I was to meet you, I was in the dungeon but I could still see the moon. I spoke to it as if I was speaking to you." He felt her stiffen in his arms and looked at her wide eyes. "What is it?" He asked.

"I went out that night ready to take my place as your

mate," she started. "I stayed out there all night until Gowan found me. But before he did, I swear to you I felt you pull me into your arms and tell me how sorry you were and how much you loved me."

"I suppose the moon carried my message to you," he began. "We did mate under the Hunter's Moon, after all."

"What does that mean?" She asked confused.

"It means that we were blessed. Had we had a child from our union that night, he or she would be very special."

"Special how?" She asked and Weylyn could feel her body tense even more.

"Pups conceived under the Hunter's Moon have special abilities. Their wolf abilities are enhanced or they are able to learn quickly. It varies from wolf to wolf," Weylyn explained. "The only wolf that I ken of in the past is Marrock. He was conceived under the second harvest moon and it was the blood moon's eclipse. His skills are unmatched." When she did not answer, Weylyn massaged the back of her neck and gently held her to him. "Enough talk of me. I want to ken of you."

She relaxed a moment and shrugged.

"No' much to tell," she answered. "Gowan and I raised our son, Aedan."

"Who is Gowan?" He inquired.

"The man I married," she replied simply.

An unconscious growl escaped his lips. She looked back up at him and breathed a laugh. Looking away, he realized he had no right to his response. She was his as a wolf only and he knew she married again, but hearing it from her very lips, the lips he had just kissed as they made love, did not sit well with him.

"He was my best friend," she went on pulling his face

back to hers. "He found me half-dead with heartbreak at the spot I was to meet you. He carried me home. He was such a good man and I do miss him terribly." When he did not respond, she kissed the corner of his mouth. "It is nae what you think. He... he helped me, Weylyn."

"I remember when I heard you were to be married again; I went to the woods, the closest I could be to you without breaking Marrock's order. You were walking with several other women up the hill to the stones. The wind whipped around you, you paused and turned. You looked into the woods as if you felt me. The wind brought your scent to me and in that moment I let you go with a full heart even if it was broken. Then my father heard that the blacksmith's daughter had died in childbirth and... I thought."

"My sister, Gwen," she answered. "No' me."

"I am sorry for your sister. But I am so very glad it wasnae you. The gods have seen fit to give us this time. But I understand now, your scent is mixed with... your husband's that is why I did nae recognize it immediately," Weylyn said.

"We had been married for nearly thirty years when he died ten years ago," the sadness in her voice nearly undid him. Wanting to give her something to put a smile back on her face, he took a deep breath. Celt. Highlander. Warrior. Animal hide. Male. But there was something else. Something he could not place.

"His scent is all over this house," Weylyn revealed.

"Is it?" She looked around. "Good. He build it for me on our spot so I would have a part of you always. He was always so thoughtful of me... of us. He kenned, you see. I told him everything."

Weylyn let a soft snarl escape him.

"Did he think I abandoned you?" he demanded. "Took your virtue and left you destitute?"

"Nay!" she sounded insulted at the suggestion. "Nay, he kenned well enough that you were a wolf. He was the one who told me that it must have been an alpha order to keep you from me. He was a good man, Weylyn. I loved him very much."

"You never do anything halfheartedly, my love," he said. "Forgive me. I did nae think before I spoke. What of your son?" He finally asked. "Tell me about him."

"Aedan is a good, strong and handsome man, just like his father," she replied leaning forward out of his hold to set her drink on the table near them. "Does Alexina ken?" She asked.

"I have nae told her," how could he tell her that her husband was being tortured?

"Told me what?" They heard Alexina's voice from the doorway. Weylyn and Brietta jumped and quickly stood away from each other. "Where are we? Who are you?" She asked looking at Brietta. "Weylyn?" She turned scared eyes up to him.

"'Tis all right," he said soothingly raising his hands towards her. Alexina went to him as quickly as her tired body would let her and held on to his hand.

"What is going on?" Alexina asked. "I donnae remember anything."

"This is Brietta, my mate. Do you recall I spoke of her?" Weylyn replied. Brietta looked at him loving him all the more. "She offered a dry place for you."

"You said she was dead," Alexina said eyeing Brietta with distrust.

"It was a miscommunication, my dear," Brietta said. "I had a sister and it was she who died no' I."

Alexina still did not seem to accept the new truth.

"Weylyn, how long have I been asleep?" she asked turning from Brietta.

"The moon still lights the ground, Alexina. It has nae been very long," he answered, his gaze on Brietta. *Thank the gods she had been asleep.* "I found shelter for you and went to hunt. I was within hearing distance of you the whole time and when I returned, Brietta entered her barn and found us. She offered us a place to rest and most importantly a place for you to be dry and safe."

Alexina's gaze flew to the woman; her eyes on Weylyn with a look Alexina knew well. Love.

"Thank you," Alexina finally breathed.

"You should nae be up, my dear," Brietta replied stepping towards her. "Here I have something for you to eat." She reached for the plate of food and made her sit in the seat she and Weylyn had just vacated. Weylyn stoked the fire as Alexina ate ravenously. At their chuckle, she looked up guiltily.

"Forgive me," she said. "I suppose I am very hungry."

"Your child needs sustenance as do you, dear, donnae worry," Brietta replied. "We have all experienced this." A sudden pang in Weylyn's chest caused him to reach up and rub the spot that hurt. He had never seen Brietta heavily swollen with child, his or Gowan's. That thought hurt more than he was willing to accept but he knew she would have looked beautiful.

Noticing that her plate was empty, Weylyn looked over at his mate. She read his mind. "I have some meat gutted and draining in the woods west of the barn."

Weylyn nodded and crouched down to Alexina.

"You are safe," he said. "I will be but a moment."

Her eyes went to Brietta but finally she nodded.

"Be careful," she begged.

"I will be, I promise," he replied touching her cheek in a fatherly gesture. With a final look at the women in the cottage, Weylyn opened the door and headed out into the cold wintery air.

Breathing in the cold wintery air, Weylyn cleared his mind and body of their lovemaking. He still had a commission from his Alpha, but his entire being did not want to leave his mate. They were still well within Marrock's territory though only a half day at most. After that, they would be beyond his clutches and into another's. Druids ruled the land beyond.

The child would be there very soon, mother's and child's scents were distinctive. The thought of leaving Brietta again nearly gutted him, but he could not ask her to come with him. She had her son to consider.

Half-phasing, he let go of the perplexity of the situation and held on to the familiarity and peace his wolf-self gave him. Following the smell of draining meat, Weylyn found three red deer hanging in the woods near the barn.

Catching a scent he did not know, he looked around only to realize that the foreign scent clung to the deer. Taking a step closer, Weylyn made a mental image of the owner of the scent. Male, warrior, wolf's bane, Celt, highlander, human… mixed with… what? It was that same scent from the cottage that he could not place but he did have to admire the way the man, he assumed was Aedan; Brietta's son, prepared the meat. It was ready to be cooked.

Breaking off two legs, enough for the three of them, Weylyn found a fragrant plant with small stalks and leaves, leeks and wild mushrooms daring the cold and sprouting through the snow. Heading back to the cottage, he phased back to his human form before entering.

Brietta greeted him with a smile that made his heart soar. Alexina sat on the bench wrapped in a blanket with a mug of tea in her hands.

"I gathered some herbs as well," Weylyn announced. Brietta helped him and brought the food over towards the fire. After a little while, Alexina turned to Weylyn and took a deep breath.

"I want to ken. I need to. What is it you have nae told me?" Her voice caught. "Is Tristan all right?" Brietta shook her head ever so slightly telling him not to say anything. Seeing the exchange, Alexina pressed. "Please, Weylyn."

"Alexina, you must remain calm. This is nae good for your child," he said.

"What is happening to Tristan?" She asked once more. "I need to ken! Tell me."

Brietta closed her eyes as she basted the meat and turned it over the spit. Weylyn looked at her back, sighed and looked down.

"He is being... tortured," Weylyn said. "I donnae ken much more."

"But he is alive?" She asked.

"Aye," he answered.

"Is he in pain?" She asked.

"Donnae make me answer that," he said softly.

A cry escaped her lips and immediately Weylyn crouched down in front of her taking her hand.

"All I hear is him begging me is to keep you both safe," his gaze was intense on her. "That is what I am going to do."

"Thank you for telling me," she replied as tears ran down her cheeks. "Can you give him a message?" She asked.

"Anything," he answered.

"Tell him I love him and to remember the day we named the First of Spring. He will ken what I mean and it may give him some strength," she pleaded.

"I will, but right now, you must eat," he said. Taking a portion of the meat on a serving plate and handing it to Alexina. "For your child's sake, eat." She nodded and began pulling the meat apart.

After they ate, Brietta helped Alexina back into the bedchamber leaving Weylyn to phase and relay the message to his Alpha. A brief flash of understanding from Tristan flittered across Weylyn's mind and he felt the message give Tristan strength just as he felt a hot branding iron on the tender flesh of his stomach. Feeling what his Alpha felt, Weylyn cried out and fell to the ground, phasing back to his human form and ending the link between the wolves.

Weylyn lifted himself slightly from the ground utterly spent as pain washed over him. Brietta rushed out of the room and ran to him. Getting him up from the ground to sit on the wooden bench in front of the fire, she stroked his hair as he leaned forward and rested his forehead on her chest just above her heart.

"Gods above," Weylyn panted. "How has he survived?"

"What are they doing to him?" Brietta asked gently stroking his jaw.

"You donnae want to ken," he replied. Breathing deeply, he cleansed his mind and body of the pain.

Almost immediately, he sniffed the air and stood in one swift movement. All pain forgotten as his warrior instinct took over. Pushing Brietta behind him, he whispered.

"Someone is coming."

She peeked out around him and snuck to the window.

"I donnae see anyone," she said.

"They are too far away," he replied taking another deep breath in and letting it linger. "A woman, a man… no two men."

"Human?" She asked.

"With the snow it is difficult to tell. All I can sense is male and female," he answered. Brietta looked out the window again. "Do you see them?" He asked.

"Och, 'tis only my son and his wife but I donnae ken the other man," she said.

"Maybe I should go," Weylyn replied. Brietta looked at him confused. "I can stay in the barn… a strange man in your house, a woman with child in your room, she is acceptable, I am no'."

"Nonsense," she said. "You are an old friend and we are above impropriety." She walked back to him, grasped the nape of his neck and kissed him. Resting his hands on her hips, Weylyn returned her kiss. Pulling away slightly, she smirked.

"Or have you forgotten?" she asked breathlessly her eyes trailing to their place before the fire.

"Minx," he grinned using the same word he had used years ago. "Do you honestly think I could?"

Kissing him again, she walked to the door and opened it.

Chapter Eight

"The gale ended and I wanted to make sure all was well with you," Weylyn heard the man say to Brietta as she opened the door and greeted her son and daughter-in-law. "It will be turning into a rather cold night." Weylyn heard someone laugh. "Isla, my love why do you still laugh at me? I ken 'tis nae going to be pleasant I can sense it."

"We both wanted to be sure you have enough peat and food," a female voice said.

"Och darling, thank you!" Brietta smiled embracing them. "Aedan, an old friend and his ward came to visit me today. Let me introduce Weylyn," she turned, stepped aside and Weylyn finally got a good look at her son.

Something about him startled Weylyn. Aedan was tall with dark auburn brown hair touching his shoulders but some of it was braided at his temples. His eyes were dark and his features were defined. A rough bit of stubble covered his face almost in the exact same way Weylyn's face was covered. Strikingly handsome and somewhere in his very early thirties,

Aedan wore the same clan colors draped over his shoulder that Weylyn had seen in Brietta's drawer earlier that evening; her husband's plaid.

Aedan locked eyes with Weylyn and they greeted each other with a nod as they assessed one another. He was built like a highlander, tall, broad with defined yet lean muscles, two daggers were in sheathes on his forearms, a sword at his back, another dagger strapped to his right calf and another on his left hip. Clearly, he knew how to use the weapons. If the scars on his body were any indication, he was a warrior.

Weylyn finally took his eyes off Aedan and focused on the others coming into the room. Brietta was speaking to Aedan's wife, Isla and all Weylyn could see was a flash of fiery red hair and a glint of light brown eyes.

"This is our good friend Maelogan," Weylyn heard the female say, her voice accented by their northern region in Alba.

"Welcome," Brietta greeted.

Maelogan; a common enough name, but one that held history with Weylyn. Seeing the highlander was about the same age as Aedan with long dark hair braided at his temples and beaded at the tips, he knew that it was not the same man.

Maelogan's dark brown almost black eyes were penetrating. He was tall but not as broad as Aedan and clearly was not build for warfare but more as a scholar. Even still, Maelogan wore a bow and a quiver of arrows on his back and a knife strapped to his calf. Weylyn took in a long breath, closed his eyes and held the scent.

Human.

So not the same man he knew many years ago… but there was that other scent again.

"Isla, this is Weylyn. Weylyn, my son's wife, Isla and their friend Maelogan," Brietta introduced.

Isla came fully into the room and Weylyn was hit with the scent. Finally he placed it. The scent of his enemies. The scent of the Druids. Weylyn opened his eyes and they burned yellow. Isla screeched, pulling out a flower from her pocket. The smell caused Weylyn's nose and mouth to burn and after his night filled with that flower, his wolf-self overtook him and uncontrollably he half-phased.

"Wolf's bane," he snarled as his lip drew back over his teeth.

Aedan pulled out a knife from the sheath on his forearm. Weylyn snapped his teeth as Aedan raised his weapon. Pushing his wife and mother behind him and closer to Maelogan at the door, Aedan lunged at Weylyn. Claws extending from his fingernails, Weylyn slashed at the knife. Maelogan notched an arrow and let it fly missing his target as Weylyn jerked to the side. Growling at the bowman, Weylyn barked a warning. Aedan's knife connected with Weylyn's arm and he cried out but knocked the dagger out of Aedan's hand before another blow.

"Stop it!" Brietta yelled, stepping forward and standing between them. "Isla, put that flower away. Weylyn, phase back. Aedan, sheath your knife."

"Mother, you can see what he is!" Her son cried, another knife already in his hand.

"Aye, but he is also my friend," she said.

"Are you mad?" Isla demanded. "Has he cast some sort of spell over you?" A growl rumbled deep in Weylyn's chest.

"Stop it!" Brietta ordered her daughter by marriage. Everyone went quiet as she took a step towards Weylyn and took his injured arm in her hand. Their eyes connected and he nodded. Brietta inspected the wound and kissed above it, the wound having already started to heal. "Are you all right?" she asked him. He nodded and phased back into human form.

"Merely a cut," he said. She held his arm and turned to her family. Aedan's jaw hung open as he watched his mother.

"Now, Weylyn's ward is about to deliver a child. Either you will help us or not. If not you can leave now," Brietta said.

There was a pause and Isla touched her husband's arm coaxing him to put the knife away. Aedan snapped his mouth shut and sheathed his dagger. Isla turned to Weylyn and spoke low, her eyes drifting to the curtain covering the bedroom.

"Your ward... is she wolf as well?" She asked.

"She is human. The child is that of my Alpha. He is being held by another alpha and my former pack. There are several wolves hunting us," Weylyn explained.

"And you are expecting to use my mother's home as your defense?" Aedan demanded as his hand shook with suppressed anger. "That is nae going to—"

"Aedan," Brietta snapped. "It will be all right. Go out to the barn and get your father's reserve weapons. Isla, come with me, see if we can help Alexina."

"I will head home, Aedan," Maelogan said.

"Aye, my thanks, Logan," Aedan clasped his arm in a warrior's shake. Just as he turned, Weylyn stepped forward.

"We will need as many arms as possible," Weylyn replied. "Are you good with that bow?"

Maelogan raised his head proudly. "Very good," he answered.

"I cannae promise a reward," Weylyn said. "The only thing I can promise is that they will sing songs about this battle."

"Sounds like my kind of battle," Maelogan replied. "I will stay."

"I thank you," Weylyn stated.

Suddenly, Alexina cried Weylyn's name. He raced into the room, ripping the drape back and seeing her clutching at her stomach, water soaking the bed sheets. He swallowed hard and locked eyes with her.

"'Tis time," Weylyn breathed.

Chapter Nine

"Tristan," a soft familiar voice called from out of the darkness. "Tristan..." it called again. Tristan groaned but could not move. The voice became more insistent. "Tristan, lad, are you awake?"

He moaned again a little louder. The door to his cell opened slowly and someone walked in. In his current state, Tristan could not defend himself. The person approached him and put a hand on his shoulder. Weakly he batted him away.

"Nay," he breathed. "Nay, stop, please."

"An alpha never begs," the voice said. "Listen to me, lad, you must eat."

"Faolán?" Tristan's voice was soft. "Is that you?"

"Aye," the voice continued. Faolán leaned over him and offered a hunk of bread. "'Tis me, lad. You must eat."

Tristan eyed him warily.

"You have every right to be wary of anyone," Faolán started. "But you can trust me."

"You could be killed for helping me, Faolán," Tristan

said.

Scoffing Faolán pressed the bread to Tristan's lips, as he took a small bite, he continued. "I died already, just a day ago." Tristan chewed and swallowed even as pain scratched his throat.

"I heard about Heledd," Tristan started. "Faolán, I am so very sorry."

"She made her choice," he answered pressing him to eat more. "I ken what it is you are going through. I would join you and Weylyn if I could but I think it would be more prudent if I stay connected to Marrock's pack. I can give you information to pass on to Weylyn."

"If my father finds out, you will be killed," Tristan said.

"Then I will join Heledd," Faolán replied. "Donnae fear for me, my friend. All will be well but you must eat to keep up your strength if you are to survive. I will return when I can."

Weylyn stepped out of the cottage and into the brisk winter night. The pup was coming and he was of no use to Alexina. As a healer in the pack, Weylyn had attended many women when they whelped, and some were not strong enough to bring forth the life within them. Closing his eyes when he heard Alexina cry out again, he prayed the gods would be merciful.

Looking around, he saw Aedan and Maelogan close to the well having a low and intense conversation. They stopped speaking when he walked up.

"Is the woman all right?" Aedan asked.

"Alexina," Weylyn replied. "Her name is Alexina. And I would nae ken. I am no midwife."

"No' a man's place," Maelogan grunted.

"I am her protector," Weylyn explained. "I can do nothing to help her now. Do you realize what that does to me?"

"She is having a child," Aedan said. "As Maelogan says 'tis no' a man's place."

Weylyn stared hard at the man before him. His was the scent that clung to the red deer hanging in the woods but he was not certain if he was friend or foe. Sensing the tension between the two, Maelogan pulled out one of his arrows and tested the sharpness with his thumb.

"I am going to go to the barn," he said. "I need to sharpen these."

Aedan and Weylyn said nothing as the third man left the group. They stood together in silence staring at each other. Standing eye to eye, their gazes were hard and their jaws were set.

"How do you ken my mother?" Aedan finally asked.

"We met over forty years ago," Weylyn replied.

"You did nae answer my question. How do you ken her?" Aedan demanded.

"Why do you ask?" Weylyn asked.

"Were you lovers then?" Aedan asked.

Weylyn's eyes twitched. "That is a question you should ask your mother," he replied.

"I am asking you," Aedan replied forcefully.

"Is it that important to you?" He asked.

"Aye," Aedan replied.

Weylyn looked into the Highlander's dark brown eyes and sighed.

"Aye," he finally said. "We mated."

Aedan's jaw clenched and he took a deep breath before continuing.

"I thought wolves mated for life," Aedan said.

"We do," Weylyn looked at him deliberately. "But your mother is nae a wolf and our love was a wolf bond no' a human one. She was free to marry your father."

Again they fell silent their eyes falling from each other's to the woods around them. Interested in the man before him, Weylyn continued the conversation, "how long have you and Isla been married?"

"Nearly ten years," Aedan answered.

"Do you have any children?" He asked.

"No' yet," Aedan answered.

"How old are you?" Weylyn asked.

"How old do you think I am?" Aedan asked.

"You donnae look a day over thirty summers but I ken your mother said you were older than that," Weylyn answered.

"I am turning forty-one in two moon cycles," he replied.

"How do you look so young?" Weylyn asked. Aedan shrugged.

"Good bloodline, I suppose," he said.

Weylyn looked over and observed his profile. Feeling his eyes on him, Aedan sighed and looked over.

"What is it?" Aedan demanded.

"Nothing," Weylyn replied. "I am sorry... Your mother told me what happened to your father. I am very sorry for it."

"When I find the dog that did that I will kill him," he said fingering the knife strapped to his forearm. "Mother always taught me to love and respect your kind," Aedan began. "But when my father was killed by one that was it. I kenned there was no good in any of them. You are all animals and should all be hunted down like the dogs you are."

Rumbling started deep in Weylyn's chest and grew

louder. Aedan looked over at him and saw his nose scrunched up and his lip pulled up away from his teeth. Weylyn's jaw was set in an unconscious warning to Aedan. Wrapping his fingers around his dagger, Aedan prepared for battle. Fortunately, Brietta's voice broke their focus. Weylyn looked over at her, her eyes going from one to the other concern deepening her brow. Trying to smile, Weylyn nodded.

"She is asking for you," Brietta went on.

"I am coming," Weylyn said. "Ken this, lad," he turned back to Aedan. "I have lived long and I have seen many things, donnae test me." Weylyn walked away from him and headed towards his mate leaving Aedan standing alone.

"Alexina, Weylyn is here," Brietta's soft voice soothed her. Slowly opening her eyes, Alexina saw Weylyn standing beside the bed.

"Weylyn," she said softly smiling.

"How are you?" He asked gently. She let out a small breathy laugh. "I ken, foolish question, I am sorry." She reached out for his hand, her fingers like ice against his hundred and two degree skin. He sat down on the side of the bed and clutched her hands in his to warm them. "Should we move you to the fire?"

"Nay, I am well," she said. "I wanted to thank you, Weylyn for being so kind to me."

"There is no need," he said.

"There is need," she interrupted. "I also have a request."

"Name it," he offered. Before she spoke, her face contorted in pain as her body clenched in another contraction. Gripping his hand tightly, Alexina cried out. Isla reached over and soothed her hair out of her face. Once the pain subsided, Alexina opened her eyes again.

"I am sorry," she said releasing her grip on Weylyn's hand.

"'Tis all right," he replied not removing his hand from hers. "What is your request, Alexina?"

"'Tis rather… personal," she began. "My husband is nae here. I ken he desires to be, but he cannae. Could you… stay with me? Just for a little while?"

"Aye of course," Weylyn replied knowing Tristan would want him to help her.

Helping lift her, he slid in behind, angled on the bed with his back resting against the wall and his legs over the side. He pulled her gently back to him so that her back rested on his chest. She was far too warm, he thought as he felt her heat against his tunic. Her hands were cold but the rest of her was burning. Moving her hair from sticking to the back of her neck, he felt her relax against him as she leaned her head back onto his shoulder, closed her eyes and sighed.

"You were right, Brietta," Alexina said softly. "He *is* very comfortable."

Brietta laughed when his eyes flew up at hers.

"I told her you were a very comforting and gentle man," Brietta said. "And I see age has nae changed you."

He did not know what to say but as soon as he opened his mouth to respond, Alexina's body clenched again. She cried out and he held her close to him rubbing her arms gently.

"Shh, shh," he soothed. "'Tis all right. It will soon be over."

The pain subsided and she laid her head back on his shoulder and released her grip on his knee.

Looking up at Brietta, realizing the pain that she must have gone through bringing Aedan into the world, Weylyn's heart clenched with fear and for a moment, he was glad their union had not been blessed with a child. He was not sure he would have been able to survive seeing her in so much pain.

Chapter Ten

An hour or so later, Weylyn stepped outside. Alexina had released him when the contractions started coming closer together and she saw the desperation in his eyes. He did not know what to do. Thinking a long run would clear his head, he decided to run the perimeter once more. Aedan looked up from his seat, an old tree stump between the window to his mother's room and doorway of the cottage where he sharpened a rough looking knife with a stone.

"How is she?" Aedan asked testing the knife's sharpness.

"Soon," Weylyn answered. "It willnae be long now. I am going for a run through the woods," Weylyn said.

"Desire companionship?" Aedan asked not looking up at him.

Weylyn looked over and eyed him up and down as if assessing him.

"Do you think you can keep up?" Weylyn asked and half-phased.

Aedan did not look up as he slid the knife into the sheath

on his calf. Finally looking at Weylyn, he stood, determination written on his face.

"Lead on," he replied. Weylyn chuckled silently knowing no human could run at wolf speed.

Bounding off at his usual pace, Weylyn sensed Aedan running right behind him, but for only a moment.

"Brietta," Isla's voice from the doorway startled her. Turning from the fire, her hand clutching a leather strap, Brietta locked eyes with her daughter-in-law. "I am sorry. I did nae mean to startle you," Isla continued.

"Nay, my dear, 'tis quite all right," Brietta answered. "How is Alexina?"

"She is resting for as much time as she is able," Isla replied. "I am afraid I have little experience in this."

"You are a wonderful help," Brietta said.

"No' being a mother somewhat hinders my help," Isla replied.

"Och, my dear," she said cupping her daughter-in-law's face. "Your time will come."

"I want to give Aedan a son," she looked down. "But you ken the reason behind my reticence."

"I do," Brietta replied twisting the leather strap in her hand.

"What is that?" Isla asked.

Brietta smiled and held it out. The leather bracelet was carved with interwoven designs and fringe ties on the end; it was brown in color and well cared for.

"This was Weylyn's wedding gift to me," Brietta explained. "It was something I would wear to show the world that I was taken. That I was his."

"There is a carving on it," Isla replied. "What is it?"

"It is our names woven together in the language of the wolf," Brietta answered.

"You kept it all these years?" Isla asked.

"Of course," she said. "Imagine something that Aedan gave you at your wedding or on your wedding night. Do you still have it?"

Isla smiled. "Aye," she replied.

"Well then," Brietta answered. "I loved… love Weylyn just as much as you love Aedan."

"You only had one night together?" Isla asked sitting on the wooden bench in front of the fire.

"Then, aye, one beautiful, wedding night," she answered.

"And now after all these years," Isla said. "Do you think he will be able to stay with you finally?"

"Look at me," Brietta replied. "And look at him. He is still young, I am… He is so wonderful to tell me that I am still beautiful but the truth is he sees me as I once was."

"How can you be so sure?" She asked. "Would he no' see you as the woman he kenned you would become? A wonderful mother, and an extraordinary woman, one that I pray I can emulate?"

"Och my sweet girl," Brietta sighed as tears threatened her eyes. "There is so much I want to tell you…"

"About what?" Isla asked gently.

"About…" Brietta started. She could not continue as they heard Aedan and Weylyn coming back from their run.

"How could you possibly go that fast?" Aedan asked, panting. Weylyn chuckled.

"'Tis a gift," he replied. Aedan bent over, put his hands

on his knees and breathed deeply.

"Whoo," he sighed. "And I am the fastest in the village."

"Well I was going as fast as I could... just to show off," Weylyn winked putting a hand on Aedan's back. For the first time, Weylyn heard Aedan laugh.

"I am beginning to like you, Weylyn," he said.

"Good," Weylyn smiled. "Aedan, I—" Before he could continue, Maelogan came out of the barn and headed towards them. "Any change?" Weylyn asked Maelogan as he approached.

"No' that I am aware of," Maelogan said. "How was the perimeter?"

"Quiet," Weylyn replied. "But I am sure it willnae be long before they find us."

"When they do, I will take the roof of the house," Maelogan said. "I see better higher up."

"I work best hand-to-hand," Weylyn explained. "Aedan?"

"I am the same," Aedan replied looking at Weylyn.

"Knives?" Weylyn asked.

Aedan pulled them out from the sheaths that were strapped to his forearms and handed them to Weylyn.

"You may want to rub some wolf's bane on them," Maelogan offered.

An unconscious snarl escaped through Weylyn's teeth as his eyes snapped up to his.

"It will do more damage," Maelogan said. "My arrow tips are already coated in them."

At that moment Weylyn could smell it and it made him sick.

"I am famished," Aedan said. "Let us go inside, eat and gain strength for the fight."

"I ate earlier today," Weylyn stated. "You two go."

They both headed into the house just as another crippling scream came from Alexina. Weylyn took a deep breath. Maelogan walked out of the house almost immediately with a platter of food. They locked eyes and Maelogan shook his head.

"I cannae stay in there," he said. "No' with the child coming. I will go eat in the barn." Maelogan walked past him.

Weylyn paced up and down waiting, hoping, praying all would be well. It was only a few moments later when a scent tickled his nose; the scent he had tracked hundreds of times; the stench that churned his stomach.

Druid.

Weylyn whipped around abruptly, his eyes yellowed. He was not quite in a full half-phase, but he was ready to pounce on whomever it was sneaking up behind him. Isla stood just outside the cottage door with a cup of something steaming in her hand.

"Brietta thought you might like something to drink," she offered the cup to him. "I thought you might want something hot... In case you were chilled," her breath swirled in front of her.

"You ken better than that," Weylyn's eyes still burned yellow as he stared at her.

She looked down and set the drink on the stump of the tree beside the house.

"It was merely an offering, refuse it if you so wish," she said and turned to go back inside.

"I ken the kind of offerings you do," he replied harshly taking a step towards her. Turning, she defended herself.

"My sisters and I –" she started.

"There are more of you?" Weylyn's voice was low but intense. "This is *our* land!"

"My sisters live northwest on Skye," she went on. "I met and married Aedan ten years ago. I have lived separately from them for all that time."

"Does he ken?" Weylyn hissed.

"What?"

"Does Aedan ken what you are?" Weylyn demanded. She looked up at him and he saw the truth in her eyes: she had never told him.

"He is special, certainly you have seen it," she replied. "I did nae find it necessary to tell him."

"Another Druid lie!" He rebuked. "How do you think he is going to react when he does find out? Because he *will* find out."

"Please," she begged, her voice low as she took a step closer to him. "He does no' and I would like to keep it that way."

"I could smell it on you the moment you entered the room," Weylyn said. "Your red hair and honey brown eyes, I have kenned several druids in my day they were always beautiful. Is that how you ensnared Aedan?"

"They say that is where you wolf people get your beauty," she answered. A deep, menacing growl from Weylyn's chest stopped her from continuing.

"We have nothing to do with you," he replied harshly.

"Nay?" She asked. "What about all of my kin that were killed by yours?"

Weylyn took a step closer to her, his yellow eyes blazing.

"What about all of mine your kind roasted on a spit while they were still alive and ate just to satisfy your deranged ideas of what the gods wanted you to do?" His voice was low and intense.

"It has been a long time since that has happened," she

said.

"But it happened," he replied.

"Aye, but your kind also killed countless druids," she answered.

"It was war," he growled.

"Aye it was," she replied. "A bitter, bitter war. One I hope will be over very soon." She took a step closer to him. "But as much as my kin hates yours, Brietta trusts you with her life, loves you," Isla said. "And that is enough for me. I am willing to overlook our kin's history with each other if you are. That woman in there and her unborn child need both of us."

"You could ease her pain," he murmured.

"No' without revealing who I am," she admitted.

"So you will let her suffer?" He demanded.

"Aedan means more to me than anything," she finally answered. "I ken you will never trust me, but I ask you to join me in overlooking our strained history and help those we love. I love Aedan and Brietta," Isla went on. "And if Brietta loves you that is enough for me. I will do what I can starting with this." He watched her as she bent down and gathered an amount of small white flowers at his feet. "Do you ken what this is?" She asked

"Moon flower," he replied.

"And do you ken what it does?" She asked.

"It is tea," he answered.

"Aye, but as it is boiled down in the water for tea it becomes a very powerful weapon, one that no' many people ken how to use," she explained. "It gives wolves the ability to handle the smell of wolf's bane. But it only works on the senses. Pour it on a piece of cloth and wrap it around your mouth and nose, you cannae smell the poison. It does nae work internally. If you are poisoned it cannae stop the progression to your heart." She reached for the mug she had brought out with her.

"Do you have a cloth I could use?" She asked. His brows pulled together but he ripped a piece of his tunic and handed it to her. She stared at him as she pushed the cloth into the mug. "I brought this drink out for two reasons," she went on. "One, because it is awfully good tea, but also to show you that I want to help," twisting the cloth, she wrung it out drying it almost completely.

"Wrap it around your nose and mouth." He looked at her skeptically as the voice inside his head that had never lead him astray told him that he could trust her and for some reason he listened to it. Taking the cloth slowly, he raised it to his nose and sniffed. It smelled of flowers, the smell was enchanting. He held it to his mouth and nose and watched as she slowly pulled out the wolf's bane she had from earlier. His eyes widened and his body convulsed into a half-phase.

"Be easy," she said gently. "'Tis only a test. Can you smell it?"

He waited, hesitant to breathe in, but finally, he took a deep breath, brows furrowed and he shook his head. She looked directly into his eyes and raised the flower higher. Instinctually, he took a step back.

"And now?" She asked. Again he took a deep breath through the cloth and shook his head. "And now?" She placed it directly under his cloth covered nose.

His eyes grew wide as he shook his head again. She smiled and lowered the flower.

"So you ken I am no' trying to trick you with a different flower, I will put it in my pocket. Take the mask off," she said. "Can you smell the residual?" He removed the cloth, took a deep breath and groaned. The smell was intense, it burned his nose and throat. "There," she grinned. "Shall we call it a truce?"

"Stalemate," he replied.

"Whatever you wish," she replied.

"I still donnae understand why you are doing this," he said.

"Honestly neither do I," she answered. "All my life I have been at battle with your kind. But I have a feeling you and I will need each other again soon."

A cry from Alexina stopped them, Weylyn started towards the door, but Isla held him back as Brietta called through the window.

"Isla, it is time, I need you."

"Please donnae tell my husband," she said.

Weylyn's yellow eyes faded and his brown human eyes returned.

"You have my word," he said.

"Thank you," Isla reached out and touched his arm. Flinching, he drew back and Isla turned away heading back into the cottage.

Chapter Eleven

Weylyn blocked out Alexina's screams as she delivered the child. She cried out for Tristan several times as Weylyn paced outside the window wishing he could help her. Feeling the moon's rays on his back, he turned and looked up. The snow clouds parted and the moon shown down on his face. Aedan walked out of the cottage and took a deep cleansing breath.

"Hoo," Aedan let it out. "I am very glad I am nae a woman." Weylyn was too focused on Alexina's cries to reply. "Where is Maelogan?" Aedan asked.

"Barn," Weylyn answered simply as another cry came from the house.

"Are you warm enough?" Aedan asked as he pulled his cloak tighter around him.

"Aye, I am fine," Weylyn replied closing his eyes as he turned up to the moon.

"What is it about moonlight?" Aedan sighed. "It feels so warm. Warmer than sunlight, truly."

Weylyn looked sharply over at him, brows drawn down at him surprised.

"Is something the matter?" Aedan asked.

"That is a surprisingly accurate remark," Weylyn said. "How is it that a human can feel that?"

"I have always loved the moon," Aedan replied looking up. "There is something about it that has always called to me."

Weylyn tilted his head watching him. Aedan closed his eyes and took a deep breath.

"You are a very strange human," Weylyn said.

"And you are a very strange wolf," he replied.

Just as Weylyn chuckled, letting some of the tension ease from his shoulders, he heard a baby's cry from the cottage.

"Thank the gods," he sighed.

"All is well," Aedan slapped his shoulder. "Praise be to the gods."

"Weylyn!" It was Brietta calling to him from the cottage. "She is well and asking for you."

Leaving Aedan outside, Weylyn entered the room where Alexina lay with her back against the wall holding an infant. His breath caught when she looked up at him and grinned, she glowed. Isla and Brietta smiled up at Weylyn and took the linens to be washed, leaving the room and the two of them alone.

At Alexina's beckoning, Weylyn sat on the edge of the bed. She looked back down at her child and raised her arms so Weylyn could see.

"'Tis a girl," she grinned.

Weylyn smiled looking at the tiny sleeping baby wrapped in a blanket.

"She is beautiful," he replied.

"I want to name her after my mother, Giorsal," she said.

"Do you think Tristan would be all right with that?"

"I do. I think 'tis very appropriate," he answered.

"Can you...?" She asked tentatively.

"I thought it scared you," he said smiling slightly.

"No' anymore," she replied. "I want him to see our daughter."

Weylyn smiled and stroked the little girl's cheek. Waiting until he was sure the baby was asleep before he phased, his body convulsed and he felt the hot spike run through Tristan's side. Biting his tongue to stop his cry of pain, Weylyn spoke to his Alpha.

Tristan, he called. *There is someone who I am sure you will want to see.*

There was no answer as Tristan screamed.

This is your daughter. Weylyn opened his eyes and looked down at the baby in Alexina's arms. He felt every pain Tristan felt melt away when he saw what Weylyn showed him. Tears streamed down Tristan's cheeks.

She is so beautiful, Tristan whimpered.

Aye she is that, lad and Alexina is doing just fine. She had such strength. She wanted to tell you something, Weylyn said.

He looked at Alexina and nodded. She stared into Weylyn's yellow eyes and spoke to her husband.

"Tristan," she began. "This is your daughter. She is so beautiful and a fighter, like her father. I need to tell you how much I love you and I want you to fight. You have to hold her. You will survive this. You are strong. Husband, ken that I love you and I will see you again very soon. Until then, remember us and fight with every fiber of your being. Stay alive, my love. Please, for us."

What is her name? Tristan asked.

"He wants to ken her name," Weylyn said to Alexina.

"If 'tis all right with you, husband," she started. "I want to name her after my mother; Giorsal."

Aye, Tristan answered. *That is a perfect name for our lass. Alex, I love you and I swear I will fight.*

Weylyn spoke his words aloud for Alexina to hear then gave his pupil words of his own.

I am coming for you soon, Weylyn said.

Gods, nay! They are coming for you! Tristan screamed. *Marrock just order twenty wolves that were following your scent to a cottage west of Aberlyall. He kens where you are!*

How? Weylyn demanded.

Someone you are with. Donnae trust anyone, Weylyn. And Weylyn... If I donnae make it out of here alive... promise me you will take care of them, Tristan begged.

As my own, I swear it, Weylyn promised.

Give her your love and name, for me please, Tristan pleaded.

To both, I swear it, Weylyn said. *You will survive and you will have a long life with your wife and daughter.*

Weylyn heard another cry from Tristan as his flesh was ripped from his shoulder and dangled in front of him tauntingly.

"What is wrong?" Alexina cried when Weylyn shouted in pain. "Weylyn? Is Tristan all right?"

Go now, protect her. They will be there in a very short time, Tristan ordered.

Weylyn bowed his head hearing his Alpha's command.

Nay! No order, Tristan's mind yelled. *I am sorry. No order. Just go please.*

I promise you, Tristan, I will protect your Queen and your child. On my life, I swear it, Weylyn promised.

Wait! Let me see her once more, please, Tristan begged.

Weylyn looked down at the tiny sleeping baby in her mother's arms and Tristan took a long look.

Thank you. Tell my daughter that I love her… and please tell Alexina I love her more than the heather on the hills. She will ken what I mean. His mind cried as tears ran down his cheeks.

I will. I must go now, Weylyn said.

Weylyn phased back to human form just as Tristan screamed again. Weylyn paled and covered his mouth feeling like he was going to vomit.

"What is wrong?" Alexina asked. "Is he all right?"

"He saw his daughter, heard what you said and he told me to tell you both that he loves you and to tell you that he loves you more than the heather on the hills. He said you would understand what that meant," Weylyn said.

Tears streamed down Alexina's face as she nodded.

"Is he in a great amount of pain?" She asked.

Weylyn looked at her and, knowing she was strong enough to handle the truth, answered.

"Aye, but he is strong." She closed her eyes causing the tears welling up to spill down her cheeks. Weylyn gently brushed them away. "But now, we must prepare. Marrock has sent twenty wolves to our location."

"How did he ken where to find us?" She challenged.

"I have an idea," his words burned with hatred as his eyes turned towards to the living room where Isla stood with Brietta talking softly. "We need to get you away from the window and somewhere you will be safe. If we can douse you with wolf's bane, it might help dissuade them from coming to you."

"What about Giorsal?" She asked concerned looking

down at her child. "Will that hurt her?"

"I am no' sure. I have nae dealt with a half bre— wolf before," he said checking his language before he offended her.

"Giorsal will be fine," they heard Isla say from the doorway. "Wolf's bane only affects those wolves who have phased before. Since she is a newborn, she willnae be affected by it. It would be best to cover you in the oil."

"What about you?" Alexina looked at Weylyn.

"I will be fine," he replied. "Brietta, Isla, take care of her. Aedan! Maelogan!"

Weylyn went outside and was greeted by the two men.

"How is she?" Aedan asked.

"She is doing very well," Weylyn said. "She has had a daughter."

"A female?" Maelogan asked surprised. "'Tis a shame."

"Logan!" Aedan was shocked. "Women have every right to be born."

"But what good can come of it?" He asked. "She cannae fight."

"Enough," Weylyn ordered. "Now, there are about twenty wolves headed our way. How are you stocked?"

"I have enough," Maelogan said gesturing to his arrows.

"Good," he replied. "Aedan?"

"Sharp and ready to go," he replied touching the handles of his knives strapped to his forearms.

"Good," Weylyn replied. "Your claymore willnae be of any use to you. The wolves will attack too quickly for you to utilize the long blade. Knives will be best." Aedan nodded once and took off his broadsword. Disappearing inside the cottage for a moment, he immerged without the weapon. "Maelogan, you take up high. We have below covered," Weylyn directed.

Maelogan nodded and went to climb up to the roof just as they heard a howl in the distance.

"They are closer than I thought," Aedan replied twisting his neck back and forth loosening his muscles. Feeling something cold and wet hit his cheek, he looked up and saw more snowflakes had begun to fall. "At least it is snowing. That might slow them down."

"I doubt it," Weylyn said. "They are no' affected by the cold. Are you ready?"

Aedan pulled out his knives and twirled them around with some flourish. He took a stance when they heard another howl from the woods, much closer that time. Weylyn looked back at Maelogan who nodded once drawing back his bow. Weylyn's eyes caught Aedan's.

"If I donnae make it through this, Aedan," Weylyn began. "Could you do me a favor?"

"Namely?" Aedan asked.

"Tell your mother I love her, now and forever, please be sure to say those words," Weylyn said. Aedan took a deep breath but nodded and pledged that he would. "Then with that, I say to battle." He stretched his arm to Aedan in a warrior's salute. Aedan stared at it for a long moment but accepted his offering in a firm shake. As soon as they let go, Weylyn convulsed into a half-phase.

"They are coming," Weylyn's voice was gruff, as he flexed his claws and took a deep breath coughing when he caught the scent of wolf's bane inside the house.

"Weylyn!" Isla yelled a moment later. Turning in time, Weylyn caught the towel she threw to him. The familiar scent of moon flower clung to it. Glaring at her, Weylyn gritted his teeth against her feigned confusion.

Tying the towel around his nose and mouth, Weylyn turned away from her as she shut the door and barred it. Aedan leaned over to him without taking his eyes off the forest.

"What do you see?" Aedan asked.

"About twenty fully phased wolves," Weylyn answered, his voice muffled by the towel and the half-phase.

"Are they more dangerous fully phased?" Aedan asked.

"Nay," Weylyn replied. "Less dexterity but more unpredictable."

Aedan did not answer as the snow began to fall heavier around them and the wind bit sharply.

"Are you well?" Weylyn asked seeing he wore nothing but his thin tunic and leggings.

"Aye, I never wear my furs to battle, they have only gotten in the way," Aedan answered, his breath swirling before him. "They are here," Aedan went on. Weylyn saw the yellow eyes of the wolves glaring at them still in the cover of the woods. Turning back to Aedan, Weylyn did not question how the Celt Highlander could see them so far away and focused on the battle. There would be plenty of time after the fight to talk to Aedan. The wolves were stalking them, keeping mostly to the shadows of the trees and out of the moonlight. Weylyn's claws clenched and unclenched waiting for the twitchy newer wolves to break ranks.

He knew them all.

Finally exactly what he expected to happen, happened; one impatient wolf charged them.

"Scrymgeour," the leader, still in the trees, bellowed. "Hold!" But the wolf did not and Weylyn sent him flying back to the woods with a single backhanded strike across his snout.

"Conchor," Weylyn growled.

"You ken the leader?" Aedan asked.

"Aye, my father trained him," Weylyn replied.

"Is he a good warrior?" Aedan questioned.

"He is ruthless," Weylyn said.

"Glad to see you remember something about me, Weylyn," the voice from the woods called. Weylyn did not answer.

"Protect Alexina and the child at all costs," Weylyn called. Aedan took a stance beside him, his knives in hand.

"My mother and my wife as well," Aedan said through clenched teeth.

"Agreed," Weylyn answered.

Immediately leaping into action as two wolves charged them, Aedan and Weylyn stood back to back. Aedan's skill with the knives was impressive. Weylyn moved with him in harmony as if they were dancing.

Maelogan stood on the thatched roof of the cottage firing a slew of arrows from his bow. Weylyn did not have time to watch him but saw his aftermath. Several wolves fell before they reached the two men. Their cries as they felt the wolf's bane coated tips ram into them made Weylyn hate what was happening.

But as wolf after wolf charged him, all he could think of were the lives Marrock had taken or destroyed. *No' today...* he pledged. *No' ever again... never again will Marrock hurt those I love.* With that as his battle cry, Weylyn fought.

Chapter Twelve

After some time had passed, the wolves retreated into the woods to regroup. Panting from exertion, Weylyn and Aedan paused for a moment by the well taking the bucket they had filled earlier and dumping the icy contents on their heads. The shock to their overheated bodies cleansed them of the fatigue they were experiencing. A scratch just above his eye bothered Weylyn as his blood dripped down, blurring his vision.

Aedan tore off his tunic and stood in his leggings bare-chested. Tanned, muscled, scarred, Weylyn saw the warrior in him. But what concerned Weylyn was the blood dripping from a large gash on Aedan's forearm.

"I am all right," Aedan replied waving him off.

"Aedan, let me look at it," Weylyn demanded. Showing his arm to the wolf, Aedan kept his eyes on the woods. "Did they bite you?"

"Aye, damned animals," Aedan answered. When Weylyn did not answer, Aedan looked over at him. "Does that mean something?" Aedan asked. Weylyn did not speak. "Tell me!" he barked.

"You will turn," he said.

"Turn? Turn into a wolf?" Aedan asked. "Like you?"

"Nay, no' like me," Weylyn replied. "When a human is bitten by a wolf, they cannae phase back into human form after their first phase. They lose all sense of humanity and become wolves, actual wolves no' wolf-men." Without missing a beat, Aedan pulled his arm from Weylyn's grasp and grabbed his tunic. Ripping the tunic into strips, he wrapped a strip tightly around the wound.

"How long do I have?" Aedan asked, devoid of emotion.

"'Till moon rise tomorrow night," Weylyn replied.

"Incoming!" They heard Maelogan yell.

"Donnae tell Isla," Aedan ordered.

"She needs to ken," Weylyn replied.

"I said nay!" Aedan cried as he fought the next wolf to appear.

Crying a battle cry Weylyn had never heard, Aedan swiped his knife across the wolf's throat with a snarl and a satisfied grunt. Weylyn watched the human's strength in shock but quickly focused on the battle and continued to fight.

Again the wolves retreated into the woods.

"I am impressed, Weylyn," that same silky voice called. "I can hardly believe that three men were able to defeat twenty of the best."

"Come on out yourself, Conchor," Weylyn called.

"Och," Conchor said. "Now now, you ken a leader does nae get his hands dirty."

"What do you want?" Aedan demanded.

"'Tis very simple. Marrock wants that whore of a human and the half-breed spawn," Conchor said.

"He cannae have them," Weylyn replied simply.

"You ken whatever Marrock wants, he gets. Faolán can attest to that," Conchor said.

"You can have them over my dead body," Weylyn replied.

"I believe Marrock would agree to that," Conchor said just as another five wolves jumped through the threshold of the forest in a surprise attack. Maelogan killed two of them before they reached Weylyn and Aedan. When those were killed or mortally wounded limping back to the pack, Weylyn phased to his human form and held up his hands.

"Conchor, stop this now," he pleaded. "I donnae want to kill any more of my brothers. Go back and tell Marrock that he cannae have her or the child."

"Always the diplomat, Weylyn," Conchor answered. "So she has given birth, then? Good. Marrock will be interested to ken that." Weylyn's eye twitched. "What is it, Weylyn? A boy? A weakling of a girl? Marrock has said what he would do to half-breeds. You above anyone should remember. How is that whore of a human you mated with, hmm? Thanks to you every mate we take has to be accepted by the Alpha and if he does nae like the match then he forbids it, and 'tis all thanks to you."

"That is in the past," Weylyn said feeling Aedan's eyes on him. "You ken very well that she died in child birth with another man's child."

"Did she?" Conchor asked. "That is unfortunate… I was hoping you would introduce us since you were always so close." Weylyn felt the charged air around the human beside him. Luckily, Conchor went on. "Very well, Weylyn, we will return to Marrock, but your Alpha will pay for those you killed here today."

"They are retreating," they heard Maelogan say as he crouched low, still on the roof.

Once they were sure the wolves would not attack again, Aedan looked to Weylyn and asked the question that had been burning in his heart since he heard the wolf speak.

"Because you loved my mother the Alpha changed the laws?" Aedan asked quietly.

"Aedan, I love her more than life itself," Weylyn replied. "But no wolf had mated with a human before and Marrock is a tyrant for tradition no' to mention he hates all humans. He also did nae ken what a child from our union would be."

"That was invigorating," Maelogan said smiling as he walked up to them.

"Aedan," Weylyn reached for his arm bleeding through the bandage. "How do you feel?"

"I am fine," Aedan waved him off. "It does no' even hurt."

"That is nae possible," Weylyn said shaking his head.

"What?" Maelogan asked looking from one to the other.

"Nothing," Aedan replied. "Can you go inside and make sure the women are all right?"

"Of course," Maelogan answered and headed towards the door.

"Let me see your arm," Weylyn said. Aedan sheathed his knives and showed him. Taking it gingerly in his hand, Weylyn unwrapped the cloth. "I thank you for your assistance this eve. You fought well," Weylyn complimented.

"It was war. I am fairly adept at fighting in a war," Aedan answered.

"Have you fought in a war before?" Weylyn asked.

"Aye, I have," Aedan replied and from his tone, Weylyn knew he would speak no more about it.

"Your father would be proud of you," Weylyn said.

"You ken nothing of it," Aedan shouted harshly.

"I meant no offence. Merely that any father would be proud to call you his son," Weylyn answered. "There is no need to be angry with me."

"Is there no'?" Aedan asked. "Because of you I am to lose my humanity tomorrow. To never again see my wife or even ken who I was. None of this would have happened if you had just left when we arrived."

"You are wrong," Weylyn said. "If we had left, the wolves would have been here still and killed your mother and that I couldnae allow. I am truly sorry for it."

"Sorry?" Aedan demanded.

"Aye, trust me if I kenned how to reverse the process I would," Weylyn replied.

"Or would you let me die? I ken your kind. You have no love of humans. All you have ever wanted is Mother. You. Cannae. Have her."

"That is nae true," Weylyn said. "'Tis true I love your mother but I would never sacrifice her only son just to be with her! What can I do to convince you?"

"Get out and take that half-breed with you!" Aedan cried.

Weylyn's hand swiped across Aedan's face in a hard slap. Aedan looked back at him stunned.

"That is my Alpha's wife and child you speak of," Weylyn snapped. "I ken you are angry but I donnae think you are in any danger."

"What do you mean?" Aedan questioned.

"There is no sign of the poison," Weylyn explained. "Wolf saliva carries with it a poison to humans but only when we bite. It discolors the skin leaving it red and the veins that carry the poison to the heart turn red as well. You have no sign of discoloration."

"Maybe I wasnae bitten then," Aedan said, his voice suddenly lighter.

"The teeth marks are clearly visible," Weylyn replied observing the wound. Touching Aedan's arm, Weylyn felt the heat radiating off it. "Are you feeling all right?" He asked touching Aedan's forehead. He was far too warm especially standing in the snow without a tunic. He burned with fever.

"I am fine. I have never been better actually," Aedan said not pulling away from him.

"You are very warm," Weylyn replied concerned.

Aedan pulled his arm free and took a step back. "Am I infected or no'?"

"I donnae ken," Weylyn said.

"Then I would like to go see my wife now," he said turning away from Weylyn and heading into the house.

Aedan went straight to Isla and kissed her. Stunned she looked up and stroked his face. "Are you all right?" Isla asked.

"Never better," Aedan replied. "I love you."

She looked up into his brown eyes concerned but smiled and gently kissed him back.

"I love you, too, Aedan," she said. "You are hurt." Seeing the wound rewrapped in strips of his tunic, she looked up at him worried.

"A scratch," Aedan answered. "It will heal."

Weylyn entered, nodding to Maelogan who stood by the door. Brietta rushed to him and wrapped her arms around him holding him close to her.

"Is everything all right, my love?" She asked him.

Weylyn nodded.

"Can I take this off?" he asked indicating his mask.

"We got rid of the wolf's bane when we heard Maelogan jump down from the roof but there may be a residual smell," Isla turned from her husband and explained. "I used moon flower on the places we had the wolf's bane to counteract the smell."

Weylyn untied the towel around his face and took a deep breath. Smiling at Alexina who sat resting on the wooden bench in front of the fire; her daughter asleep in her arms.

"Is everything all right?" Brietta asked. Touching his forehead to hers, he kissed her gently.

"Aye it will be, once *she* is gone," Weylyn said turning to look at Isla.

"Excuse me?" Isla asked seeing Weylyn look at her.

"You told Marrock where we were," he said pulling away from Brietta.

"What are you talking about?" Aedan demanded, wrapping his arm around Isla's waist pulling her closer to him.

"I ken it was you," Weylyn went on. "Tristan told me that someone in our group told Marrock where we were and only a *Druid* would ken how to communicate with the Alpha of a pack."

"Weylyn!" Isla and Brietta cried together.

"What?" Weylyn demanded taking a step closer to her. "'Tis true, is it no'? Donnae deny it. You would do good coming clean."

"I have nothing to hide," Isla said.

"Besides being a Druid?" Weylyn demanded, his eyes flaring yellow.

"You gave me your word!" she cried.

"This changes things, when you betray those I love, things change," he said taking another step towards to her.

"Isla..." Aedan said softly looking down at her and slowly

removing his arm from around her waist. "Is it true?"

"Aedan," she started turning towards him.

"Tell me," he said quietly. She was silent and looked from one face to another.

"'Tis true I am a Druid, but I did nae do what he is accusing me of doing," she said.

"You lied to me?" He stated backing away from her slowly.

"Aedan, I love you. You ken who I am," she said stepping closer to him only to see him step back.

"Do I?" he asked. "You are a druid… that is important… why did you never tell me?"

"Because I…" she tried to think but all she could do was to look over at Brietta helpless. Brietta stepped away from Weylyn and went over to her wrapping an arm around Isla's shoulders.

"I told her no' to, son," Brietta answered.

"Mother?"

"Brietta?" Aedan and Weylyn said together.

"I kenned," Brietta replied simply. "She told me what she was when you first brought her here. She kenned you were falling in love with her as she was with you. She wanted to tell you, but wanted my advice on how to do it. I told her it did nae matter and that you would love her no matter what but to no' say anything for the sake of your position in the village."

"Did nae matter?" Aedan cried. "She is a druid!"

"Brietta, do you no' ken what her kind did to mine?" Weylyn asked.

"Aye, I do," she answered. "But we are all guilty of things, Weylyn," Brietta went back to him and touched his chest over his heart. "Was I to judge her? The sins of her kin were nae to fall on her shoulders, no more than the sins of yours falls on you." She reached up and gently stroked his face. He leaned in to her touch wanting so very badly to kiss her again.

"I swear to you both," Isla said looking at Aedan and Weylyn. "I did nae tell *anyone*. I was with Alexina the whole time."

"It is true, Weylyn," Alexina said from the bench where she held her daughter. Weylyn turned to her. "She was with me the whole time, apart from the few moments she was out with you. It couldnae have been her."

"If it was no' you..." Weylyn started, looking at Isla. "Then who told Marrock where we were?"

A quiet chuckle from behind him made him turn. Weylyn came face-to-face with Maelogan's bow with an arrow nestled and drawn back. He stood by the door a few feet from Weylyn.

"Me," Maelogan replied and let the arrow fly.

"Nay!" Brietta screamed stepping in front of Weylyn, her sharp gasp echoed in Weylyn's ears.

"Brietta!" Weylyn shouted.

The arrow had pierced her chest and forced her back into Weylyn's arms.

Maelogan ran out of the house. Aedan followed, his knives already drawn. Searching the area for his traitorous best friend, Aedan could not see anything. His breath swirled in front of him, his body shook, his mind raced and his heart pounded as he gripped his knives tightly. He had known Maelogan for over twenty years, he had welcomed him as a brother, had entrusted his wife's life to him, had fought with him, laughed with him and he had betrayed him more brutally than any enemy ever could.

Hearing a whistle from the rooftop, Aedan turned and looked up to see a half-phased wolf on the roof, bow raised.

Maelogan smirked and widened his eyes so Aedan could see that they flared yellow. Maelogan let loose the arrow just as Isla ran out and threw herself on Aedan. The arrow landed in the grass beside them and Maelogan bounded away.

Isla looked up from her position on top of her husband and watched Maelogan disappear into the woods.

"Are you all right?" she asked Aedan looking down at him.

He nodded.

"Aye, are you?" he asked breathlessly.

"Aye," she answered.

"Maelogan is a—" Aedan started.

"Apparently," she said.

"Did you ken?" he flashed angry eyes towards her. She shook her head.

"Nay," she breathed.

"I must go after him," Aedan said getting up and heading towards the woods.

"Aedan," Isla pulled on his arm. "Your mother needs you."

Aedan's eyes grew wide as he remembered and ran back into the house, Isla close behind him.

Aedan's breath escaped him as he saw the scene before him; Weylyn cradled Brietta in his arms beside the fire, he was looking into her eyes as she struggled for breath, her blood soaked the front of her gown and the arrow still protruded from her chest. Alexina had rushed to Weylyn's side, one hand clutching Brietta's and the other resting silently, comfortingly on Weylyn's forearm. Aedan raced to her side opposite Weylyn as Isla knelt beside her husband. Aedan's pounding heartbeat rang in his ears and he almost did not hear Weylyn's soothing voice.

"'Tis all right," Weylyn said to her. "You are going to be fine, my love." Brietta looked into his eyes gaining strength from him. "Can you do something? Anything?" Weylyn begged Isla. "I will do anything, just save her, please."

Isla met his eyes and shook her head.

"I am sorry," she said as tears streamed down her cheeks. "'Tis too late."

"Brietta," Weylyn called softly to her, his voice shaking. "You are strong, stronger than me. You will survive this. Gods, why?" he demanded. The sound of her struggling to breathe was almost too much for him. He clutched her tighter in a subconscious attempt to take away her pain.

"This is your fault!" Aedan yelled at Weylyn. "If you had nae brought your curse here none of this would have happened!"

Weylyn looked over at the man kneeling beside Brietta. He would have happily taken that arrow considering what the alternative was; his mate was dying. He had no time to react as Aedan grabbed his knife from its sheath at his forearm and swiped at him catching Weylyn's cheek. Blood splattered on Brietta's face.

"Nay!" Brietta cried. Weylyn dodged the next attack but released his mate in order to defend himself.

"Aedan, stop this!" Isla cried holding Brietta. Ignoring his wife's pleas, Aedan charged Weylyn with the knife in his hand. Weylyn threw him off and toward the opposite wall.

"Make him stop," Brietta gasped.

"Aedan! Please! Your mother needs you!" Isla cried.

Aedan lost no time. When he righted himself, he grabbed a vial out of his pocket, gripped the cork in his teeth and pulled.

The smell of wolf's bane oil burned Weylyn's nose. Aedan poured it onto the knife just as Weylyn's body convulsed in a half-phase. The infant cried beside him and it distracted him just enough not to see Aedan's attack. Reacting too slowly, Weylyn cried out as the burn of wolf's bane made his arm go numb for a few seconds, fortunately not enough of the poison had gotten inside the wound.

"*Sguir dhth!* Please stop this," they heard from Brietta. Both men froze. "Aedan, stop now. Put it away. Weylyn, my love, I need you."

Both men looked at each other and when they saw the other comply, they did as well. Back in human form, Weylyn raced to her holding her close to him.

"Come here, please, both of you," Brietta's voice was weaker now. "My brave men, my lads…"

"Please donnae fight," Brietta said. "Donnae ever fight. I couldnae bear it."

"Mother, he brought this on us," Aedan replied.

"Nay," she reached up and stroked her son's cheek. "Nay, son he did nae."

"Look at what has happened to you," Aedan said realizing his eyes were filling with tears.

"It was nae his choice," she replied. "If you must blame someone, blame Marrock. None of this would have happened if we were allowed to be together."

"But you were no'. He left you," Aedan said through clenched teeth. "And look at you. Do you think, if Father was alive, he would have let this dog into our lives?" Weylyn snarled at him.

"Aye, he would have," she replied. "Because he kenned…" she could not breathe but forced the words out. "How much Weylyn means to me."

"My father was a good man. He would never have put your life in danger," Aedan bit out.

"Nay, Aedan, your father *is* a good man," she stressed. "And I am so very sorry..." her body reared back in pain. "You donnae ken... This is nae Weylyn's fault. I did this. I stepped in front and I would gladly do it again."

"How can you defend him to me?" Aedan demanded. "Look at you!"

She closed her eyes for a moment. When she opened them, she looked straight into the eyes of her son.

"Because Weylyn is your father," she answered.

"What?" Aedan breathed. Weylyn froze. "What are you saying?"

"Gowan, my husband, the man you thought was your father, was my best friend. He married me kenning full well that I was with child, with you, son," she said. "Weylyn is your real father. You were conceived on our wedding night. He never kenned of you. Gowan took you as his own kenning you to be Weylyn's. You are a wolf, son, just like him. I am so sorry. I did nae tell you but Gowan wanted you as his own. He was so proud of you and loved you very much."

Aedan's breathing increased and he felt lightheaded. Looking over at Weylyn who knelt, stone faced, staring at Brietta, it was clear that Weylyn never knew either.

"Consider it, my dearest one," Brietta went on, struggling for air. "You are handsome, brilliant, fast, and you have the ability to see, hear, and smell things before anyone else. That is the wolf in you..." she closed her eyes against the pain. "You never phased, you donnae ken how. That is why, as Isla mentioned, you have no aversion to wolf's bane. And I am so sorry... Weylyn," she reached for him. Finally, he moved and inched closer to her, clutching her hand tighter and raising it to his chest. She felt his heart beat pounding as she reached up with her other hand and cupped his face. His rough prickly jaw scratched the palm of her hand in that all too familiar way. "You remember our night together, the night we pledged our love to each other and married under the moon? You told me wolves mate for life..." he nodded reaching up with his other hand and covering hers with his. He nuzzled his cheek against her hand and she smiled at the feeling. "My husband was such a good man and I loved him dearly. We never had any children but he took care of your son as his own. Forgive me, I was unfaithful to you."

"You are no' a wolf, Brietta," Weylyn said. "You were no' held to our pledge. I am glad you did nae waste your life waiting on me."

"I did love him, but it was a different type of love," she revealed. "He understood... and he still loved me. Donnae be angry with me for no' telling you about our son."

"I am no'... I am no' angry, Brietta, I promise," Weylyn said softly kissing the palm of her hand.

"I have always loved you," she said her eyes focused on him. "Always."

"And I have always loved you," Weylyn choked out as his tears welled in his eyes but he pushed them away. He wanted her to see him strong, not crying, even though his heart was being so cruelly ripped from him. "Donnae leave me... no' when I have finally found you again."

"Oh my love," she sighed and stroked his bristled jaw. "I am sorry, but Fate has a different path for me." Her eyes turned to her son then back at Weylyn. "Look at the two of you..." she said. "You look like brothers. Every day I could see him grow more and more like you, my love. It kept you with me always." Taking her hand back from Weylyn's face, she reached for her son. Aedan took his mother's outstretched hand. She gasped for air as tears ran down her cheeks.

"I donnae have much time. Alexina, it was such a wonderful joy to meet you... keep that little one safe. She is a fighter, just like you," Alexina nodded through her tears.

"Forgive us, Brietta, if we had nae come here," Alexina began.

"Shh," she soothed. "If you hadnae I would never have seen Weylyn again and my son would never ken his father." She turned to Isla and called to her. "You have been a wonderful addition to our family, my dearest," her tears rolled down her cheeks faster. "You have made my son happy and you have been an absolute treasure to me..." Isla wiped her tears from her eyes.

"It was an honor, Brietta," Isla said.

"Now my lads... my beautiful, beautiful lads... Forgive me... Aedan, every mother wonders what she will say to her son when she kens her time has come. Just ken that I love you so very much. You stay the good man and the good husband that you are. Donnae let this change you. You will be a wonderful father when your time comes. Listen to your heart," her hand went down to his chest where she felt his heartbeat. "It will guide you. I love you more than my own life, my darling boy. Donnae be angry with your father... or me. My love... Weylyn..." she clutched his arm as if her life depended on it.

He moved closer to her so she could see him and took her in his arms gently. She locked eyes with him. "Take care of our son," she said, her speech was soft and no longer broken with pain. Her body relaxed resigning to its fate. He nodded softly.

"I will. I swear to you, Brietta," he said.

"Kiss me, my love... one more time." Leaning down, he gently placed a kiss on her cold lips. He lingered just above her staring down at her, giving her strength. "*Tha gràdh agam...*" she whispered her love to him. He looked directly into her eyes.

"I love you too," he replied. "Always and forever." She tried to smile. "Be at peace, my love, you have done your family proud."

She took one more gasp of air and as she let it out, her hand slowly slid down his face and fell limp on the ground. Her eyes stayed fixed on his and he watched as life left them.

End of Part One

Part Two

Chapter One

Oblivious to Isla's and Alexina's cries, all Weylyn could hear was the pounding of his breaking heart. He leaned down to kiss Brietta one more time but there was no kiss back. Sitting back, he closed her eyes with a shaking hand.

Everything disappeared around him. There were no people, no cottage, no fire, just Brietta. The memory of their time together came back to him and he recalled the moment he first saw her, holding her in his arms as she slept with him in the woods on their wedding night, how she woke that next morning and kissed him as his wife. How they made love in the woods and how they never wanted to part.

Slowly, reality came back and his senses were heightened beyond measure; the women crying, the crackling of the fire, and the blowing of the winter wind and he was shaking. Shaking like a leaf in autumn just waiting for the wind to blow it down. Strong and weak at the same time. He knew what was coming and he had to leave. His wolf form refused to be suppressed. Rushing out of the cottage and into the cold air, he filled his lungs with the burning cold air. Tears stung his eyes as they froze to his skin.

Snow was falling in large flakes but the clouds parted for a moment revealing the moon high in the night sky. It was brilliantly white and, for the first time, felt cold to Weylyn. Everything around him was bitter and empty.

He felt it coming and did nothing to stop it. With a loud cry of despair, his complete phase overtook him and he burst into a wolf.

It felt strange being on four legs again but it was oddly comforting. Rearing his head back, a long, mournful howl escaped his mouth. His body trembled as he continued to weep. The low soft whimpers that escaped him sounded strange and he collapsed into a heap on the ground curled up in his own fur.

Brietta had been in his thoughts every moment of every day since. All those years he thought she was dead, only to be given half a day with her; he felt cheated. Why had he been able to find her just to lose her again and this time for forever?

Weylyn, I am so sorry, he heard Tristan's soft voice in his head.

Weylyn shook his head and blocked Tristan out. He wanted to be alone. He needed to be alone.

Soon after, Weylyn heard someone calling his name. Turning his massive face back to see who broke through his grief, his sad, yellow eyes looked full into Aedan's dark brown ones. He did not know if he had the strength to stand as tears glistened off the brown fur around Weylyn's eyes.

His son said nothing only looked deep into his eyes. That thought… *his son,* forced Weylyn to move and pull himself up to his full height. Towering over him, he stood over eight feet tall from paw to ears and over ten feet long from snout to tail.

So much about the Highlander before him made sense then, his ability to run faster than any human, to see the wolves in the woods when no human could have, the way he fought, the reason the wolf bite did not affect him, everything about him screamed wolf but Weylyn had been too blind to see it. How could Brietta have never told him he had fathered a child?

"Weylyn," Aedan said softly. "We must speak."

It took him a moment, but finally Weylyn phased back to human form but when he did, he wrapped the bit of plaid Aedan offered around his waist and took the buckle he had discarded.

"Isla and Alexina are taking care of Mother," Aedan stated.

"I never meant any harm to come to her," Weylyn said. "I would have given my life for her. As much as I wish to the gods that I had never come here, there is nothing I can do to fix it. And if I never did, I would never have kenned I was a father."

"You may have fathered me, Weylyn, but you are no' my father," Aedan replied. "Gowan was my father and when he died I strived to be just like him. I donnae ken who you are. To be a father means more than just fathering a child."

"Aye, I understand, but if you would allow me, I donnae want to replace Gowan, but I would like for us to be friends," Weylyn said.

"I can agree to that," Aedan replied. "Father was a good man and he took care of me and Mother. When he was killed by a wolf, I hated them. Mother had always taught me to care for the wolves. Now I ken why, I am one of them."

"I donnae ken who killed your father, Aedan," Weylyn said. "But I will help you find him. And when I find Maelogan, he will pay for what he did."

"I have lost my mother and my identity in one eve," he

said finally. "Who am I?"

"You are my son," Weylyn replied. "And I will be here for you... if you want me, that is."

Aedan looked at him.

"And if I donnae?" he asked.

Weylyn took a deep breath and nodded.

"As soon as Alexina is healthy enough to travel, we will leave and I will nae bother you again," he said softly. "But I ask you to let me mourn my mate properly. Give me until the next full moon to leave and allow me to tell you a little of your heritage."

"I want nothing to do with being a wolf," Aedan said.

"'Tis who you are, Aedan, you may no' desire it, but 'tis who you are," Weylyn replied.

"I never wanted any of this!" Aedan shouted. "I was perfectly happy until—"

"I came here," Weylyn said softly.

"Aye!" Aedan replied turning away from him and back towards the cottage. He was silent for a long moment before he took a deep breath. "I was a man, a highlander. I had an identity. I was a leader among my clan, respected, honored even. I was a son, a husband, a friend. Now I donnae have a mother... or a wife."

"You still have a wife, Aedan," Weylyn snapped. "And you are still a son. My son."

Aedan did not turn around and he did not move but after several moments, he nodded.

"You may stay for a moon's cycle. One. And that is all," Aedan said.

"And may I train you?" Weylyn asked.

Aedan did not answer for a moment but finally he

turned around.

"Aye," he said. "You may train me to phase."

Chapter Two

Brietta was laid out in her best gown, a thin veil covered her face and a wreath of moon flowers crowned her head. Weylyn stood beside her burial mound looking down at her lovely face. As was custom in their village, the family was having a private moment before the mound was covered.

"Weylyn," he heard Isla call at his elbow. He turned and looked down at her seeing her offer him something wrapped in a cloth. "Brietta would have wanted to be buried with this. I saw her looking at it the other day. She told me what it was. I think it is only right that you be the one to place it on her wrist."

He looked at her confused but took the small package. When he opened it, he felt his breath stop. Taking the leather bracelet gingerly in his hands, Weylyn rubbed a thumb over the engraving.

"What is it?" Aedan asked, having never seen it before.

"I gave this to her as a wedding gift," he explained looking over at Isla. "Thank you," he breathed. "It was an indication that she was mine," Weylyn explained reaching up to his collar and pulling out the medallion he wore around his neck. "This was her gift to me. Her father, the blacksmith, made it for her thinking it was a trinket for her to wear. We exchanged these gifts as we professed our love to each other," leaning down into the mound, he whispered something none of the others could hear.

Gently taking her hand in his, he wrapped the bracelet around her wrist and tied the strings together, knotting them. "Until we meet again, my love. Carry this in remembrance of me." Feeling Aedan walk up beside him and kneel at his mother's grave, Weylyn did not turn towards him only spoke low. "I ken you may no' think it, Aedan," Weylyn started. "But I loved your mother. I still do and I always will."

"I ken," Aedan replied. Not saying anything more, Aedan clutched his mother's cold hand and squeezed. "*Slán*, Mama. *Tha gràdh agam.*" Leaning down, he kissed her forehead. Both men stood and walked to Isla and Alexina.

"The clan is coming. We should agree upon a tale for who you two are," Isla said looking at Weylyn and Alexina.

"Aye, tell them that I am Brietta's cousin, Kinnon," he looked over at Alexina who held Giorsal in her arms. "And she is my—"

"Wife and Giorsal is your daughter," Alexina said walking over to him. "If you say sister they will wonder where my husband is and the speculation would be worse than the truth, if that is at all possible." Weylyn looked down at her and took her hand. "I have lived with this sort. I ken how they think. And I am sure my husband willnae mind, if you donnae, Weylyn." He waited a moment then agreed.

"I think that is probably for the best," Isla said seeing the group approaching. "You are up from Edinburgh for the birth of your child and Brietta died unexpectedly while at peace. She is with her husband now."

Weylyn could not suppress the growl that escaped him.

"For their sakes only, Weylyn," she clarified.

Alexina stood beside Weylyn as Giorsal slept wrapped tightly against Alexina's chest in a sling around her. Weylyn took a deep breath smelling the wolf's bane that lingered on the villagers as they approached. Swallowing, Weylyn trying hard to suppress his shudder. Alexina's grip on his hand increased and he gave a quick pulse telling her he was all right just as the clan's chief approached Aedan and conveyed his condolences.

Chapter Three

"Nay, Aedan, again," Weylyn's voice outside the window startled Alexina. It had been five days since Brietta passed and every morning Weylyn and Aedan trained outside. Having just fed Giorsal and put her back down for a rest, Alexina slowly crept to the window to look out. Dawn was cresting above the trees as both men stood outside in the winter chill, stripped to the waist. Snow still blanketing the ground and the mist from the men's breath swirled before them as they breathed. Aedan was concentrating on something while Weylyn held a switch behind his head resting on his shoulders, his brown hair tied back by a leather strip.

"Good morning," Isla called as she walked past the bedroom curtain.

"Good morning," Alexina replied smiling. "They are out there again early this morning," Alexina said as she walked out of the room and set Giorsal down on the wooden bench by the fire, surrounding her with pillows then going to the fire to warm herself from the chill.

"It has been only a few days," Isla sighed pouring some tea she had made. "I hope Aedan learns quickly. I ken Weylyn wants to go for Tristan soon."

Alexina's body stiffened with emotion as she stared into the fire thinking of her husband.

"Och, I am so sorry," Isla said. "It must be so difficult for you."

"'Tis," Alexina replied. "But at least he is alive. I donnae ken what I would do if Weylyn could nae communicate with him. He has told me that the torture has stopped, thank the gods, but they have chained him to a stake and are barely feeding him."

"At least he kens you are safe," Isla tried to give comfort.

"That is what gives me strength," Alexina replied. "Weylyn says that Tristan keeps asking how we are... he shouldnae be so worried about Giorsal or me. We have Weylyn to protect us. Tristan has no one."

"I ken it seems like he is the one needing protection," Isla said. "But honestly, he is a man and above all he is a husband and a father. He wants to make sure you two are safe. He can handle anything as long as you are safe and he needs that assurance constantly."

"But there is only so much a body can go through," she replied.

"What can I do?" Isla asked gently.

"Nothing," Alexina said. "I just need him. I need to see him. To hold him. To love him. I—" she cut off as her emotions overtook her.

Isla reached out and hugged her friend.

"I ken," she said. Alexina held on tightly. "You must stay busy. Now what needs to be done?"

"I was going to wash Giorsal's blankets. She has been fed

and sleeps well," Alexina answered looking over at her daughter. "I found some materials and thread in the room. Do you think Aedan would mind if I use some of Brietta's supplies to make Giorsal some clothes?"

"I think he would be perfectly happy with you using them because it is exactly what Brietta would have wanted," Isla replied. Alexina smiled slightly. "I am sure you are as hungry as I am. I will go and ask the men to hunt." Heading to the door, the winter air drifted in and Isla gasped at the sudden chill.

Before she could gather her wits, she heard Weylyn shout "Good!" and watched as he fully phased into a dark brown wolf. Her eyes flew to a massive reddish brown wolf shaking its head and looking down at its paws.

"Aedan?" she questioned. Both wolves looked over. The reddish brown wolf locked eyes with her and raised his head puffing out his chest. Her breath caught as he turned away and looked towards the woods.

They had not spoken since the night Brietta died and she knew he had not forgiven her for lying to him. Closing her eyes against the pain that welled in her chest, Weylyn barked at her. Looking over at him she fought against the tears that threatened.

"I was hoping you could get us something with which to break our fast," Isla called. "Alexina and I are rather hungry."

Weylyn dipped his head in acknowledgment and let out a strange hissing bark when he turned back to Aedan. Aedan did not look back at her as he followed Weylyn into the woods.

When will I learn to half-phase? Aedan's mind asked Weylyn as they walked quietly though the woods. Their immediate mental connection surprised Weylyn but as father and son he supposed it was to be expected.

No' for some time, Weylyn replied.

Why? Aedan asked.

Because it takes years to learn how to half-phase, Weylyn explained.

Why? Aedan asked again.

Because 'tis nae our natural state. It is the most common state for those who have learned how to do it, but for pups it is difficult, Weylyn said.

I am hardly a pup, Aedan replied.

It is your first phase... you are a pup, son. Weylyn said. Aedan let out a scoff but said no more. *Gods, you remind me so much of me when I was your age,* Weylyn went on. *My father must have had his hands full.*

Aedan looked over at him.

Your father?

Aye, Weylyn stated as flashes of his father's face flittered across his mind. *Gods, he was the best father a wolf could have and my mother was an incredible woman.*

Are you the only child they had? Aedan asked.

I am, Weylyn replied. *It was odd for wolf families to have only one child but the gods did no' grant them anymore. My father held a high rank within the pack. He always had kind and instructive words to say and my mother loved him fiercely.*

You speak of them both in the past tense. Have they died? Aedan asked.

Unfortunately they have. But they died together and at peace without pain. They would have nae wanted it any other way. I strive every day to be like him. I kenned, with him, there was no judgment, no envy or anger. I could tell him anything and he would always counsel me, never condemn me, Weylyn said. *I hoped once to tell my son that as well. Even if I was angry, my father would come to me and we would talk or even go to the training field and fight together.*

Weylyn, a soft voice startled them from their communication.

Who is that? Aedan asked raising his lip and barring his teeth in a growl.

'Tis Tristan, Weylyn replied. *What is it, Tristan? Are you all right?*

Is my family safe? Tristan asked weakly.

Aye, both Giorsal and Alexina are safe. Why? Weylyn asked.

Good, Tristan responded. *I donnae ken how much longer I can hold on. They are starving me. What little food I do get, I get from Faolán, without Marrock kenning. He tells me that my father is angry at you for killing some of the wolves that were after you. He is getting everyone together and planning a massive strike on the village.*

When? Weylyn asked.

Soon. That is all Faolán said. I am worried he will be caught helping me. Tristan said.

That is his choice, Tristan, there is nothing you can do, Weylyn told him.

You need to get everyone to safety, Weylyn. I cannae have other deaths on my conscience. If I hadnae wanted Alexina so much... Weylyn saw himself in Tristan's mind. He recognized the agony he felt when Brietta died.

Hush, Tristan, it is all right. Brietta was no' your fault, son. None of this is your fault. Weylyn said.

Is it no'? Tristan asked.

Nay, Aedan replied. *It is nae* your *fault.* Weylyn felt the animosity toward him and it made his heart heavy.

Aedan, is it no'? Tristan asked. *I am glad Weylyn has you.*

My mother's death is on you, Aedan continued.

Weylyn, if I donnae make it out of here alive, please come for me. Donnae let them leave me out here as food for birds. Please.

'Tis nae going to come to that, Tristan. We will no' let you die. You have nae held your daughter yet. We are coming for you. Weylyn said.

Please... Tristan's plea was faint and then ended all together.

What happened? Aedan demanded.

We need to hurry. Let us get something to take back to the women. Now, focus, close your eyes, take a deep breath, what do you smell? Weylyn immediately began Aedan's training.

Pine... berries... snow... something delicious... Aedan stressed. He opened his eyes and looked at Weylyn. *What is that?*

That is a red deer, Weylyn explained.

Nay, that cannae be, I have had venison before it did no' smell like that, Aedan said.

That is because you are smelling it as a wolf for the first time. Deer are our primary source and favorite food. Now, follow my lead, son, Weylyn replied.

Chapter Four

A day after his first phase, Aedan followed his wife silently through the woods. Careful not to let her hear his approach, he stayed far behind. Losing her once, he tracked her to a small clearing but unsure as to what she was doing, he watched and waited.

Slowly she began to sway, her hair was lose and her gown billowed about her. Had he not been so angry or curious as to what she was doing, he would have gone to her and told her how beautiful she was.

But then she began to move more actively. She jumped and swirled around, her arms moving in a dance of their own. No move was repeated. When she raised her arms up towards the sky, Aedan saw the light of dawn break through the shadowy curtain of night. Once Isla was standing in full sunlight she stopped, her hands extended up towards the heavens. Then slowly she lowered them and with it, bowed her head mumbling a prayer or a chant he was not sure. When she was still for a long moment, he decided to approach her.

"Isla," he called. She gasped and turned. "What are you doing?"

She stared at him, her eyes wide and wild.

"I… I was… I was welcoming the dawn," she said.

"Do you do that often?" he asked, taking one step towards her.

"It is the largest snowfall we have had," she answered. "I suppose I do it often enough though. I leave our bed when you are still asleep."

"You never told me," he stood with his feet apart and arms down at his sides, still an intimidating pose.

"I couldnae," she answered.

"Why?" he demanded.

"Aedan," she sighed. "Would you have understood?"

"You think me ignorant?" he demanded.

"Nay, never!" she replied.

"Then why?" he cried.

"Because I did nae want to lose you," she said. "But it does nae matter now. You have no' even spoke to me since you found out. You sleep every night on the hay in the barn and no' on our pallet with me."

"I am dealing with the loss of my mother, I am nae going to get into bed with you while I am in mourning," he replied.

"I lost her too, Aedan!" she cried. "I am in just as much pain as you are and I need you. She was my confidant, my friend. And I feel like I did nae just lose her, but my husband as well."

"She was my mother!" he shouted. "How do you think I felt? My wife has lied to me, our marriage built on lies and I find out my own mother was behind it?"

"That is no' true!" she said.

"Stop," he shouted. "I cannae talk to you, witch."

Her eyes widened and she let out a cry. Aedan bit back the words the moment he said them but in the village that was what Druids were. Isla rushed passed him but his hand shot out to grab hold of her wrist. They were side by side and she leaned into him for a moment.

"I ken you did nae mean it, Aedan, but it still hurt me," she said. "I love you."

He wanted to say it. He did. He tried, even opened his mouth but the words were dry on his lips. Turning his head away from her he swallowed against the lump in his throat. Isla twisted out of his grasp and rushed through the woods.

Her heart was going to explode within her, that was the only explanation. She could not breathe, could not speak. He did not mean it, he could not! She ran until her chest ached and her legs nearly gave out. Stopping up short at the well on Brietta's land, she remembered how Aedan had kissed her there, at the side of the house and inside the barn. They had made love against the barn's outer wall and had talked about a future with children all while eating in the courtyard between the cottage and the barn on a blissful summer's day. Her eyes blurred with unshed tears. Wiping her hands across her cheeks, she let herself cry.

"Isla?"

She groaned and wanted to scream. Looking over, she saw Weylyn standing in the doorway of the cottage.

"What do you want?" she demanded.

"Are you all right?" he asked. "What is wrong?"

"What is wrong?" she repeated his question dumbfounded. "What is wrong?" her voice rose as he took a step towards her. "What is wrong is that because of you my husband will no' even look at me. He does no' even speak to me. He has no' acknowledged my existence since Brietta died. And it is all because of you!"

She marched over to him and struck his chest. He grunted and she found she liked the sound of him hurting. Striking him again and again and again she released some anger. He did nothing to stop her, he let her hit his chest. Frantically striking him again and again as tears streamed down her cheeks, Isla hated what she was doing but could not stop. Eventually her strikes grew less and less powerful and she felt his hands come up to her wrists as he pulled her into him. She cried against his chest and buried her face into his tunic giving a scream that could have woken the dead.

"Why?" she cried. "Why did you have to tell him?"

Weylyn did not answer and that made her cry more. Finally she controlled her actions disgusted with herself at the outburst she had allowed. Pulling away from Weylyn, she took several steps back.

"I should see to Alexina and the babe," she said and before he could stop her, she rushed passed him and into the cottage.

Weylyn took a deep breath, and let it out slowly. Isla's tears were his fault and he hated himself for it. He had denied her request that he not tell Aedan what she was. And now his son would not talk to his wife. Aedan's scent filled his senses and he looked over. He stood at the edge of the woods, how much of the exchange he had seen, Weylyn did not know.

"Aedan?" he called to him and took a step forward. Aedan held up his hand shaking his head and phased into his full wolf before bounding off into the woods. "Aedan!" Weylyn shouted after him. Half-phasing he tried to communicate with him but Aedan blocked him out. Phasing back to his human form, Weylyn gave a shout and hurried into the woods. He lost Aedan after a league and let out another shout.

"What am I supposed to do?" he cried to no one. Looking up at the heavens. "I am no father. I never was, this was forced upon me. I donnae ken what I am doing. Father, you have to help me. What do I do next?" When there was no immediate answer, Weylyn ran his hands through his hair. "You swore you would be there for me! You swore! And you are no'! You promised me I would ken what to do. You told me that it was all instinctual and that with the right woman by my side it would be a pleasure. 'Tis no'. I am nae a father! I donnae ken what to do. You promised me you would help me! You promised me and where are you now? You have left me! I have no one! What am I supposed to do?" Falling to his knees Weylyn closed his eyes. After a moment, he heard a voice he had not heard for two years.

"Weylyn," the voice called. "Weylyn, get up." The voice was comforting and Weylyn kept his eyes closed hoping that if it was a dream he would not wake. "Weylyn!" The voice was more forceful. Weylyn opened his eyes and looked in the direction of the voice.

"Father?" Kinnon stood before him beside a large oak tree. Standing slowly, Weylyn raced to him. Kinnon took a step back.

"Nay," he said. "You cannae touch me for I am no' of this realm."

"Father," Weylyn nearly sobbed. Gods, how he had missed him. "What am I supposed to do?"

"Get up and be the wolf I trained you to be," his father's voice was not harsh. "I did nae raise a whelp, a pup. I raised a wolf. You are grown. Act like it. Be the father I ken you can be. Mend the bond between Aedan and Isla. The rift is there because of your words. You have to mend it."

"How?" Weylyn asked. "I am no' a father. I never was. This is all new to me."

Kinnon looked down.

"No' a moment goes by where I donnae regret telling you a falsehood, Weylyn," Kinnon said. "I truly believed that it was Brietta who died."

"I donnae blame you," he said taking another step forward. "Brietta and I were only meant to be together for a short time. Perhaps Aedan has some part to play in the gods' plans."

"'Tis no' the life I wanted for you, but it is the life you have been given, live it to the fullest," Kinnon replied.

Weylyn looked down.

"Are you with mother?" he asked.

"Aye," Kinnon revealed. "We are together as always."

Weylyn smiled slightly grateful for that.

"What do I do with Aedan? I am his father but I cannae raise him the way I need to raise him," Weylyn said.

"He is a grown man. Guide him. Donnae raise him," Kinnon said.

"What is the difference?" Weylyn asked.

"When you learn that, then you are truly a father," Kinnon replied.

"Did you learn that?" Weylyn asked.

"Aye, around your eightieth winter," Kinnon teased. Weylyn grinned.

"You were the best of fathers," Weylyn said.

"And you my son, be an even better one," Kinnon replied.

"How? Without you to guide me?"

"I am always with you," he stated. "Always in your heart. Listen and you will hear me speak to you." Kinnon looked behind him. "I must go."

"Nay!" Weylyn stumbled towards him. "Please! Donnae leave me!"

"You be the wolf I taught you to be, Weylyn," Kinnon said. "I am so very proud of you, son. Ken that."

"Father! Please stay!" Weylyn begged. Kinnon smiled, stepped forward and helped his son stand from where he stumbled. The feel of his father's hand on his arm shocked him. Weylyn looked up into his father's brown eyes.

"I love you my lad," Kinnon stated and wrapped his arms around his son holding tightly. Weylyn embraced him in return and after a moment Kinnon vanished.

Chapter Five

Weylyn reached the cottage as smells of stew billowed out of the chimney. Hearing shouting coming from the barn, he sent a silent prayer to the gods hoping Aedan and Isla were not arguing over the past. Before he could approach, Alexina came rushing out.

"Weylyn?" she called and raced to him. He wrapped his arms around her and held her close to him.

"Are you all right?" he asked concerned.

"Aye," she replied. "But I fear for them. They have been screaming at each other for a little while now."

"Hush, lass, 'twill be all right," he stated. "How are you?"

"I am well rested thanks to Isla, but I fear for my friend. She loves him so and I worry that he will—"

"My dear one," Weylyn stated. "I promise all will be well." At that moment, Aedan stormed out of the barn, his claymore strapped to his back. Weylyn called to him but he did not respond as he headed into the woods. Alexina looked over at the barn to see Isla weeping at the doorway watching her husband leave. Squeezing his arms, Alexina raced to her friend. Isla nearly collapsed in Alexina's arms as she wept. Weylyn rushed to her as well. "What has happened?"

Isla looked up at him and weakly slapped his face. Weylyn closed his eyes and turned away.

"He has left me," Isla cried. "Thanks to you!"

Weylyn gritted his teeth and looked out into the forest.

"Alexina, get her inside," Weylyn said. "There is some whisky in the cupboard give her some. I will return."

She nodded and helped Isla up. Weylyn went towards the woods and half-phased.

Aedan's scent was easy enough to find and Weylyn tracked it quickly. Aedan was walking away from the cottage and the village.

"Aedan," Weylyn called when he was within hearing distance. Aedan froze and turned clutching the claymore in his hand. "Where are you going?"

"Away from here," Aedan said. "Away from this, away from you and that lying witch who claims to be my wife."

"Why are you doing this to Isla? She loves you. There are several things people want to keep hidden from each other, several things that they want no one to ken," Weylyn replied. "Why are you really leaving? Running away?"

"I am no' running away," Aedan shouted.

"Then what is it? Are you frightened?"

"Frightened of what?"

"Of the truth?" Weylyn asked.

"Stop speaking in riddles," Aedan shouted.

"I felt what you felt, remember?" Weylyn said. "And I remember how it was for you. Your first phase. You were always taught that it was wrong to be something different, but it felt right to you. You finally felt a part of something. It felt freeing, liberating but you were confused. You did nae understand what was going on. That is why I am here, Aedan. You will always have me. I am your father whether you like it or no', son and you willnae lose me. Isla is your wife and she loves you. She did nae tell you what she was. She had her reasons. Your mother did nae tell you the truth because she did nae want you to look upon Gowan as anything less than the man who raised you, the man I am envious of and the man you strive to be like. Aedan, you have to understand this is who you are now. You cannae run from it, you cannae change it, and you cannae go back to the way it was. So be the man you are now and accept it."

Turning away from him, Weylyn headed back.

"Weylyn," he heard Aedan call. Stopping he turned back. "I am no' afraid."

"Then prove it," Weylyn stood arms wide as he phased into his half wolf. Aedan watched as he shifted but did not move. "Prove to me you are worthy to be part of my pack."

Aedan's mind warred with itself. He wanted to forget any of this happened. He wanted to go back to a few days ago where he was nothing and no one special. Son of Gowan and Brietta, husband to the most beautiful woman alive, war chieftain of his clan, right hand to the chief. Why could he not be that again? The other part of him wanted the freedom of the wolf. Weylyn was right, he had never felt like he belonged anywhere. He was either too good, too handsome, or too lucky.

When he was a wolf, he was more and he felt like he belonged. He was a wolf. Weylyn was right. He may have fathered him, but Gowan would always be his father. Thanks to the highlander who took his mother in and raised him, he was who he was. Gowan always told him to stand up straight and be who he was meant to be. *Could he have kenned? Of course he did,* Aedan thought. *Father, I have always strived to be like you and make you proud. But today I must leave that behind. You and mother will always be in my heart but in order to survive this, I must become something else. Forgive me.*

As soon as the words were said, he felt his father's and mother's presence all around him, the wind rustled the trees and he felt their comfort. With them surrounding him, he phased into his wolf-self and looked at Weylyn, a smile tipping up the edges of his mouth.

This was right.

This was who he was meant to be.

His heart lighter as he felt his parent's blessing on his new life, Aedan walked with Weylyn back to the cottage. The women stood in the doorway watching them approach, his wife's eyes red from crying, he felt a gut wrenching ache. Locking eyes with Isla, he opened his arms to her. She hesitated for a moment.

"I am so sorry," he whispered. Covering her mouth as another sob escaped her, she raced to him. Catching her as she threw herself into his arms, he held her tightly to him and lifted her off the ground. "Forgive me, my love. I donnae deserve your forgiveness, but I ask you to give me a chance to prove how sorry I am. I love you so much, I couldnae imagine my life without you. I was angry and hurt and upset, I should never have taken it out on the one who loves me the most."

"You kenned I could handle it and love you still, Aedan," she sobbed. "'Tis true, but I cannae lose you."

"And you never will," he said. "I swear it to you." Locking

eyes with his father, Weylyn nodded and Aedan carried his wife to their room in the barn.

"All is well?" Alexina asked Weylyn.

"All is well," he confirmed. "Now to get Tristan."

Isla traced the strips of scars on her husband's chest as they lay together on their pallet, the bed clothes pushed down to the end, their own clothes lost somewhere between the door to the barn and their bed. His arm stroked her bare back as her leg rested snugly between his. Her head on his shoulder, she sighed contented.

"I wish to stay in your arms forever, my love," he said softly.

"Then you shall," she grinned kissing his chest lightly.

"I was a fool," he breathed into her hair as he kissed it. "Forgive me."

"We all go through grief differently, my love," she said. "I lost her too and I felt like I lost you as well."

"You did for a moment," he confessed. "Only because I lost myself. I did no' ken what to think. My life was turned upside down."

"You loved Gowan, but Weylyn is also your father," she said gently. "And you are a wolf, my love. Wolves and Druids donnae mix well."

"Why?" he asked.

"No one kens what began the feud but it has been going on since the dawn of time," she explained. "There is a legend about the very first alpha and his mate. She was a druid and her father did nae approve of the match. They were star-crossed lovers, doomed to never be together. Some attribute that as the origin of the war."

"How did Weylyn ken you were a druid? Did you tell him?" he asked.

"Nay, he could smell it," she replied. "Humans, wolves, and druids all have very distinct scents and within that, wolves can tell what gender the person is. He could smell my druid blood." Aedan took a deep breath burying his nose into her hair.

"You have always smelled of heather to me," he said. She smiled and snuggled deeper into his arms. "Isla, is there anything else I need to ken about you?"

"Oh my love," she sighed and stroked his jaw. "Aye, but I am concerned of your reaction."

"I was told by my dying mother that the man I thought was my father was in actuality no' and the man who did father me was a wolf. I have phased into a wolf three times and hunted a red deer while on all four legs. The fur is itchy and the sounds I hear are so odd that it nearly drove me insane the first time. I believe I can handle what you have to tell me," Aedan convinced.

"Very well then," she started. "As a Druid, I am immortal and have lived in this world for three hundred years already." Aedan said nothing as he heard her confession. "I was born a druid. Both my parents were and I was blessed with long life," she went on. "When I was accepted into the order, I was gifted with immortality for as long as I wished it. When I fell in love with you, I kenned you were special as you have no' aged in all the years I have kenned you. I stand ready to give up my immortality and become human at any moment to be with you. But now that your ancestry is kenned, I am glad that I did nae give it up yet."

"From now on," he started. "Nothing is a secret between us."

She let out a strangled sigh and nodded kissing his

shoulder.

"Aye, my love," she replied. "I will tell you all."

"Tell me about your home," he said.

"What I told you when we met was true, I have three sisters," she explained. "They are related no' by blood but by bond. They live on the Isle of Skye."

"What is that like?" he asked.

"'Tis the most beautiful place in all the world," she said. They spoke long into the day, pausing only to eat and make love again. Aedan listened as she described the sheer magnificence of her home. She told him how their high priest whom they all called father was killed by Marrock. He asked her questions about what she had seen in all three hundred years of walking the earth. She had traveled far and wide and found none but Alba to her liking. Toward gloaming, they rejoined Weylyn and Alexina inside the cottage for supper where the women entertained them with songs and legends.

Weylyn lay on the wooden bench in the main room of Brietta's cottage, staring into the peat fire. The turf sizzled and the flames jumped as the fire raged and slowly his eyes closed.

"Weylyn," he heard someone call. The voice was soft and beside his ear. Turning, he saw Brietta resting beside him, the same beauty he remembered from over forty years ago. Her light blue eyes mesmerized him, her blonde hair was long and hung down to the middle of her back, and her eyes sparkled with the youth he had found so intoxicating.

"This is a dream," he said softly feeling her fingers on his jaw.

"Aye, my love," she answered gently. He did not care that it was a dream as long as she was there with him. Taking her in his arms, he held her close to his chest. It felt real enough to him.

"Can you ever forgive me for what happened?" he asked, his lips kissing her hair.

"It was my choice to take that arrow for you, Weylyn and I would do it again," she replied clutching his upper arms as he held her close to him.

"I wasnae strong enough to fight for you. How can you ever forgive me for leaving you alone and with child?" he pleaded.

"Because I love you," she replied simply. "I have always loved you. You had no choice, Weylyn."

"Why did you no' tell me about Aedan?" He asked.

"How could I?" She asked leaning up and looking down at him, her blonde hair touching his face and chest. "You always warned me to never come to you... I did no' ken how to get a message to you."

"But why did you no' tell me when I asked you about him while we were in the cottage together?" He asked.

"Think of how that conversation would have gone, my dearest love," she said. "We just met again for the first time in years, made love before the fire, and then talked low together for only the gods kenned how long we had. How was I to tell you that you fathered a child and he was married to a druid?"

He did not say anything only breathed deeply and moved a piece of her hair back behind her ear, swallowing the lump that rose to his throat.

"I would have wanted to ken," he said. "I would have been able to watch over you both. I thought you were dead for forty years and when I finally found you again, you died in my arms with an arrow that was meant for me. How is that fair?"

"There was nothing you could have done, my love," she

answered. "It was my choice and I would do it again." He closed his eyes for a brief moment but asked her a question.

"You said your husband kenned about us... about Aedan being mine. How could he accept that?"

"Gowan and I grew up together," she replied. "He was my best friend. He kenned everything... I told him everything. He warned me about you, but I told him I loved you. When we married, he was very happy for us, until he found me that next evening half frozen and crying waiting for you." Weylyn closed his eyes.

"I donnae tell you this to make you feel guilty," she continued. "Merely so you understand what Gowan did for me. When I told him I was pregnant and that you must be dead or something had happened to you, he took me in his arms and told me he loved me and would do anything for me. He kenned that I was yours, but he told me that for the child's sake – for Aedan's sake – he would marry me with no desires upon me, just to give us companionship and to give our child his name.

"We married later that moon cycle and we did nae consummate our marriage until Aedan was nearing three summers. I fell in love with him and I couldnae deny him the joys of our marriage. He was the most remarkable man I have ever kenned. To take another man's child and raise him as his own to be his father. Aedan and I were both highly blessed to have him in our lives. When he was taken from me, I mourned heavily."

"Do you ken who killed him?" He asked.

She shook her head and continued. "Aedan found him in the woods..." she broke off as tears welled in her eyes. "I heard Aedan's cry when he found him... so did half the village. He carried the body of his father to our door. Gowan wasnae a small man, but with the strength of the wolf in him, Aedan brought him back to me. Since Gowan died, I have been alone."

"You were in my thoughts every moment of every day," Weylyn whispered.

"As you were in mine," she replied. "Watching Aedan grow into the man he is, I saw you in him. He is so like you. Like the man you were when I kenned you. No' the man you are now. My love, you take things too seriously. I remember a wolf who was always laughing and finding the joy in life."

"It was easy to find it when I had it in my arms," he said wrapping his arms even tighter around her.

"Promise me two things," she said. "Promise me, you will take time to be happy and laugh like you once did."

He took a deep breath and shook his head.

"There is no reason to laugh anymore," he said. "My happiness was stolen from me."

"Promise me you will try," she begged. "And promise me that you will move on. I ken they say wolves mate for life, my love, but I am nae a part of your *life* any more. You need someone. You donnae deserve to be lonely."

"That I cannae promise," he said firmly. "I willnae."

"Please, love," she replied.

"Nay, Brietta, why would I move on now? I have lived with this pain for forty years I can live with it another forty. I will have no other take your place in my heart."

"Nay, of course no'," she said gently reaching out and touching his chest where his heart beat under her fingers. "I am just giving you permission that if you ever do find someone to care for, you willnae think of me."

"I cannae promise that," he said shaking his head.

"Perhaps no' now, but when it happens ken that I am happy for you. And do me one last favor," she said.

"Anything," he replied.

"Take care of our son," she said.

"You ken I will," he replied softly.

"I ken you are training him to be ready to fight Marrock's army, but ken this, he will be ready thanks to your talk in the woods this morning. You need to go for Tristan. He willnae stay alive much longer. He is your Alpha," she said.

"Aye... but Aedan is my son," he replied. "I cannae risk his life."

"He will be fine," she answered. "It will be a frightening situation, but you always have a plan. You must go. 'Tis your destiny.

"You ken I donnae believe in destiny," his disdain for the word came across a little too harshly.

"I ken," she replied. "But was it no' destiny that brought you to my barn? You would never have kenned of your son if you hadnae."

"And you would still be alive," he said clutching her to him.

"You would never have kenned that, either," she answered.

She kissed him gently and moved his hair off his forehead.

"This is how I want you to remember me," she said. "The way I was when we pledged our love to each other, when we created our son."

"I will always remember you," he replied. "Both ways, as the girl I fell in love with and the beautiful woman I found again."

"Ken that I love you, Weylyn and, though there is nothing to forgive, for your own sanity, I forgive you wholeheartedly, my darling. Be at peace," she smiled and kissed him once more.

"Well, done, Aedan," Weylyn said when Aedan phased back to human form quickly. Aedan smiled at him and pulled on his tunic. Alexina averted her eyes, but his wife's brazen study of his naked flesh caused him to smirk and wink at her.

"Aye, well done," Isla grinned. Aedan barked a laugh.

"Little minx," he called back. Weylyn laughed along with his son remembering his repartee with Brietta.

"Come now, Aedan," Weylyn smiled. "Put your need for your wife on hold, I must train you on using your wolf form in a fight."

"Is it similar to knife fighting?" Aedan asked.

"Similar, aye," Weylyn replied. "Perhaps that is why you are so adept at it."

"I never did like the bulk of the claymore," Aedan said. "It was too cumbersome to use in tighter spaces."

"But effective when swinging coming down a hill," Alexina offered.

"Aye," Aedan replied. "You ken of fighting, lass?"

"My father taught us all, my two brothers and myself," she answered glad that her voice waivered only a moment. Catching Weylyn's eyes, she tried to smile.

"Phase, Aedan," Weylyn ordered. "Let me show you how to fight."

Aedan phased into his full form, shaking his head clearing the confusion he sometimes felt. He watched through his wolf eyes as Weylyn phased into his half form, and communicated his thoughts. Out of the corner of his eye, he saw Alexina stand and pick up her daughter, Isla walked with her to the cottage and he swore he could smell pain and the scent of tears but his thoughts were not his own as Weylyn rushed him and threw him to the ground.

"Is everything all right, my dear?" Isla asked as she helped Alexina sit at the bench and took Giorsal from her mother's arms. Once the baby was well situated, Isla returned to her friend.

"Aye, forgive me, I grew weak," she said. "I fear for Tristan is all."

"Is it?" Isla asked. Alexina looked up at her and her knowing eyes startled her. "I ken grief, my friend. And you have such grief in your heart."

"My family was killed by the alpha Marrock," she revealed. "Tristan and I found their bodies and I couldnae bury them." Tears rolled, unchecked down her cheeks.

"Oh my dearest," Isla sat beside her and wrapped her arms around her. "All that you have suffered."

"For love," she replied. "I hate myself sometimes, but I wonder if I had never met Tristan, would my family still be alive? I betray my husband." She sobbed.

"Nay!" Isla cried. "It is purely natural to question after a tragedy!"

"But no' my love for my husband or his love for me!" Alexina wept.

"Listen to me, Alexina," Isla began. "You are nae the first nor the last woman to question her bond with her husband," her face clouded. "But the fact that you still have the love in your heart for your child and your husband should tell you that no matter what trials you go through you will always have him. Hold to the bond you have with him."

"Our bond is a human one, no' a wolf," she sobbed.

"Your bond is reflected in your child," Isla replied looking her in the eyes. "You cannae doubt your husband's love for you, it will tear you apart."

Swallowing, Alexina finally nodded.

"The pain is so much," she cried.

"Here," Isla stood and went to the cupboard. "I donnae condone drinking to lessen pain, but sometimes it is the only thing that will help quickly. Drink," she poured a small amount of the whisky into a cup and handed it to her. Sniffing, Alexina's face puckered in distaste. "I ken, but try it." The drink smelled of earth, peat and fire. Certain she would not like it, she took a tentative sip and closed her eyes.

"Oh dear gods, that is the nectar of the heavens," she whispered as she felt the burn of the drink down to her toes. Instantly she felt warm and soon after she felt her pain ease from her chest and she could breathe. Isla poured herself some and gave Alexina a wee bit more.

"Well, done, son," Weylyn praised as he phased back to his human form and wiped a small trickle of blood from his eye. "Now, follow me."

"Did I harm you?" Aedan asked as soon as he phased.

"Och, nay," Weylyn smiled as the cut healed itself nearly immediately. "'Twas just a scratch."

Aedan wrapped his plaid around his hips and looked over at Weylyn. "Where are we going?"

"To bathe," Weylyn answered heading towards the woods. "You stink."

Aedan laughed. "You donnae smell much better yourself."

"Aye, trust me I ken, but I donnae have a beautiful wife I

want to sleep beside this eve," Weylyn smiled ducking into the woods.

Looking back at the house, Aedan did not see the women but the sounds of laughter and the comfort of the peat fire billowed out.

Finding Weylyn waiting for him a few steps away, they walked side by side.

"Is there a burn we can wash in?" Aedan asked.

"'Twould be cold," Weylyn replied.

"Aye, but I have bathed in winter's chill before," Aedan said.

"Would you nae rather submerge in a warm pool?" Weylyn asked.

"Och, aye, but there is no' a chance for the water to be anything but icy in this weather," Aedan replied.

"You would be correct," Weylyn answered. "And as wolves the cold would be a shock but nae unbearable as our internal heat does nae drop much below our current state."

"Isla does seem to enjoy my new found heat," he replied. "She curls up against me like a cat seeking warmth from the fire."

"I guarantee that is nae a hardship," Weylyn winked.

"Och, nay," Aedan grinned suggestively. "Of course, I do tell her that she would be warmer if we were skin to skin."

"And what male wouldnae?" Weylyn laughed. "I am glad you spoke," he went on. "It did my heart good to see the bond mended between you."

"Aye, it was an adjustment, but your guidance assisted me in my darkest hour," Aedan said. "For that I thank you."

"My moon's cycle is nearly finished," Weylyn replied. "If it is still your wish, I will leave and you shall no' be bothered by me again."

"I do believe you ken the answer to that," Aedan admitted. "I would be lost without you."

"You desire that I stay?" Weylyn asked.

"Aye," he answered. "I wish you to stay. And I want to go for our Alpha soon."

Weylyn's heart expanded with pride. *Our Alpha,* he had said. Taking a deep breath for a moment, he felt his father surround him and he smiled.

"Aye, son," Weylyn replied. "I wish that too." The men stared at each other for a long moment, Weylyn's heart opening to him. Before he could stop himself, Weylyn stepped forward and embraced his son.

Aedan's initial reaction was to push him away as his entire body stiffened. But after the first moment, he wrapped his arms around him and returned the embrace.

"Forgive me," Weylyn said after he pulled back. "I overstepped I am sorry."

"Nay, 'tis all right," he answered. "I was nae expecting it."

"Aye, I ken," Weylyn replied and after a moment, he nodded towards a pool behind Aedan large enough for nearly five people to stand without touching, nestled at the base of a mountain. The pool had no ice crystals as so many burns in the woods would have at that time of year. Aedan rubbed his hands together, though not cold, his mind played tricks on him. Weylyn pulled off his tunic. "Let me get in first and see what it feels like," Weylyn said as he sank into the water. "Hoo, 'tis cold," Weylyn replied. "But 'twill soon warm and help with your aching muscles, get in."

Aedan nodded, pulled off his plaid he had wrapped around his waist and stepped in opposite his father letting out a small yelp when he felt the cold water.

"Aye, 'tis frigid," Aedan replied. "But oddly, I am no' as cold as I thought I would be."

"That is the wolf in you," Weylyn answered. "We are born to withstand the elements."

"I have noticed that I am no' as affected by them as I once was," Aedan admitted.

"Aye, come nearer to me son, you are directly under the spout," Weylyn said.

"Spout?" Aedan asked turning to look up and seeing a stone that jutted out of the mountain base. "What is going to happen?"

"Watch," Weylyn motioned. Aedan waited to see a small waterfall start and the pool water instantly began to warm. Fascinated with the new found discovery, Aedan stepped forward and ran a hand beneath the boiling hot waterfall.

"Did you ken this was going to happen?" Aedan asked.

"Aye," Weylyn replied watching his son and feeling a sort of love he had never felt before.

"How did you ken this was here?" Aedan asked.

"I have been here before," he replied simply.

"When?" Aedan asked.

"You probably donnae desire to ken," Weylyn answered chuckling.

"You and Mother?" He asked gently.

"Aye," Weylyn answered. "There is an above water geyser inside that mountain. After your mother and I would meet, I would submerge in here to wash her scent from my clothes. I was traveling with other wolves and my father so it was essential to keep her safe."

"Would you tell me the story of how you two met?"

Aedan asked as he tilted his head back under the waterfall.

"Come now, and get out of there. Let your old man have a go," he grinned pushing his son out from under the waterfall. Aedan laughed and moved aside. The pool water was the perfect temperature as the steam rose into the cold air. "The very first moment I saw her," Weylyn began. "I was leading some of the pack through the outskirts of Marrock's land. He hadnae conquered the whole of the wood yet and I was sent ahead of the others as a scout.

"I caught a scent. It was strange and it called to me. I had always been fascinated with humans so I crept up to see a group of the village women gathering heather on the mountain no' far from here. I saw your mother. She was the most beautiful woman I had ever seen. The wind whipped around her and she held her hair back with one hand. I caught her scent and realized that was the one. She had called to me without words. I thought my heart would stop, when she greeted me, I did no' ken the human language; Gaelic, fluently then, but I kenned enough to understand what she was saying and to speak to her."

"How old were you?" Aedan asked.

"About seventy-five," Weylyn answered.

"Which is what?" Aedan asked.

"Roughly early twenties certainly no more than twenty-three," he explained. "We talked... well... she talked I just stood there like a fool." Aedan chuckled. "When her sister called to her saying they were heading back down the mountain, she smiled and said goodbye, but before she had gotten too far away she came back and offered me a sprig of heather... I still have it." Aedan looked at him. "I snuck away from the others in the scouting pack that night and followed her scent to the village. She was at the well with her sister, your aunt. We went for a walk and ended up here. She had figured out what I was. I remember it was the first time she kissed me."

"*She* kissed you?" Aedan asked surprised.

"Your mother was very unconventional," Weylyn grinned and stepped away for Aedan to have a chance to use the waterfall. "We met here every night until we..."

"Mated," Aedan replied.

"Aye," Weylyn answered.

"Then what happened?" Aedan asked.

"Then I went back to Marrock, told him I found my mate and was forbidden to ever see her again and punished for telling a human what I am," Weylyn said devoid of emotion. Thinking over what Weylyn had just told him and flinching when he turned his back on the hot water, Aedan looked behind him. "Are you hurt?" Weylyn asked concerned.

"I donnae believe so, but my back does ache," Aedan replied.

"Let me see," Weylyn offered. Aedan turned around revealing a large bruise that had formed on his son's back between his shoulders. "Did you fall on something?" Weylyn asked gently prodding the area.

"No' that I recall," Aedan said.

"Let the water sooth you," he replied. "Perhaps Isla has some herbs to help with the pain. Your healing should begin very soon."

Aedan nodded as he relaxed against the stone and felt all the tension ease from his muscles.

"I am growing tired," Aedan revealed.

"Aye, you have worked hard, lad," Weylyn answered. "Harder than many. You have had to learn quickly. But you are my son and you were conceived during the Hunter's Moon."

"Mm," Aedan replied as his exhaustion overtook him and he closed his eyes.

Weylyn watched him fall asleep and smiled fondly. Aedan had yet to call him father and that troubled him but knowing his son needed more than just a moon's cycle to adjust, Weylyn waded over to him and lifted him out of the pool. Wrapping him in his plaid, Weylyn carried him to the cottage.

The women were still within and if the sounds of laughter were any indication, they were feeling rather intoxicated. Weylyn carried his son to the barn and laid him out on the pallet in the loft room. Aedan moaned but did not wake.

"Sleep, son," Weylyn whispered stroking his forehead. Tucking the blanket around him, Weylyn went back down the ladder, across the courtyard and into the cottage. The women were, in fact, drunk. As he opened the door they looked over at him and laughed. "Glad to be of some amusement to you ladies," he said, only causing them to laugh more. "How are you feeling, Alexina?"

"Ooh," she grinned and laughed at the same time. "Utterly and unbelievable," she hiccupped and laughed again.

"I would assume so," Weylyn said. "Isla?"

"She needed time away from males fighting, Weylyn," she slurred her words as well. "And Gowan wouldnae mind us breaking into his reserve."

"How much have you had?" Weylyn asked.

"I am older than you," Isla went on. "Sho," she slurred. "Donnae be disciplinin' me, laddie." Alexina and Isla both giggled hysterically.

"I merely wondered how much I need to imbibe to be able to participate," he grinned and grabbed the container at their elbow and took a long swig. "Och," he said when he lowered the bottle as his face twisted. "I never had whisky until Brietta gave me some. 'Tis good."

"Aye," Isla raised her cup and took a drink. "Och, where is my husband?" Isla asked taking the bottle from him and filling their cups again.

"Aedan is in your room," Weylyn said as he sat down beside Alexina. "He was tired."

"Ooh," Isla grinned and looked over at Alexina who nodded vigorously. "I should go then." She stood, wobbling on her feet as she headed to the door. Turning around suddenly, she had to clutch the wall. "I am all right. Are you feeling better Alexina?"

"Aye, thanks to you," she replied. "Get some sleep."

"Oh no sleep," she grinned. "I am going to my husband."

Weylyn watched as Isla stumbled out the door and across the courtyard to the barn.

"Are you all right?" Weylyn turned to Alexina as soon as they were alone. "You seem worried."

"I am," she answered. "Weylyn, I donnae want anything to happen to you, Aedan or Isla. I feel like I am betraying my husband but I donnae believe we should go back for him without more help than the two of you."

"That is why you drank nearly this entire bottle?" He asked.

"I donnae normally drink, but it has affected me. I cannae restrain my words," she said.

"You were in need of female companionship. I am glad Isla provided that for you," Weylyn said. "But trust me, my dear, I swore to you that I would get Tristan back for you. I will keep that promise and I willnae allow anything to happen to us."

"You cannae ken that for certs," she said. "Anything can happen and if Marrock is as evil as Tristan and you have said, then we are dead for sure."

"Nay," Weylyn replied taking her in his arms and holding her close to him. "I do ken it, because we have right on our side. I would be lying if I said I was no' worried either. But in truth Alexina, Tristan is so important to all of us that we all want to help him. I will be approaching this with the desire no' to go to war. We will get him back. I will sacrifice myself if need be to get him safely back to you."

"I ken you would and that is what I am worried about," she said. "You have a family now."

"So does he," Weylyn answered looking at the sleeping baby in her bed of blankets and pillows. "Everything will be all right. You need to get some sleep. I will stay up and make sure Giorsal is safe. You have nae slept well."

"I donnae without him," she replied.

"I understand," he answered. "But now try and sleep. Everything will be all right." She nodded and wished him goodnight as she stumbled to the bedroom.

Weylyn stoked the fire and put another peat log on the flame, it crackled and snapped as the fire caught it. Giorsal woke up and looked over at him. He smiled down at the babe and she squealed. Putting his finger to his lips, he slowly and gently picked her up. She clung to him as tightly as her little frame let her. He stood and walked around the room with her.

"Now, my dear one, where were we?" He asked. "Och aye I remember... the handsome wolf-man had just killed the evil shape-shifting Druid and had reached the room where his love lay... Well this wolf kenned that the spell would only be broken by true love's kiss. So, he looked down at her and saw she was just asleep. Leaning down, he kissed her gently. No' a moment later, her eyes fluttered open and she smiled up at him. 'I kenned you would come for me,' she said to him. 'Always and forever,' he replied. She kissed him again and he helped her sit up. 'Where is the Druid?' she asked for she kenned that the druid would never allow her handsome wolf to save her. 'She will never harm you again,' he answered. They walked to the window of the tower to see dawn breaking through the clouds.

"They both took a deep breath sensing that the evil had ended and they kenned that all would be well in their land. You see, this tale has been told to every generation of my family and I wanted to tell it to you, Giorsal because it is a story every beautiful princess should ken and you are such a beautiful princess, dear one. One day a man will come and sweep you up... but he will have to get past your father and me before that happens." Giorsal squealed and wrapped her fingers in Weylyn's hair. She gave one strong tug and tears stung his eyes as the pain registered. Nuzzling her nose, he reached around and unhooked her hand from his hair. "As long as he treats you well and loves you, he will pass the first test... but he may no' pass the next." He winked at her and sat down on the bench.

Alexina tried to hold back tears as she watched her child in Weylyn's arms. She did not know that Weylyn took care of her child every night. He seemed so comfortable with Giorsal and she was so thankful that Weylyn was there to protect them. To see the man she looked up to as her protector, melt and be so gentle with the tiny baby in his arms, was such a fascinating and beautiful sight. She watched as he gently sat down on the bench and held Giorsal upright close to his chest as his thumb ran across her tiny back.

"I promise you I will never let anything happen to you," Weylyn went on. "I love you, Giorsal. I hope your father does nae mind if I look upon you as my granddaughter." Covering her mouth as a sob attempted to escape, Alexina felt the tears streaming down her cheeks. "But I want to be a part of your life. Your father will be your protector, rightfully so, but I will always be there for you."

Looking down at her, Weylyn smiled seeing she had fallen asleep on his shoulder sucking her thumb.

"And the wolf and his mate lived happily ever after," he whispered kissing her cheek

Alexina watched as he stood and placed the sleeping baby on the bench, surrounded her with pillows and covered her with a blanket.

"Sleep well, my princess," he whispered as he kissed her hair. Sitting down with his back on the pew, facing the fireplace, his hand rested on the seat and covered Giorsal's arm. Alexina snuck further behind the drape so Weylyn would not see her watching him. After he yawned, he checked on Giorsal once more then lay down on the floor before the fire and closed his eyes.

Alexina waited and when his breathing slowed to a steady pace, she snuck back out into the room, pulled a plaid from the back of the bench and covered Weylyn. He stirred for a moment but did not wake, sighing and muttering something in his sleep, all she understood was the name Brietta.

Alexina watched him for a short time. He looked so young with his eyes gently closed and his body relaxed. She turned and checked on her daughter.

Heading back to her room, Alexina took a final look at

Weylyn and smiled slightly then she lay down on the hay filled mattress, turned on her side and closed her eyes. Deep sleep claimed her.

Chapter Six

Early that next morning, Weylyn woke to Giorsal's cries of hunger.

"I am sorry," Alexina said as she bounced the baby up and down on her hip. "She must be hungry."

"Aye," he stretched. "'Tis all right." Standing he went over to her and stroked Giorsal's cheek. "You are well, little one. No need for such racket."

Almost instantly, the baby quieted and looked up at him. Reaching towards him, she cried out when he did not take her immediately.

"I do believe she wants you," Alexina smiled.

"Aye, my women like me," he winked. She laughed but passed her to him. "Shh, me wee lassie, I am here."

"She wants your protection," Alexina said.

"She will always have it," Weylyn replied kissing the baby's plump cheek. "She is so very beautiful, Alexina, you have done well."

"I thank you," she looked at her baby with pride. "She

takes after her father."

"Donnae discount your contribution, Alexina," Weylyn said. "The baby looks much like you."

"I appreciate that, Weylyn, thank you," she replied. "You are so very good with her."

"I have always wanted to be a father," Weylyn explained. "But now, I will have the joys of being a grandfather to Aedan's children."

"No' just to Aedan's," she said as Weylyn's eyes locked with hers. "My parents are dead, Tristan's father wants nothing to do with him anyway," she went on. "You have been more a father to my husband than anyone and you have protected me and my daughter almost to the death. I believe that qualifies you to be a grandfather to my child."

"Thank you," he said softly. Giorsal squirmed in his arms and he looked back at her and smiled. "But now, I need to wake Aedan so we can hunt. Keep the fire going? When we return we will need to eat and gather our strength. Alexina, I donnae ken what the future will bring, but ken that I will do anything in my power to bring him back to you."

"I ken you will," she smiled up at him. "Just be careful, I beg of you."

"Aye, lass, I will," he promised as he passed Giorsal off to her mother and headed outside to the barn.

Chapter Seven

"Aedan," Weylyn called quietly up to the loft. "Aedan," he called again and heard something rustle above him.

"Weylyn?" Aedan called confused as he looked over the edge of the loft.

"'Tis dawn we must hunt for the women to break their fast," Weylyn said.

"Can I no' this morning?" He groaned. "I… uh… did nae sleep much last night."

"Nay," Weylyn raised an eyebrow. "Since you are tired 'tis essential to take you hunting."

"Weylyn, please," he moaned. "I am in no state to hunt at the moment."

"You have a few moments," Weylyn said. "Or I am coming up there, and I donnae really think I desire to."

"Nay, you donnae," Aedan agreed. "And I am a grown man, no need to be scolded…" Weylyn raised his eye brows at him. "Och, fine," Aedan sighed and ripped the blanket off of himself.

A great yawn over took Aedan as he walked into the sunlight. Weylyn was leaning against the well waiting for him. The ground glistened with snow and the sun was bright... *too bright,* Aedan thought. The temperature had dropped drastically and was below freezing. Aedan saw the look of mild amusement on Weylyn's face as he walked towards the well.

"Breaking our fast?" Aedan asked as Weylyn stood and faced him fully.

"Aye," Weylyn answered.

"Does that mean if I am nae hungry I donnae have to go?" He wondered if the Fates would be so kind.

"Nay," Weylyn replied. Aedan huffed but finally nodded. Weylyn pulled off his tunic and beckoned his son to do the same. Turning away from his father to set his tunic down inside the barn, he heard him continue. "Where is your bruise from the other day? Did it heal that quickly?"

"Nay," Aedan answered walking back over. "Isla healed it for me last eve."

"What do you mean she healed it for you?" Weylyn asked his eyes narrowing on his face.

"I mean she used her Druid power of healing to heal my back," he answered. "It feels better."

Weylyn pursed his lips together as an uncomfortable growl escaped him.

"I ken wolves and druids donnae care for each other, but she is my wife," Aedan said. "And she healed me last night so I am better today."

"I understand," Weylyn finally said. "I am glad you are feeling better."

"A stiff compliment, Weylyn," Aedan drolled. Weylyn

took a deep breath. "I ken I will never see you happy with a druid," Aedan went on. "But my druid makes me very happy."

"Apparently," Weylyn answered. "But you must get your mind off of her and focus."

They phased together and trotted off into the woods.

Father and son crouched low stalking a mountain goat. They could smell them as soon as they passed the pool at the base of the mountain they had visited earlier. As they waited to attack, Aedan let his mind drift. It was a few moments later when he heard his father's voice in his head.

Aedan, stop...

What? Aedan asked him.

You do realize I can see *and* feel *everything you are thinking of right now...* everything... Weylyn stressed. *And 'tis no' something I really need or want to see.*

I am sorry. Obviously now you ken why I am tired this morning. I cannae help my thoughts as they drift to my wife, Aedan explained.

Well, then, Weylyn paused and deliberately thought of he and Brietta on their wedding night.

Och... that is just... Aedan shook his head trying to rid himself of the image he just saw in his father's head.

Agreed, Weylyn replied. *Now you ken how I feel. Keep that out of your head while you are phased unless you want your entire pack to ken your wife intimately.*

'Tis nae my fault. You woke me too early this morn. I am still recovering, Aedan said.

Clearly, Weylyn replied. *Focus.*

Och, I am, Aedan smirked as another flash of memory from that previous night crossed his mind.

No' on her! On what we are doing here, Weylyn said.

Aedan let a low growl escape his lips.

I am tired! He wanted to yell.

Fine, Weylyn replied and pounced on him. *This should wake you up.*

They wrestled together for a time. Weylyn attempted to get Aedan to focus but he made careless mistakes and once allowed Weylyn to slash his face. Aedan yelped and cowered low.

Aedan, are you all right? Weylyn cried.

Nay! You slashed me! Aedan turned away from his father.

I am sorry, you normally pull back, Weylyn apologized.

Weylyn, Aedan turned back to him. *Right now, I am nae in control of my own thoughts how do you expect me to be able to fight you?*

Forgive me, son, but you need to learn how to keep focused on the problem at hand, Weylyn said.

I have never had that problem before. I willnae have that problem. Today I am more tired than usual. I have nae trained this hard since I first joined my laird's guards. I am trying to learn quickly, Weylyn but at the moment I merely want to curl up with my wife and have a repeat of our night, Aedan revealed. Weylyn was quiet. *What is it?* Aedan asked when he had not spoken for some time.

Tristan is dying. We need to go to him and soon. Weylyn explained.

When? Aedan asked.

As soon as possible, Weylyn said. Aedan took a deep breath as all thought left him. *That is why I am trying to train you as quickly as I can, son.* Aedan was quiet as he heard the desperation in Weylyn's voice.

I am sorry, I will focus, Aedan promised.

Let us get something to break our fast and hurry back to the women. When we return we will speak more on this, Weylyn offered. They both turned when they heard the baying of a mountain goat, crouched down and pounced killing the animal in one swift movement.

"That was an extraordinary meal," Aedan complimented pushing back from the table and wiping his mouth. His wife came over and refilled his water and he wrapped his arm around her, tugging her down onto his lap. Smiling at him, she swatted his arm and stood away from him. Heading over to Weylyn to refill his cup of water, she approached slowly. Weylyn pushed back from the table as well allowing her to reach his cup.

"I never realized that phasing and hunting could make one so hungry," Aedan smirked.

"Indeed," Weylyn chuckled. Aedan's smirked widened as he winked back at his father. Shaking his head, Weylyn turned to the women. "Thank you both," Weylyn said changing the subject. "It was wonderfully prepared and flavorful."

"It was our pleasure," Isla stated. "A little something so you ken your druid daughter-in-law is no' attempting to murder you."

"No' at the moment," Weylyn had a smirk toying at the corner of his lips.

"No' ever," Isla snapped. When all eyes turned to her, she looked down. She eventually cleared her throat and looked back at Weylyn; her voice was lighter and more playful. "Besides I am afraid I would have Alexina's wrath if I tried."

Alexina looked up from changing her daughter's clothes

and grinned.

"Aye, you would," Alexina teased and grinned at Weylyn. "And I donnae think anyone wants that."

Isla set the pitcher of water on the table, went back over to her husband and slid down on his lap as he nuzzled her neck.

"No' to put a damper on our spirits but before Aedan and I go out to train—" Weylyn started.

"More training?" Isla asked pulling from Aedan and looking at both of them.

"Of course, Aedan is doing extremely well. We need to keep training," Weylyn said looking over at his son who grinned and reached for his water. "But before we go, we must speak about Tristan," Weylyn replied. Alexina stiffened behind them and almost on cue, Giorsal began to cry. Alexina picked her daughter up from the pillows and held her close to her.

"I think it is time to go," Aedan said. "I donnae think it is right that any man be held against his will. We need to save him. He is your Alpha."

"He is yours as well, Aedan. He became yours when you could hear him," Weylyn explained. "You pledged loyalty to my pack by accepting me as your... father but more accepting who you are. Tristan is the leader of my pack so he is your Alpha."

"Well," Isla said. "If we are planning to go into the heart of Marrock's land we may need some assistance."

"Druids?" Alexina asked making sure Giorsal was tucked safely on the wooden bench. She stood and walked over to them. Isla nodded.

"I donnae think so," Weylyn replied harshly.

"Weylyn, please, let her speak," Aedan asked. "I am sure she has an excellent idea."

Weylyn growled softly. But Alexina put a hand on his

shoulder and he calmed instantly. With barely hidden frustration, he motioned for her to continue.

"My sisters and I have been at war with the wolves for far too long," Isla started. "They have no love of the tyrant; Marrock and his war mongering. But, I have spoken to my sisters about you, Weylyn and told them how you saved us all and your loyalty to Tristan, Alexina and Giorsal. The little I ken of Tristan, he seems like a fair leader. That is all we want. We want someone we are able to speak with. We want to end this bitter feud between our two kinds. We believe that you may be just the man to follow against Marrock."

"I have no desire to start a war," Weylyn said.

"Of course no'," Isla answered. "And that is what my sisters and I find so appealing about following you."

"For those who donnae ken, my love," Aedan began. "Tell them about your sisters."

"There are four of us," she replied. "Myself, Labhaoise, Geileis, and Eithne."

"Are they on Skye?" Aedan asked.

"Aye, but there is a little kenned passageway that we are able to utilize that transports us from Skye to the heart of the Highlands within a moment," she said. When they did not respond and merely looked at her confused, she continued. "'Tis Druid... you would say *magic,* but we call it artifice. Each Grove has their own entrance and exit from their land to the main land."

"Grove?" Aedan interrupted.

"A group of Druids is called a grove, no' a coven as is commonly misconstrued. We are healers and mystics no' witches, there is a difference," Isla explained. Weylyn scoffed and took a drink of his water. Isla pursed her lips together hearing his sneer. "The entrance to our land is no' easily found. We have protected it against the wolves."

"How?" Aedan asked.

"It is in an area where wolves cannae go," she said cryptically. "If I call for my sisters, they will come to us and we can face Marrock together."

"Isla, you are my son's wife and therefore I *tolerate* what you are," Weylyn began. "But your sisters are another issue. I ken nothing of them. One Druid is enough and if we have any chance of living through this, then one of you is plenty."

Isla stopped herself from saying something she would regret.

"They were nae overly enthusiastic to find out about Aedan's... parenting. But, as has been said, *the enemy of my enemy is my friend* or at least ally. All I am saying is that we need a plan of attack if we are going to step into the wolf's lair," she went on. "The four of us willnae be enough against the entire pack."

"I am no' going to pick a fight," Weylyn said. "I believe we can live in peace with one another. I will tell Marrock that I donnae want a fight."

"But they will," Isla went on. "Donnae be so foolish as to think Marrock will no' kill you both on site, let alone what he would do to Alexina, Giorsal and myself. And you must think of Tristan."

"I have lived under Marrock's tyranny for a hundred and twenty years, Isla. He has dictated every aspect of my life. Donnae think me blind to his ways," Weylyn replied sharply.

"Then what are you going to do, Weylyn? Tell me, because I would be fascinated to ken. Appeal to his human nature? He is an animal," Isla asked.

"Isla," Aedan spoke sharply looking at his wife.

A low, menacing growl resonated deep in Weylyn's chest. Alexina's grip on his shoulder increased but it did little good. Weylyn and Isla locked eyes, his eyes had flashed to yellow and Isla looked down. She did not want to fight with him, but he was making it difficult.

"I will speak to him as a father," Weylyn explained. "If he has any instincts to protect his child, maybe I can use them. Tristan is the only child from his true mate and queen. That has to mean something to him."

"I respect your suggestion, Weylyn but honestly, Marrock has been torturing his son for fun," Aedan replied. "He has been stabbed, branded, flayed, beaten and now starved; do you truly believe that Marrock has any fatherly compulsion left?"

A small cry escaped Alexina. She covered her mouth quickly taking her hand from Weylyn's shoulder and rushed out of the house.

"Oh well done, Aedan," Weylyn rebuked as he stood and followed her.

"Forgive me," Aedan said softly as his father walked out.

Chapter Eight

Weylyn followed Alexina out of the house and to the well where she stood, shaking with silent tears. Reaching her, he placed his hands on her shoulders and squeezed lightly. She turned into him and he held her close, her face buried into his chest. He said nothing only gently rubbed his hands up and down her back trying to comfort her. Finally releasing the weeks of torment she had kept secret, she wept.

He felt every pulsating heave as she could be silent no longer. It broke his heart to hear her sobs, but he never stopped his gentle soothing. Without his arms around her, he was not sure she would be able to stay standing. He said nothing and only held her close to him banishing all her fears and demons. Finally she pulled away and looked up at him.

"Is it true?" She got out between hiccups for air. "What Aedan said? Is that what has been happening to Tristan?"

Weylyn took a deep breath. He would not lie to her.

"Aye, lass," he replied softly. She let out a wail of undefined torture.

"Please can you save him?" She begged between sobs. "Please?"

"I will do my utmost," he answered pressing her head into his chest.

"You saved me," she wept. "Promise me you will save him."

"I cannae promise that, Alexina," he replied. "You would always blame me if I couldnae. But I will do everything I can to get him back to you."

"I ken you will," she replied calming. "What can I do?" She asked.

"Just be there for him when we do get him back. He will need us both, but you most of all," he said. "He will need your nursing and your love."

She nodded into his chest.

"He has always had it," she pledged. "Thank you. I ken you will save him."

"I will do what I can," he replied.

"I ken," she answered. "Forgive me for crying so hard," she soothed the front of his tunic, wet and wrinkled from where she had cried and held onto him.

"Donnae fash, lass," he said stopping her hand and tipping her head up to him with two gentle fingers under her chin. "I am always here for you. And you never need to hide your tears from me."

"What a wonderfully lucky woman Brietta was," Alexina said. "To have had you as her mate. If this is what you do for me… I can only imagine what you do for those you love."

"I have grown to love you, Alexina," he admitted. "Tristan is like a son to me, but in the short time I have kenned you, you have become a daughter."

She looked up at him and tried to smile.

"I love you too, Weylyn," she replied. "You have been so kind to me. I ken now why Tristan loves you. I would be honored to be your daughter."

"The honor would be mine, dear one," he said kissing her forehead. "Come let us go back inside, you will freeze out here."

"No' with you here with me," she smiled up at him clutching him closer.

"Still," he answered. "'Tis going to snow again. We need to make sure there is enough peat for the fire. You and Giorsal must all stay warm while Aedan and I train."

"We will be fine," she said. "You need no' worry about us."

"That is never going to happen," he grinned. He put his arm around her and helped her back into the house.

"Nay, again!" Weylyn's voice pierced through the dusk and snow.

"I am trying," Aedan's exasperated voice replied.

"Again," Weylyn ordered sharply.

Isla went around and pulled the shutters to block out some of the noises from the training and the icy wind as the snow fell softly to the ground. The women sat before the fire sewing new clothing for Giorsal and Isla mended one of Aedan's tunics that Weylyn's claws had slashed through the day before.

"They are working so hard," Alexina sighed taking a moment to stretch her back.

"I think Weylyn is a little concerned about taking us to battle without Aedan being well trained," Isla replied.

"But he *is* well trained," Alexina protested. "He was able to fight the wolves that came for us nearly a moon's cycle ago."

"In human fighting," Isla agreed. "There is none better. He is War Chief of the clan. But this is a completely different form of combat, one that he is still learning."

"How will the clan and your laird handle it if he disappears for some time?" Alexina asked.

"The clan is greatly understanding when it comes to grief," she began. "He is no' their laird so he is given more time. These last several days I ken Aedan is anxious to return to his duties, but I do believe he will no longer be happy there. And there is wolf's bane to consider now. He is no longer immune to the smell."

"How is he handling it?" Alexina asked.

"He does nae speak of it but I ken he willnae return, whether or no' he believes it, och, I pray he will be happy in his new life and no' pine for the lost one," she explained.

"Will you miss it?" Alexina wondered as she stitched the sleeve of her daughter's new gown.

"I may miss the friends we had, but I willnae miss the deception," she said.

"What do you mean?" Alexina asked.

"The entire time I lived in the village, I couldnae practice my calling, I couldnae be a druid and I shamed the gods by falling away. But the clan has very strong feelings against Druids and if I had revealed who I was or even the faintest hint of what I believed and practiced they would have burned me at the stake. So I donnae miss the pain of worry and the fear of discovery. I left my sisters in Skye because when I traveled through the village with them, I met and fell in love nearly instantly with Aedan."

"Tell me," Alexina smiled.

"Och, he was so handsome," she began. "The true look of

a highlander. He stood head and shoulders above the rest, even the laird who is a large man. The first moment I saw him, he was walking through the square with his claymore strapped on his back, the snow had fallen fresh that morning and he walked with his cloak over his shoulders. His hair was loose and flowed down to his shoulders, he walked with such confidence and strength that I instantly took notice. I stopped with my sisters as they passed a street merchant selling herbs and oils. I remember he looked over at me and stopped. We were across the courtyard but we locked eyes. I removed my hood and gazed at him. Taking two steps towards me, Aedan let a small smile quirk his lips and I was in love. My sisters and I were just passing through but I stayed at Aedan's request. We married but a short time later."

"And were your sisters happy for your choice?" Alexina started tentatively.

"Eithne was, dear lass that she is, she is the youngest of us and her mother was a good friend," Isla explained. "She is a romantic at heart. Labhaoise and Geileis were understanding but did nae approve. We had lost our father nearly forty years ago then and Geileis's mate had been killed by Roman legionnaires many years ago. So they were no' as supportive as I would have hoped."

"And now that we ken he is a wolf?" Alexina asked.

"They have no love for the wolves but they donnae hate them. Geileis's mate was killed in an ambush by Roman mercenaries. We were taught to hate wolves since we were born but over the years we have come to realize that no' all wolves are like Marrock," Isla explained.

"Have you been able to contact your sisters?" Alexina questioned.

"Weylyn approved of my contacting them regarding the

rescue and I was able to speak with Eithne last night. She conveyed my message to the other two and they agreed to be on hand if needed but they would no' engage in a war," Isla explained.

Alexina nodded.

"Do you think we are prepared enough?" She asked.

"I think that even if we were no' Weylyn would still do what he thinks is right," Isla said. "He wants to save Tristan and I believe he kens what he is doing. He is very good at distancing his emotions from his decision making."

"Again!" They jumped when they heard Weylyn's yell outside and an answering snarl from Aedan.

"I hope this does no' affect his relationship with Aedan," Alexina said. "They are on such rocky ground and I pray they donnae fall away from each other."

Isla leaned in to her as if sharing a confidence. "Have no fear of that, Aedan told me the other day that he has never felt more alive than when he is training with Weylyn."

"Truly?" Alexina asked hopeful.

"Aye, but donnae tell him I told you," she said.

"Again!" Weylyn snapped. They heard a snarling bark in response and a menacing growl. "I said again!" There was a flick of the switch that Weylyn held during training. Jumping when they heard Aedan yelp, Alexina covered her ears and Isla rushed to the window.

"Stop it!" Aedan's human voice yelled.

"Then do it right," Weylyn shouted, his tone was harsh. "Donnae walk away from me! Get back here! Aedan!" There was a snap of the switch again and Aedan cried out.

"Stop this, Weylyn!" Isla shouted from the window.

"No' until he does it right," Weylyn yelled back and

snapped the switch again. Aedan cried out and clutched his arm where a red welt began to form. "Again!"

Aedan growled a deep menacing growl and looked over to Weylyn, both still in human form. With a loud snarl, Aedan charged his father. Weylyn half-phased and threw Aedan to the ground behind him. Getting up, Aedan shook with anger. Roaring, he charged him again. Just as he reached Weylyn he phased into a full wolf and Weylyn ducked between his legs, sliding to safety behind him. Aedan turned back and phased to his human form. Without a breath, he charged his father again, this time running as fast as he could and throwing punches at him. Weylyn blocked Aedan's hands with his claws unable to take the time to phase back to his human form.

Weylyn's claw connected with Aedan's shoulder slashing a gaping wound. Aedan shouted and stumbled away. Concern ripped through Weylyn as he saw his son bleeding. Aedan looked up at his father, anger in his eyes. He phased into a full wolf as he charged Weylyn. This time his head connected with his father's chest and Weylyn was sent flying towards the barn. Landing on his stomach with a thud a few feet away, Weylyn got up and shook his head clearing it. He looked up just in time to see his son charging him again.

Aedan knocked him down again and this time stood over him, his teeth barred. Weylyn felt his hot breath on his face as they both looked into each other's yellow eyes and, after a moment, Weylyn began to laugh. He phased back to human form beneath Aedan's gigantic wolf form. Aedan looked down at him confused, took two steps back and let Weylyn stand. Aedan phased back to human form and yelled.

"What is the laughing matter?"

"'Tis about time," Weylyn replied. "It only took me

swatting you with a switch."

"What do you speak of?" Aedan demanded.

"You were phasing slowly, too slowly," Weylyn explained. Aedan went back to the side of the well and shook out the plaid blanket. "I had to get you to tap into your anger more and here you are, phasing fast, while running, jumping and fighting. That is what I was trying to get you to do." Aedan wrapped the blanket around his waist and belted it.

"This whole thing was to make me angry at you?" Aedan demanded turning back to his father.

"It was successful," he said. "You were furious at me. Now that you are able to phase completely quickly and without restraint, we can train you on half-phasing and how to fight without the constraint of full wolf form." Weylyn dusted himself off. "Well done, son, you are learning quickly, very quickly. I am very proud of you." Without waiting for an answer, his eyes turned up to the moon. "'Tis time for bed. How do you feel?"

"My arm really hurts," Aedan said sarcastically seeing the red welt from where Weylyn had struck him with the switch. "And my shoulder burns."

"'Tis sorry I am," Weylyn indicated his shoulder. "We will get something to stop the bleeding."

"Did you have to actually strike me?" Aedan questioned.

"In my defense, you were supposed to step away," he said.

"Weylyn, I am a War Chief. I serve my laird, well and proudly. I am a warrior. I attack. I do nae ken how to fight in this war," he replied. "Stepping away is nae what I was trained to do. When I am fighting, and I was fighting you, I donnae run away."

"I ken," Weylyn answered. "And I am sorry for hurting you. You have done extremely well, son. 'Tis proud I am to ken you are my son. You rose to one of the highest ranks in human society and you did so at such a young age. I have much to thank Gowan for; teaching you to be the man you are is one of them. Let us go inside. I am certain Isla can put something on your shoulder to help it heal. We have a dangerous day tomorrow."

"Are you all right?" Isla demanded rushing to her husband as soon as they turned toward the cottage. Her red hair billowing behind her, she ran to Aedan and shot Weylyn an angry look. Stepping around them, Weylyn walked into the cottage.

"Ahh, gently, gently," Aedan said as Isla reached for him. "My shoulder hurts a great deal."

Isla kissed near the wound and looked up at her husband.

"And my arm hurts," he said showing her the welt on his forearm. Her eyes softened to a sensual heat as she kissed it too. "And my jaw hurts," he said brushing his fingers over his jaw where a fresh bruise formed. Reaching up to kiss his jaw, she giggled when Aedan snaked his arm around her waist and pulled her to him, his lips descending onto hers.

Weylyn whistled from the doorway causing Aedan to break away and look back. "You need your rest. We rise with the sun. Isla, can you heal him?"

"Aye, come with me, my love," she replied although she sent a glare in Weylyn's direction. They walked together and disappeared into the barn. Weylyn turned back to Alexina, his expression questioning.

"Promise me one last thing, Weylyn," she started.

"And what is that?" he asked.

"Promise me that no matter what happens, if we cannae get Tristan away from there, if I give Giorsal to you, you run and you save her. Swear to me that if I ask, you will take my daughter and protect her," she said.

Weylyn took a deep breath and let it out slowly.

"Alexina, that willnae happen," he said.

"If it does," Alexina said. "Donnae look back. Swear to me, Weylyn."

"Aye," he sighed. "I promise, lass."

Chapter Nine

"Alexina, wake up," she heard Weylyn's panicked voice break through her sleep. She heard her scream echo before she gasped awake.

"Tristan!" she shrieked.

"Alexina, wake up!" she swore it was Tristan's voice but when she looked up Weylyn stood before her.

"Weylyn?" she wheezed, her throat sore. "What happened?"

"Are you all right?" He asked his face a mask of terror.

"Aye," she answered controlling her ragged breathing. "What happened?" she asked again.

"I was going to ask you the same thing. You were screaming, lass," he said. "Were you having a night terror?"

She did not have a chance to respond as the door burst open.

"Weylyn?" Aedan raced into the room. "Is everything-?"

"Everything is fine, Aedan," Weylyn called. "Alexina had a night terror."

Aedan walked over to them looking like he had just woken up; without tunic, his eyes bright with concern, his hair tangled from sleep.

"I am sorry," Alexina said slowly sitting up. Weylyn hooked an arm around her and helped get her up as her body protested the movement. Once she was situated, Weylyn sat down beside her.

"What was it?" He asked gently rubbing his hand up and down her arm. "What was your dream about?"

Looking down she did not answer immediately.

"How is Giorsal?" she asked.

"Still asleep, somehow you did nae wake her," Weylyn answered.

"Good," she looked away. Aedan put a hand on his father's shoulder and stepped out into the main room. "Tristan," she replied in a small voice.

"What about him?" Weylyn asked.

"I had a dream he was with me," she said. Weylyn said nothing allowing her to continue at her own rate. "I felt him with me and saw him beside me. He told me that he loved me, but when I went to kiss him, he pulled away before I could and got out of bed. I followed him to the center of that room," she indicated the main area of the cottage. "He was looking toward the door. My eyes followed his and I saw Maelogan standing there," Weylyn's body stiffened but she continued. "Tristan looked over at me just as Maelogan let loose an arrow pinning him to the wall, an arrow in his hand. I screamed but saw something black flowing up his arm. He saw it too and looked at me with such a frightened look in his eyes. Maelogan pulled back another arrow and this time shot him through the chest. I screamed again."

Weylyn put a hand on her shoulder as she started to shake.

"'Tis all right, lass," he said as Aedan walked back into the room with some tea.

"Isla is looking after Giorsal, Alexina," Aedan said.

"I thank you," she replied. Taking a sip of tea, she looked up at Weylyn. "Can you make sure he is all right? Please can you phase and make sure he is still alive?"

Weylyn nodded standing from the bed and turning his back to her. Aedan sat beside her, patting her hand in brotherly comfort as his father phased. It was an agonizing few moments but Weylyn finally phased back and turned to her, his face a blank mask.

"Oh gods, what is it?" She breathed.

He looked over at his son for a moment and Aedan clutched at her hand tighter.

"Weylyn, what is it?" She demanded again looking from one to the other.

For a moment she was not sure he would answer her. "I couldnae hear him," he finally admitted.

"And what does that mean?" She asked.

"Two things," Weylyn replied.

"And they are?" She asked.

"Alexina," he began.

"Nay, tell me!" She demanded.

"Either he is no' phased at the moment... or..."

"Or?" She pressed. He did not answer her only gazed directly into her eyes. "Nay," she breathed out. "Nay, that is nae possible. Nay, he is nae phased. He is fine. He has to be."

"Alexina," Weylyn stepped towards her.

"Nay," she cried. "He is no' dead! He cannae be!"

"He may have only been in human form, Alexina," Aedan tried to comfort her. "I am sure we can check again. Donnae think the worst."

"After my dream, Aedan? I believe I have every right to think the worst," she replied.

"But it was just that, Alexina," Weylyn countered. "A dream. I still feel connected to him. If the worst had happened, I would feel a void. I donnae feel that. But I do think it would be wise no' to waste any more time. Aedan, let us go and hunt quickly. We leave directly after."

Aedan nodded and left the room but Weylyn tarried. Turning back to her, Weylyn continued. "Please, donnae think the worst, Alexina, as soon as I ken anything I will tell you," he said. She nodded slowly but did not want to know anything save her husband was safe.

Weylyn and Aedan hunted quickly and, just as they broke through the tree line heading for the cottage, they heard a different voice in their heads.

Weylyn! Weylyn froze and Aedan growled.

Who is it? Aedan asked.

Faolán? Weylyn replied in disbelief.

Aye, my friend, the voice continued.

What? How? Weylyn breathed.

I broke from Marrock's pack. I could no longer follow him after seeing what he did to Tristan, Faolán said.

Weylyn panicked.

Am I too late? Is Tristan still alive? Weylyn asked.

Just, but aye he is alive. Faolán said.

Weylyn breathed a sigh of relief. *I couldnae hear him earlier and I thought...* Weylyn's thoughts trailed off.

I ken, Faolán replied. *He has been unable to phase. Marrock has him chained and bound in his human form and if he were to phase he would choke himself on the collar that Marrock has put around his neck.* Weylyn and Aedan saw a flash of Faolán's memory where Tristan was chained and bloodied. The image made Weylyn growl.

We are on our way, Weylyn said. *We are leaving directly after breaking our fast.*

I willnae be there to help you, Faolán replied.

Why no'? Weylyn's voice was a little too harsh.

Because Marrock has decreed I am to be executed within the hour. Faolán explained.

What? Nay! Why? Weylyn cried.

Why do you think? Faolán asked rhetorically. *I am nae afraid, Weylyn, but I wanted to give you this last message before I join our ancestors.*

Nay! We are coming for you! Weylyn said.

'Tis too late. They are dragging me out of my prison cell now, Faolán replied. *This is what I want. I have had my revenge on him. I ken that now. He may have taken her body, but I always had her heart and nothing will ever change that. I left his pack to join his son. There is no greater revenge than that. I will be with Heledd now. Just remember me with fondness. You have always been my dearest friend, Weylyn.*

And you are mine, Faolán, Weylyn said.

Is this your son? Faolán asked.

Aye, Weylyn replied. *Aedan.*

Aedan, Faolán smiled slightly. *Your father is a fortunate wolf to have so great a man as his son. I am glad to meet you. Your father is like a brother to me. Be well,* Faolán said.

I am the fortunate one, Aedan replied.

Aye well I cannae argue with that. Tristan is alive. See? Faolán showed them both an image of Tristan chained, watching what was happening with a penitent and terrified look. *Be sure to come for him quickly. He willnae last much longer. I am surprised at his strength. But he is strong. Forgive me for no' joining you sooner. I thought it would be best to remain in Marrock's pack in order to get information.*

Tristan told me that you took care of him when they were starving him, Faolán. I thank you, Weylyn replied.

My time has come, Weylyn, Faolán said. *Please, my friend, donnae let this be in vain.*

Be at peace, my brother, you have done your family proud, Weylyn answered.

Weylyn and Aedan felt Faolán's relaxation and they both saw the faces of those around him. Taking a moment, Faolán looked over at his father as Cian tried to break through Marrock's guards to get to his son. Faolán smiled softly at him and told him it would be all right. Cian fell to the ground, wailing and reaching for him. Faolán's eyes turned to Heledd's children who were holding each other crying. The eldest raced to Cian to comfort him. Nodding once to them, Faolán was forced to his knees. Taking a deep breath, Faolán focused on Heledd's face, holding tightly to a memory of her smiling. Opening his eyes he saw Heledd standing by the gate to the village, she looked stunning. Her arms were outstretched towards him. Faolán reached for her, surrendering to the absolute certainty of Marrock's sword.

All went quiet.

The void grew in his chest as Weylyn let the pain surround him. Throwing his head back, he howled. Aedan felt the void grow and howled with his father. Never before having experienced that kind of pain. It was different from the pain he had felt losing his parents, not only did he lose a member of the pack, he felt his father's pain at losing his best friend.

Weylyn closed his eyes against losing the man he had shared so much with; they had grown up together, fought together, lost together and now he was gone.

Staying his emotions, Weylyn guarded his heart against Marrock's treachery and felt Aedan's strength flow into him. Finally taking a deep breath, Weylyn spoke low.

'Tis time to go.

Aedan nodded and turned to see the women walk out of the cottage having heard them both howl. Alexina looked like she was about to faint. Weylyn phased quickly to put her mind at rest.

"Tristan is alive," were the first words out of his mouth as he grabbed one of the blankets they had stashed near the barn. Alexina shuddered and fell into Isla.

"Then why were you howling?" Isla demanded holding her friend.

"A very dear friend of mine just sacrificed himself for Tristan," Weylyn said, his voice shocking everyone, including himself. He was calm, dangerously calm. "Marrock executed him." It was a statement of fact, but it was also a death sentence. Marrock had just killed his best friend and member of his pack. Weylyn's wolf-self was taking over, keeping him calm and collected as he plotted his revenge. The little known alpha blood in his veins flared requiring restitution.

"Och Weylyn," Alexina cried. "I am so sorry."

Weylyn shook his head. He could not mourn his friend, he had to stay focused.

"Are you both ready?" He asked. "We have very little

time. We must go."

Seeing the goat they had hunted to break their fast, Isla shook her head. "I will make sure we have something as we go."

Weylyn nodded. For the first time, he was glad of her abilities.

"We need to leave, now," Aedan said turning his head when he heard the townspeople leave their cottages in search of the wolves that howled. Hearing the mob approach, Isla and Alexina went inside for a moment. Alexina grabbed her daughter and some supplies, and then watched Isla speak over the fire; it went out instantly without any glowing embers.

"Isla," Aedan urged. Isla grabbed Aedan's claymore and left the house following the men into the woods before the townspeople arrived. Aedan turned back to look at the cottage through the trees. "I wish I had taken something to remember Mother by," Aedan replied. Isla called to him and handed over a trinket. Weylyn could not see what it was but Aedan looked at it and then back at his wife smiling.

"I thought you might want something of hers," she said.

"Thank you," he breathed tucking it into the sheath on his forearm.

"It would be faster if we phased," Weylyn said. "We could cover more ground."

"And the women are what? To ride on our backs?" Aedan asked.

"Aye, that seems the best way," Weylyn agreed. "Alexina, wrap Giorsal around you and tie her securely to you. You will need both hands to hold on to me. I willnae be able to hold on to you."

Aedan handed his sheaths and claymore to Isla. The wolves went behind two trees, stripped, folded their clothes neatly and phased. When Isla and Alexina saw the wolves emerge, they went over to where the men had deposited their clothing, took them and held on to them so the men would have something to wear.

As soon as the women were on the backs of the wolves and as comfortable as possible, Weylyn nodded at Aedan and they bounded off toward the Wolf Village.

Chapter Ten

Back to his human form, Weylyn led the group through the woods and to the entrance of the wolf village. The gate did not open and Weylyn looked up at the two half-phased wolves in the guard posts.

"We have come for Tristan," Weylyn called, his voice strong and demanding. One of the wolves looked at the other, nodded and ran back to the main area. "No matter what happens," Weylyn turned to his pack. "Stay calm."

Aedan nodded once in agreement and looked around at the imposing structures of his father's previous home.

The wolf bounded back and growled, "Marrock wants to see you."

"We have nae come to see him," Weylyn replied.

"He says he will let you have Tristan but you must see him first," the guard replied.

With the wolf guard as their escort, Weylyn, with Aedan by his side, started through the village. The wolves came out of their huts as they walked through the village. Weylyn blocked the memories that came back to him when he saw his kin and instead, his eyes scanned the area to see Marrock's bloody trophies, heads on spears beside his throne. Weylyn's eyes caught Faolán's head nearest to Marrock but he kept walking straight down the path from the gates to the keep. All four of them heard jeers when the wolves smelled Isla's Druid blood and many phased ready to attack.

Marrock sat twisting a sword on its tip as he sat slouched on the throne, one leg slung over the arm of the chair, his remaining mistress beside him. Wrapped in the fur pelts of his conquered enemies, his black hair was long and, even slumped, it was obvious that he would tower over everyone. His broad back and chest were intimidating and his light blue eyes danced with villainous humor seeing the prodigal wolf returning. He glanced over at his son and smirked.

Weylyn and Alexina's eyes followed Marrock's and they both saw Tristan, bloody and chained to an upright board beside his father's platform. His weak eyes locked with Alexina and filled with fear for her. Jerking back and forth, Tristan's eyes screamed when he saw his daughter wrapped in Alexina's sash. Marrock's eyes followed his son's to the human woman and narrowed for a moment when he saw the babe wrapped around her. His eyes flashed back to his son then looked over at Conchor. Standing, he backhanded his lieutenant off the platform.

"Kill him," Marrock ordered. "And let it be kenned you donnae lie to me."

Rearranging his features and sitting back, Marrock's face lightened and his eyes remained cool as the group reached the foot of the platform where Marrock's throne sat. The jeers crescendoed until Marrock raised a hand, silencing the crowd.

"Weylyn," Marrock's voice was smooth and powerful, accented from their northern Highland location. "What a surprise," his lips twisted in a smirk when he spoke. "I thought you were no longer part of my pack."

Aedan's eyes met Maelogan's as he stood beside Marrock, bow and arrow in hand. Maelogan smirked at him and his eyes flared yellow. Aedan suppressed his natural growl as Maelogan taunted him.

"I am no'," Weylyn answered. "I have come for my Alpha. My leader. Release Tristan."

"You order me, dog?" Marrock demanded. "This boy kens nothing whatsoever about leading a pack," Marrock shouted.

"He is our Alpha," Weylyn said again. "We donnae want anything from you, only Tristan. We can live in harmony with one another."

"Harmony?" Marrock questioned. "We donnae have to live in harmony with anyone. Why should we? We are victorious over everyone and everything that we meet!" Marrock's voice grew louder as he spoke raising cheers from the crowd of wolves around them.

"We donnae want a fight," Weylyn shouted over the din of noise. Marrock raised his sword towards him.

"You think you could defeat me? You bring a half-breed and a child, a human woman and a druid against me? Did you honestly expect to win?" Marrock asked. "Can the *boy* even phase?" he taunted.

"I hoped we would come to an understanding without resulting to violence," Weylyn explained.

"And yet the *boy* is armed," Marrock said indicating Aedan's weapons still sheathed. "And the Druid is carrying wolf's bane. Do you think I cannae smell it?"

The pack growled almost simultaneously when the smell reached them.

"That was only to dissuade some of the lesser self-controlled of the pack," Weylyn explained.

"You think I am a fool?" Marrock asked.

"Marrock, you ken me. I am a man of my word and I ask you, as a father, look into your son's eyes and see what he has gone through. See the pain he has endured. All he wants is to live with his family in peace. You have a granddaughter," Weylyn turned slightly indicating Alexina and Giorsal. "She is one of the most beautiful creatures I have ever seen. Please, Marrock, I beg you, release your son."

Marrock's eyes went to the baby in Alexina's arms then turned up to Alexina and saw she had not dropped Tristan's gaze. In that moment he recalled Mahb's last words.

"Donnae let this heart grow bitter, Marrock," she had said as she covered his chest with her hand. *"Swear to me, you will still be a good father to Tristan. This is nae his fault."* Haunting him with his promise, his own words came back to him.

Turning back to Tristan, Marrock saw the reflection of Mabh in his face; her blonde hair and dark eyes displayed in their son, but it was not enough; his heart grew cold once more. The whole pack was silent watching their Alpha. Finally, Marrock turned his back on Tristan and spoke low.

"I have no son," turning he motioned to Giorsal. "And that *creature* that you say is my granddaughter... you aptly named her... she is nothing to do with me." Sitting on his throne, Marrock continued. "And as for you, Weylyn... You ken what the punishment is for leaving my pack," he deliberately looked over at Faolán's head on a spike beside him, then waved his hand floppily. "Maelogan," he said.

Maelogan nodded once and raised an arrow.

"Nay!" Isla screamed and stepped forward. When the arrow was loosed, she held out her hands and her eyes changed color. Red eyes shown bright as she cast a spell and the arrow landed at Weylyn's feet.

The wolves were stunned into silence and all took a step back. Marrock leaned forward in his throne fascinated. Maelogan, eyes wide with shock and anger, raised his bow and let loose a slew of arrows but all of them landed at Weylyn's feet, except for the last one. Isla held up her hand palm outstretched stopping the arrow, then cupped her fingers together and twisted her wrist. The arrow turned around midair, frozen in time, pointed back at Maelogan, her eyes burned even brighter red. Weylyn stepped forward and whispered in Isla's ear.

"Think of what you are doing."

"He killed Brietta," she replied.

"I ken," Weylyn answered. "But this is no' the way to honor her memory."

Isla did not turn away from Maelogan as she continued.

"This may no' be *your* way, Weylyn, but he will die," she said.

"Aye, he will," Weylyn's confidence made her pause. "But no' yet. We are here to get Tristan. I willnae stand idly by and allow you to start a war."

"You would defend him?" she demanded looking up at him.

"Nay," he growled. "I want revenge more than you ken… But this is no' the way."

Isla's eyes bored into Weylyn's then she turned to Aedan

who nodded once in agreement with his father.

"I will stop it before it gets to him, just let me do this," she asked.

Weylyn took a moment but finally nodded. Her hand thrust forward and the arrow flew back toward Maelogan. Stopping it just an inch from his eye, the arrow made a thudding sound as it dropped to his feet on the wood of the platform.

After a moment of complete silence, not even birds chirped, Marrock stood, his eyes never leaving Isla's. He picked up the arrow and took Maelogan's bow. Drawing it back, he aimed at Isla. Suddenly, he turned and loosed the arrow.

Chapter Eleven

Tristan cried out as the arrow pierced his hand. Alexina screamed; her nightmare from the night before coming true and Weylyn froze as he saw the wolf's bane that had coated the arrow head begin its progression to Tristan's heart. Marrock sat back down on his throne.

"You want him now?" Marrock asked sarcastically.

"Please," Weylyn replied. "There still may be a way to save him."

"Give us the druid... you can take your pupil," Marrock said.

The vibration began deep in Aedan's chest and his lip curled up as a growl escaped him.

"Och," Marrock chuckled. "The half-breed is fond of her, I see."

Isla held her head high and took a step forward. Aedan's hand caught her upper arm.

"Nay," he whispered harshly to her.

"Aedan, let me go," she replied calmly. "My sisters can

still save Tristan. It is the only way."

"Nay," his teeth were clenched and his voice was low. "I am no' giving you to him."

Marrock watched their heated exchange with ardent curiosity until Weylyn called out.

"Marrock, that is nae an acceptable arrangement. Donnae take the lass… take me."

"What?" Aedan turned to his father. "Nay, no one is going anywhere."

"Aedan, stop it," Weylyn turned yellow eyes onto his son. They stared at each other for a long moment, until Weylyn turned back to Marrock, his eyes brown again. "Please, take me instead."

Marrock chuckled.

"Always the sacrificial one, Weylyn," he patronized. "Just like your father and you ken where it got him…" he sneered. "No… I like the Druid, and I will have her." His meaning was evident in his voice and Aedan let another growl build in his chest.

"Silence," Weylyn ordered to his son.

"That is my only offer," Marrock replied leaning back in his throne. "Besides I need someone to replace Heledd and I like her, she has spirit."

Isla looked at her husband and removed his hand from her arm.

"I will do what I have to do," she said. "I will survive, come for me."

"Nay," Aedan replied taking her arm again.

"Let me go, Aedan," she said. "It will be all right." Shaking his head, he leaned into her caress as she cupped his jaw and kissed him. "Whatever I do, ken that I love you and you alone," she said softly when she pulled back.

"Isla," his plea struck her heart.

She stepped out of his hold and looked at Weylyn.

"You donnae have to do this," Weylyn said.

"It is the only way. When you leave the woods call for my sisters like I showed you. They will be able to heal Tristan but they will have to take him to Skye," she said backing away from them. Before she reached the steps, she spoke to her husband's father. "Weylyn, donnae let him do something rash." He nodded once and she turned her gaze to Aedan. "I love you," she mouthed.

"Isla," Aedan stepped forward. Weylyn held his son back with a hand on his chest.

Isla walked up to the platform where Marrock stood, his eyes yellow, his thumb stroking back and forth over his bottom lip as he watched her. The two guards, who helped her up the steps, grasped her bosom and hips causing another snarl to curl Aedan's lip. Weylyn still held him back. Isla stood on the platform facing Marrock unafraid as he stalked around her. Isla stood straight, her head held high.

"Isla, is it?" Marrock asked mockingly.

"I am Isla Dervorgilla, High Priestess of Alba, Druidess of the Isle of Skye," she announced.

"Och aye," Marrock chuckled. "I remember your father." Her eyes imperceptibly narrowed. "We met near here many years ago," Marrock said mocking her licking his lips. "Mm… He tasted good."

"I was there, Wolf, I remember it well," she said and to her surprise Maelogan chuckled. Before she could consider why he laughed, Marrock grabbed her jaw with one of his massive hands and held it in a vise grip.

Aedan fought his father's hold on him wanting nothing more than to bound up to the platform and kill the alpha. Isla did not cry out, she only held his gaze.

"I will enjoy breaking you," Marrock taunted.

Grabbing his wrist, she twisted her head out of his grip.

"Our bargain?" She asked. Marrock smirked and gestured his head for his guards to release Tristan.

The arrow in his hand twisted and yanked out, the chains rattled and the fetters gave way, Tristan fell to the ground.

"Go to your pack," Marrock spit out the words but did not drop Isla's gaze.

With all the strength he could muster, Tristan stood. Slowly and wobbly but with dignity, he walked towards Weylyn. When he finally reached them, Tristan did not accept Weylyn's assistance. To show weakness to his former pack was the last thing he wanted. Turning back to Marrock, Tristan waited.

"Go now before I change my mind," Marrock said.

Tristan eyes turned to Isla, then to Aedan but Weylyn hurried him away and to his wife. Alexina helped him walk to the gate as Weylyn turned back to his son.

Aedan never took his eyes from his wife as he stood fixed. Weylyn tried to pull him away, but Aedan would not budge.

"Go," Isla mouthed to him.

Aedan shook with anger as he saw Marrock touch Isla's red hair and bring it up to his nose taking a long sniff.

"She can take care of herself," Weylyn whispered in his ear. "We will come back for her, son, I promise you."

Weylyn pulled on Aedan's shoulder but still, he did not move. Hearing Tristan call to him, Weylyn turned to see they were at the gate waiting. Marrock looked at Aedan finally and flicked his hand twice telling him to leave. Marrock then turned to Isla and grabbed a fistful of her hair. She cried out and reached her hand up to ease Marrock's grasp but he pulled her into him and rammed his lips onto hers in a hard kiss.

That was all it took.

Aedan let out a primal cry and, for the first time, half-phased. He ran towards Marrock, his claws ready to sink into him.

"Aedan!" Weylyn cried when he saw he was too late to stop him.

Aedan bounded up to the platform, his body flying in midair, claws out stretched, his yellow eyes never leaving Marrock. In one swift movement, Marrock backhanded Aedan and he fell on his back a little further away. Unfazed by the strike, Aedan stood and rushed the platform again, striking down any wolf who tried to stop him. Marrock picked up the sword he had been twirling when they first walked in, and leveled it at Aedan who stopped short when he felt the cold tip of steel at his throat.

"You have spirit," Marrock's smooth voice taunted him. "I can see a bit of your father in you." He looked up at Weylyn. "I assume that this is the half-breed offspring between you and that human whore you were so fond of? I kenned you were special," he looked down at Aedan. "I have not seen a half-breed half-phase so quickly for a number of years. You should be congratulated, Weylyn. This is quite the bastard you created," his eyes turned back to Aedan. "I remember the last time I saw you. What was it now... over ten years ago, was it? You came across my midnight snack, I remember... some human man encroaching on my woods," Marrock laughed. "You honestly thought *he* was your father? You are clearly so much more than a mere human."

Aedan shook again when he realized that the wolf-man standing in front of him had killed Gowan.

"Your instincts are clearly inherited from your *real* father," Marrock looked back at Weylyn.

"Marrock, please," Weylyn pleaded taking a step closer. "He *is* my son. But he is also young. That is his wife," he gestured towards Isla. "He did no' ken what he was doing. Please, I am still teaching him. Let the lad go. I am begging you as a father, let my son go."

Marrock looked at him and smirked but after a moment, he sighed.

"Nay," he answered and raised the sword ready to sever Aedan's head.

"Nay!" Weylyn yelled.

"Hold your breath!" Isla shrieked as she threw a vial down in front of the Alpha. It shattered and the smoke of wolf's bane engulfed Marrock. He choked and fell back on his throne.

Taking a knife from Aedan's sheath, Isla held it at Marrock's throat.

"This is for my father," she said as she slowly slid it across Marrock's throat. His eyes grew large as he felt the slice through his skin. His life's blood began pouring out. "You believed you were indestructible, immortal, taking it from someone who kens, you are nothing more than a parasite and history willnae remember you." Gurgling sounded from Marrock's throat as he choked on his own blood. Seeing Maelogan peering through the smoke, Aedan grabbed Isla around the waist and pulled back. They fell off the platform together and Isla landed on top of him. Quickly rolling her over just as Maelogan's arrow landed in the grass, Aedan stood, helped his wife up and grasped her hand.

"Run," he said.

All of the other wolves covered their noses and mouths unable to stand the smell. Maelogan, unaffected by the poison, watched as Weylyn half-phased and threw Tristan over his shoulder, Alexina right behind him.

As soon as the smoke cleared, Maelogan saw Marrock's eyes staring lifelessly up at him and he half-phased, howled and turned back to the pack.

"Our Alpha is dead," Maelogan announced. "Killed by the Druid filth that just escaped. Hunt them down. Kill them all."

Howling and barking in unison the entire pack emptied the village tracking the small group.

Chapter Twelve

Isla called for a stop as they reached a clearing.

"We have no time for this, Isla, the pack is still behind us," Weylyn said.

"Aye, trust me, I ken what I am doing," Isla replied as she spoke in a foreign language and motioned an arch with her hands. "There… we are cloaked," she said. "They cannae see us."

Weylyn set Tristan down gently on the ground. He groaned and Alexina raced to him and held his head.

"My sisters will meet us at the entrance to our land. They are already there, as soon as they saw we had Tristan."

"Then they donnae ken Marrock's pack is behind us?" Weylyn asked.

"Nay, no' yet," Isla said. "When 'tis safe I will tell them. Until then, we must see to Tristan while we can. The pack was no' far behind."

"What were you thinking, lad?" Weylyn, still half-phased, growled at Aedan as he slapped the back of his son's head. "You could have gotten us all killed."

"Do you think I was going to let my wife anywhere near that animal?" Aedan demanded taking a step closer to his father.

"Do you honestly think I would have allowed that to happen?" Weylyn challenged. "I had a plan."

"No' good enough!" Aedan shouted and tackled his father to the ground.

"Enough," Tristan ordered. Both father and son froze unable to go against their Alpha's order. "Aye, this time I am no' sorry for ordering you. We donnae have time for this." Slowly, he stood and looked at his pack. "You came for me, for which I am extremely grateful. Weylyn, you kept my family safe, as I kenned you would. I thank you, and you, Druid, you were willing to sacrifice yourself for me… it is odd for me to say this but… thank you. This fight is far from over and I fear that it may be the extinction of us. We need a plan if we—" he cried out feeling the burn of wolf's bane creep up his hand. Weylyn phased back to his human form and rushed to his Alpha as Alexina struggled to keep him upright. Taking Tristan's arm in his hand, he looked at it.

"The poison is spreading," Weylyn said seeing the black lines on Tristan's arm had reached the top of his wrist. Tristan locked eyes with him, his body was weak and his mind told him he could not survive. His eyes subtly went back to his wife and child. Alexina stood strong and reached for his other hand.

"There is a cure," Isla stepped forward. "We must get to the Isle of Skye."

"That is at least a five day journey by wolf speed," Weylyn said. "He willnae survive."

"I ken," Isla answered.

"So what does that mean?" Alexina demanded.

"The passageway I mentioned," Isla replied. "If we travel

fast, we could reach it when the sun is at its highest tomorrow."

"A passage?" Aedan asked. "Where is it?"

"Through Wolf's Bane Field," she answered not dropping Weylyn's gaze.

"Please tell me you are nae serious?" Tristan said. "There is no possible way we three can walk through that place. The smell alone would kill us."

"No' if you have moon flower," she answered her gaze still on Weylyn.

"What?" Tristan asked.

Slowly Weylyn nodded, "'tis too difficult to explain," Weylyn answered. "Phase with me."

After a moment, they both phased back and Tristan's gaze shot between Isla and Weylyn.

"Do you think it would be all right?" Tristan asked.

"It was when they attacked," Weylyn answered.

"But *there*, Weylyn?" Tristan asked.

"I am sorry, but for those of us who are pups at this," Aedan started. "What is Wolf's Bane Field?"

"It is just what it sounds like, a field of wolf's bane," Weylyn replied.

"Planted by my father, Gabhran, to keep wolves away from the entrance to our land," Isla explained. "But we will discuss this more later, the wolves have caught our scent and I want to leave before they surround us."

Chapter Thirteen

"It is highly unusual for a half-breed to learn to half-phase so quickly. I did nae realize you mated with your human woman," Tristan said as they walked. "I am sorry. I donnae think you ever mentioned her name."

"Brietta… and I donnae tell you everything, lad," Weylyn replied.

How do I phase back? Weylyn heard his son's voice.

The same way you did when you fully phased, he explained. *But you have to concentrate on what a normal human looks like and what it feels like to be human.*

I feel normal, Aedan replied.

Weylyn's brows pulled together.

You should no', he said. *It should feel foreign to you.*

Is there something wrong with me? Aedan asked.

I have never seen this except when my father half-phases, Tristan's voice startled both of them. *You are a very special wolf, Aedan.*

What does that mean? Aedan asked.

Weylyn, when was he conceived? Tristan asked his mentor.

Under the Hunter's Moon... Weylyn replied.

I thought that might be, Tristan said.

What in the name of the gods does that mean? Aedan demanded.

I will tell you later, Weylyn said.

Can I phase back? I donnae exactly desire to be like this the rest of my life. Aedan said.

Of course you can phase back. But right now we need speed more than beauty, Weylyn replied.

"We will stop here for the night," Weylyn called. Setting down the makeshift cot they made to carry Tristan, Weylyn turned to his son and helped him phase back to his human form. "Gather some wood for a fire, and donnae do anything rash." Aedan gritted his teeth against his father's rebuke and headed to the woods. As Weylyn dug the hole for a fire, Alexina sat beside Tristan and stroked his forehead.

"I thought I would never see you again," Tristan said softly grasping her face in his hands.

"And yet I am here, my love, with our daughter," she replied raising Giorsal so he could see her.

"She is so beautiful," he breathed.

"Aye she is," she answered smiling. "And she is strong, just like you, my dearest love."

"Were you all right?" he asked. "How was the birth?"

"I was fine," she answered. "I had Weylyn there to help me. Brietta and Isla were wonderful too. I wanted you but I kenned you were with me always."

"I wanted to be there," he sobbed. Every part of him

ached, the makeshift bandages on his injuries were not keeping his wounds clean and blood seeped through them.

"Then promise me you will be there for the next child we have," she said.

"I am afraid that may no' happen, my love," he replied as tears filled his eyes. "With the wolf's bane... there is no cure. I will be dead soon."

"Shh, shh, do you want to hold her?" She asked.

He nodded and slowly lifted himself up enough to be able to look down at her. Giorsal looked up at him and blinked. His breath caught in his throat as he felt her tiny body in his arms. Her trust in him as he held her to his chest, caused tears to well in his eyes. Giorsal reached up, intertwined her fingers in his hair and pulled. Weylyn had to chuckle as he watched the babe remembering she had done that to him multiple times.

"I named her Giorsal, after my mother. I hope you approve," Alexina said.

Tristan gazed down at her unaffected by his daughter's grip.

"Hello, Giorsal," he said softly. "I am your father."

Alexina wiped her tears from her cheeks as she watched the moment she had only dreamt of. Tristan kissed his daughter's forehead and looked over at his wife again through tears glistening his cheeks. Without question, she leaned into him and they kissed with the passion of new parents and lovers long separated.

"I love you," Tristan finally said.

"I love you, too," she answered.

"When I met you, I never realized… you would have left me. I would have outlived you, Alexina," he said. "Perhaps 'tis a good thing I am dying because I could never live without you."

"Hush, Tristan," she said. "I would never leave you."

"Aye, you would," he answered. "I am no' human. I would have lived much longer than you and I donnae ken if I could have survived it. These last few weeks have been a torment for me, no' merely for this," he gestured to his broken body. "But because I was so afraid I would never see you again. I cannae go through that again." He wiped her tears away gently and followed the tears with a kiss.

"I love you," she said. "Nothing will ever change that."

"I cannae watch you age and die," Tristan replied.

"You will no'," she said soothingly. Taking Giorsal back, she looked over at Weylyn sitting on a log near to them. Giorsal cried when she left her father's arms.

"'Tis all right, lass," Tristan called to her as Alexina passed her to Weylyn. "I am right here." Giorsal instantly stilled and quieted.

"My love, you must rest," Alexina said as she felt his forehead. He burned with fever. "I am here now," she soothed. "You need to rest."

"I need you," Tristan replied.

"I am here," she soothed again. "Rest, my dearest love. I will be here when you wake."

"Are you really here? Or am I dreaming?" he begged.

"Nay, my love," she answered. "I am here. We are together."

He said nothing more as he gave into his exhaustion and pain falling into a difficult sleep.

"I am going to hunt," Weylyn whispered as he handed Giorsal back to Alexina. Aedan appeared from the woods with a bundle of wood.

"I will go with you," Aedan offered.

"Nay," Weylyn replied. "I will be faster on my own. Build up the fire. I will return shortly."

Weylyn returned a short time later carrying a large elk over his shoulder. Isla stood, did not say anything as she approached him but her look told him volumes. His eyes trailed to Aedan breaking some twigs and stoking the fire keeping it hot, but his eyes turned to Tristan as he groaned in his sleep and tossed back and forth trying to get comfortable.

"Can you do something for his pain?" He asked Isla.

"Aye, skin the deer," she said. "I have made a baste and there is a branch Aedan has skinned to use as a spit. I will see to Tristan." Walking over to Alexina she spoke low. "I can ease his pain, but only for as long as he sleeps," Isla replied.

Alexina nodded thanking her as Isla stood over Tristan, both hands hovering over his face. She spoke softly and almost immediately Tristan stopped groaning, his breathing slowed and he fell into a deep sleep.

"I thank you," Alexina said.

Once everyone had eaten, Aedan noticed the wood had dwindled. Standing, he turned to his wife.

"We need more," he said. "I will return."

"Be careful," Weylyn called after him. Aedan froze for a moment but without another word, he half-phased and ran into the woods.

Aedan gathered wood for the fire watching any movement in front of him. Hearing rustling behind him, he turned, his body ready to pounce.

"Tis me," Isla said. Aedan phased back to human form and looked away from her.

"What are you doing out here?" He asked. "You should be helping Tristan."

"I had to come and see you," she replied.

"Why?" He asked. "To condemn me? I ken I nearly killed us all. My father has already disciplined me far more than I think I deserve."

"I am no' your father," she replied. "I am your wife. And you saved me."

"*You* saved *me*. I let my emotions control me," he said piling more wood into his arms.

"Nay, my love," she said walking to him and placing a hand on his arm causing the pile of wood to drop to the ground. "You protected me and it was your love for me that caused you to phase."

"I hated him," he corrected.

"Perhaps," she replied. "But when I looked into your eyes, it was love I saw."

"I couldnae give you up," Aedan answered. "I love you too much."

"I ken," she said. Stepping closer to him, she touched his chest. He closed his eyes when he felt her hand over his heart. "You are my husband and I love you."

"Even now?" He asked without opening his eyes.

"Especially now," she answered stepping even closer to him.

"Would you have allowed him to touch you?" He questioned.

"Is that what you are most concerned over?" she asked. When he did not answer, she took his face in her hands and forced him to look in her eyes. "Listen to me, Aedan. If I allowed him to touch me, it would have only been so that you would have been safe," she answered. "You are all I care about. You ken me well enough to ken this, my love. You are the only man who has ever kenned me as a lover, and you are the only man I have ever wanted."

Without another word, he pulled her to him and kissed her.

"The thought of his hands on you, the thought of his lips anywhere near what is mine was too much for me," Aedan said between kissing her. "I need you, Isla," he went on. "I need to prove you are mine again."

"I am yours, Aedan, but if laying claim to me will help assure you that I am still yours, then make love to me, husband," she said breathlessly.

"I thought I was going to lose you," Aedan breathed.

"Never," she whispered pulling his tunic up and over his head. "I will always be here."

"I couldnae bear losing you," he said as his lips found her neck.

"You never will," she answered. "I am yours and only yours. I have pledged myself to you. And here, under the moon, tonight, I swear my love and fidelity to you. You are my husband."

He pulled off her outer gown as he spoke.

"And I swear mine to you," he replied, lips never ceasing his attentions. "Ever since I first saw you, I wanted to be your husband. I wanted to be your partner through life."

"And you are," she said. "I am yours and you are mine. You are my soul mate, Aedan."

Pulling back slightly, he smiled down at her. "I like that," he said as he pushed a piece of hair behind her ear. "I love you, wife," he breathed.

"I will always love you, Aedan," she said sliding her hands to his shoulders. "Now make me yours."

"They have been gone for a quite some time," Alexina said smoothing her husband's forehead as he slept.

"I do believe there is an explanation for that," Weylyn replied. Alexina looked up at him surprised. Shrugging, he continued. "They are married."

"Ah, of course," she answered knowingly. Giorsal squirmed in her pouch against Alexina as Weylyn looked down at the baby and smiled. She turned her beautiful big brown eyes to him. He winked at her. She squealed with delight and squirming more attempting to reach him. Alexina smiled lovingly and pulled Giorsal out. "I do believe she wants her grandfather."

Weylyn's grin was blindingly bright as he reached for the wee babe.

"And her grandfather wants her," he said. "Come 'ere, me wee lassie," he took the babe in his arms and rocked her back and forth. "My beautiful princess, *you* should be sleeping." She squealed and he let her wrap her little hand around his finger as tightly as she could. Swaying back and forth humming a song, he watched her fall asleep.

"What song do you sing?" Alexina asked softly.

"The Wolf and the Willow Tree," he answered without taking his eyes off of Giorsal. "My mother used to sing it to me when I was a pup."

"And the story you told her?" Alexina asked. Weylyn's eyes shot up to hers in surprise. "I am sorry, I did nae mean to eavesdrop, but I heard you telling her the ending of the story of the woman in the tower."

"She liked that story," he smiled slightly, looking down at Giorsal. "It has been in my family for generations."

"In the story you mentioned a Shape-Shifting Druid... what are they?" She asked.

"They belong to the ages," he started. "My father told me about them. I have only met one. They killed my uncle before I was born by shifting into my father's - his brother's - likeness. We have been at war with them for generations ever since my - *Marrock's* great -grandfather was alpha." Alexina said nothing prompting him to continue. "They were supposedly the highest ranking druids of all. They were deadly because they were able to take any shape, from human to animal to even a tree. If you met them on the battlefield they could be any form. My father and his brother had a message for each other, so if they met on the battlefield they would ken one another. Everything would be the same, their look, their clothes, even their voice would match the form they took. If you allowed them to get close to you they would kill you before you kenned what had happened."

"Was that story about one of your ancestors?" She asked.

"A distant relative," he agreed. "But 'tis been so long that their names are lost to time." Suddenly, they heard movement in the woods. Alexina looked over sharply and put a protective hand on his leg.

"Donnae fret," Weylyn said. "'Tis only Aedan and Isla." She sighed with relief as the couple emerged from the woods. "Took you both a while," Weylyn said grinning.

Aedan chuckled.

"Sorry," he replied. "We were... talking."

"Is that what they are calling it now?" Weylyn asked playfully sarcastic as Isla smiled and looked down. "Did you at least get the wood for the fire?"

Aedan pulled the bundle off his back and set it beside the spit, noting his father holding Giorsal. He smiled slightly and looked back at Isla. He could not wait until Weylyn held *his* child with Isla. Soon, he hoped. Aedan put a few more logs on the flames and stoked it with a long branch.

"How is Tristan?" Aedan asked sitting with his back against the log angled off the one his father sat on.

"He is feverish," Alexina replied. "But I think his pain has lessened thanks to Isla."

Isla smiled and went over to Tristan, knelt down beside him and took his arm. The wound in his hand was black and his veins up to his shoulder had turned black as well.

"He only has another half-day at most," Isla said. "We are a full day from the entrance to Skye. It will be a race... and his other wounds are putrid." She noticed the discoloration on his bandages. "That is what is aiding the wolf's bane. I will set his bone now as he sleeps."

Alexina flinched when she heard the bone snap back into place. Tristan groaned but did not wake, not until she covered his forehead with her hand and took his injured hand in her other one. Closing her eyes, she spoke low. Tristan's shallow, quick breathing deepened and slowed but his eyes slowly opened and, seeing Isla over him, he flinched and pulled away from her.

"Easy, my love," Alexina said touching his leg. "She is only helping."

He stilled but watched Isla with distrust. Isla squeezed his wounded hand in hers, he flinched and they all watched as the blackness in his veins retreated back to his elbow and into Isla's hand, up her arm all the way to her neck until she opened her eyes and they burned red. Her mouth gaped and black smoke expelled from her body along with a cry. Releasing his hand, she fell to the ground weakened.

Aedan cried her name and rushed to her, holding her close. He soothed her hair out of her face and stroked her cheek.

"I am all right," she said slowly opening her eyes. "Wolf's bane does no' affect me; it merely takes a great deal of strength to perform that healing." She sat up, her back resting against her husband. "That should help slow the progression. It at least gave us another day. I feel better about the time frame."

"I thank you," Tristan leaned up now fully awake with color back in his cheeks. "I feel better."

"You are welcome," she said. "Your arm is set but we need to bind it." She tried to stand but fell back into Aedan.

"I will do it," Weylyn offered. "I was a healer in the pack."

"I thank you," Isla said. "I must rest."

"Isla," Alexina paused. "If you can draw out the poison that far, could you pull it out all the way?"

"I could but the amount of strength needed would kill me," she said. "That is why wolf's bane is so deadly, there is very little we can do once it is in the blood."

"Then what will happen tomorrow?" Tristan asked.

"We will discuss that later," Isla answered raising a hand to her forehead as her head began to ache. "I must rest."

Aedan took her hand and helped her up, leaning her body against his; her back to his chest she walked with him.

"Isla," Alexina called. "Thank you."

Isla smiled at her friend as Aedan helped her to the other log beside his father where he had sat earlier. Resting his back against the log, he beckoned Isla down to him and gently laid her head on his leg, facing him. He stroked her hair as she slowly fell asleep.

Chapter Fourteen

The moon was high in the night sky and shown down on the travelers as Weylyn and Aedan kept each other alert telling tales and trying to best each other by naming the insects they heard. After a moment of silence, Weylyn looked down at Isla still resting on Aedan's leg.

"How is she?" Weylyn asked his son softly.

"She rests, thank the gods," Aedan replied looking down at his wife.

Tristan and Alexina had long since put Giorsal to bed and rested together, his arm draped possessively around her. The chill of the bitter winter wind bit through their camp and even at their hundred and two degree body heat, it was a cold night. Aedan took the plaid his father offered and covered Isla.

"Aedan, I wish to apologize to you. I am sorry for what I said earlier, more *how* I said it. And for what I did when we left the village. I shouldnae have struck you," Weylyn said.

"I nearly killed my pack, Weylyn," Aedan replied. "You had every right to strike me. I wasnae thinking. Isla helped me understand that I shouldnae be upset with you… or myself. I admit I was angry with you for how you treated me, but I understand now. I am a weak point in this group, my anger at seeing that cur kiss my wife kenning he would attempt to – to force himself on her—"

"You have every right to be angry, Aedan," Weylyn replied. "She is your wife."

Aedan stroked Isla's long red hair absently as she slept. His leg had long since lost feeling but he did not care. He did not want to move for fear of waking her.

"Aye, but in my anger I nearly lost everyone else I… care for," he looked at his father.

"I am very proud of you," Weylyn replied smiling slightly. "You have fought to keep your wife safe. I wish you had learned that from me, but I ken you learned that from your father."

Aedan was quiet for a long moment.

"Gowan was… gods I miss him," he started. "He was a great beast of a man, stout, much shorter than you with a fiery red beard; his hair was long past his shoulders, curled and wild. He had this laugh… it was like a tree falling; deep and resonating in his chest making his whole body bounce," Aedan chuckled at the memory.

"He would always tease me about my being so much taller than he. The village men would laugh saying mother had chosen a more handsome man to be the father of her son and he would reply by saying there wasnae a more handsome man. I remember the first time I brought Isla to meet my parents. I was a little concerned due to the fact that if you did no' ken and understand Father's sense of humor you could find it offensive. But, Isla fell in love with him almost immediately. That is when

I kenned… I kenned I had to marry this amazingly beautiful, talented and loving woman."

Weylyn did not respond for a long moment, then, without taking his eyes off the fire, he asked the question that had been on his mind since Brietta had told him about her marriage.

"Did she love him?"

"I think… in her way she did," Aedan answered. "They were wonderful together, everyone said so. They were happy. And when he was killed, she mourned him."

Again, they were quiet as Aedan continued to stroke his wife's hair absentmindedly.

"Is it true what Marrock said?" Aedan asked. "You ken it does nae bother me to speak of this, but I must ken. Were you and Mother no' married? Am I… what he called me?"

"Nay," Weylyn answered. "However we were no' married in the human fashion; we were married under the moon." Aedan looked at him confused. "When wolves find their mate, there is no ceremony, there is no gathering of family or friends to witness our pledge. We meet somewhere away from the village under the moon. We pledge our love to each other, the moon is our only witness. Your mother and I were married as wolves nothing more."

"That is how wolves marry?" Aedan asked, his eyes subtly moving to his wife.

"Aye, 'tis, so as wolves we were married," Weylyn answered. "But no' as humans."

"But Mother was nae a wolf," Aedan replied.

"Nay, but as my mate she would have… should have, been accepted no matter what," Weylyn answered. "She left her race to become my wife. I would have given her the human ceremony as well had she asked… but she never got the chance. I did no' ken our union had produced you. When I went to Marrock to tell him that I had found my mate and we were one, he claimed to be happy for me until I told him what she was. He called for my capture and I was tried for breaking our most sacred law… Never reveal who you are to a human. My punishment…" Weylyn sighed. "Was grim, you have seen the scars on my back. No matter what pain he inflicted on my body, it was his Alpha order that broke me. He commanded me to never be with her again… ever… So, to answer your question, son, no, you are nae illegitimate when it comes to being a wolf. I donnae ken what other answer to give you, except that you were from love… such love."

"I donnae care if you and mother were never married in the human fashion," he started. "All I want to ken is that you loved her."

"A wolf bond is a strong one," Weylyn explained. "We donnae take it lightly. It is animalistic. We cannae mate under the moon and no' be considered man and wife."

Aedan did not answer for a moment; his eyes went to his wife.

"Then I suppose tonight is Isla's and my wedding night, as a wolf," he said softly.

"Under the moon," Weylyn confirmed. "You have had both ceremonies."

"When Isla and I do have children," Aedan started. "What will they be?"

"I donnae ken," Weylyn answered. "There has nae been anything like this before. Your mother and I conceived you under the Hunter's Moon as I mentioned earlier with Tristan. That is a very special moon to our people. It was under the

Hunter's Moon that we came into being and under that same moon, we went to war with the Druids. It is said that those who are created under the Hunter's Moon have the greatest abilities. It looks like yours is the ability to half-phase without any training, that is something even the oldest wolves have trouble with. Marrock was conceived under the Hunter's Moon; as such, his ability was great strength and command of leadership. No' only was he Alpha, he was a great warrior and the biggest of all wolves. He was a great leader and his battle plans hardly ever failed."

"Isla and I both want children," Aedan said staring into the fire.

"Of course, being a father is a blessing," Weylyn said softly.

"As is being your son," Aedan replied.

Weylyn took a deep breath reveling in the feelings that overwhelmed him. The moment he breathed in, his nostrils flared and his eyes turned yellow. Aedan stiffened and sniffed as well. When he turned back, his eyes burned yellow just as his father's did.

"What is it?" Aedan asked his father. He recognized the scent of flowers but something made his stomach churn. It was not the sweet smell that Isla had but something more sour. Weylyn stood and went to the edge of the fire looking into the woods.

"Druids," he whispered harshly. "Wake her, wake her quickly."

"Isla," Aedan gently shook his wife awake. "Isla, my love, we need you."

"Aedan?" She moaned then seeing his yellow eyes, she sat up quickly. "What is it?"

"Druids," he said simply. She got up and went to stand with Weylyn as Aedan waited a moment until feeling returned to his leg.

"How many?" She asked Weylyn.

"Two men and three women," he answered sniffing again.

"Dervorgilla! Skye!" Isla called out.

"Arc'hantael, Lochalsh," came an answer from a strong male voice.

"We are heading for my grove on Skye," Isla called out.

"May we approach?" The question came from the same voice.

"Of course," she replied. Turning to Weylyn and Aedan, her voice low she continued, "Donnae phase no matter what." They nodded their agreement just as five people crossed into the light of the moon and fire. They were dressed similarly to each other, cloaks and tunics covered their bodies. Both the men and the woman had straight, long hair, their bodies lean and slim. It was difficult to tell them apart as their features were similarly beautiful. The only distinguishing characteristic was the men were several inches taller than the women and their voices were masculine.

"My family and I were traveling to my sisters in Skye," Isla explained.

"We came to see who lit a fire on our land," the man whose voice they had heard earlier spoke. He was dressed in a long brown cloak that matched his long hair, which was braided at the temples and tied at the back of his head. He had a crown of leaves circling him and Isla bowed when she recognized his rank.

"I ask your pardon, my lord," she said. "But we have a

babe among us and she needed warmth."

"And you have three wolves with you," one of the women said tilting her head to one side eyeing Weylyn and Aedan.

"Aye," she answered. "But as you can see, they are no threat."

"A dog is a dog," the other man said. Weylyn and Aedan controlled themselves from growling.

"Cathbad," the leader warned. "Donnae."

"This is my family," Isla went on. "My husband and his father," she indicated Aedan and Weylyn.

"You married a wolf?" Cathbad spit out the words.

"Aye, he is my soul mate," she answered raising her head high. "One in our company is very sick."

"Wolf's bane," another of the women said. "I can smell it from here."

"Aye," Isla answered. "He was infected several hours ago by the Alpha, Marrock. We are being followed by his pack. Forgive us, we did no' have the time to ask your permission before entering."

"We felt the wolf pack enter our land," the leader said. "They are no' far behind you and with the moon in its second full phase tonight, we set out to check our realm. After the violation of their kind on our land we grew concerned that the historical aspects related to the Hunter's Moon were repeating. We sensed the fire and drew near."

"'Tis our fault that the wolves have entered your land," Isla replied. "We beg your pardon."

"'Tis all right, sister," the leader said. "We grant permission."

"I thank you," Isla answered bowing again.

"Have you been able to eat?" One of the women asked gently. "You all look like you have traveled a great distance."

"We were, Priestess," Isla answered. "We gave thanks to Cernunnos that he provided an elk."

"Good," she smiled. "I ken the mother could use some food if she is to keep her strength to feed the child."

"Liam," one of the women went to the leader and gently placed a hand on his arm. "Perhaps you could help the wolf? He is very sick and I sense he is the alpha of their pack; his destiny is important."

"You have far too much faith in my abilities, my love," the leader, Liam, answered. "There is only one cure for wolf's bane and it has nae been bestowed in nearly a thousand years."

"Liam Arc'hantael of Lochalsh?" Isla asked tentatively.

"The same," he answered with a bow of his head. "You ken of me?"

"Gabhran was my father-priest," she replied.

"Ah, so you knew my unfortunate birthfather?" Liam asked.

"I grieved his loss," she said.

"Aye," Liam answered. "So did all the Druid Circle."

"Is the child sick?" his wife asked and Isla noticed the slight move she made to cover her stomach as if protecting a child not yet seen.

"Nay," Isla said smiling at her kindness. "Only the alpha but I am sure the child is tired."

"Perhaps some mistletoe would no' go amiss," the woman said.

Isla hesitated. "The child is no' fully human," she said delicately but she saw Liam's and Cathbad's eyes widen imperceptibly.

"Is it wolf-kind?" Liam asked.

"Half, my lord, aye," Isla replied.

Isla felt Weylyn stiffen beside her.

"But as you see with my husband, half-breeds are no' something to fear," she went on indicating Aedan.

Isla watched as Liam's eyes turn to Aedan and appraised him. Aedan did not move.

"You are a healer, are you no'?" the first woman spoke.

"I am, Priestess," she replied.

"You are a high priestess," Cathbad said.

"I am," Isla answered.

"My father, Gabhran, was killed," Liam said without preamble. "... By a wolf," his eyes turned to Weylyn. Again, Weylyn and Aedan suppressed the growl that wanted to escape them.

"By the Alpha Marrock," Isla said quickly. "I killed him. That is the reason the pack chases us. They held my husband, his Alpha, and me captive."

"Well done," Liam answered. "I have no' had so much to celebrate during the Hunter's Moon before. You have done our order a service by ridding it of Marrock's filth. In gratitude, is there anything you need?"

"Do you have moon flower?" She asked.

"There is a field just over that hill," he stated. "You may have as much as you require."

"I thank you, my lord," she said bowing her head. When she looked up, they were gone. Turning back to Weylyn and Aedan, she took a deep breath. "That could have been much different. Thank you for not phasing or growling."

"How could it have been different?" Aedan asked.

"A wolf pack on Druid land *especially* without

permission?" Isla replied. "That is a punishable offense. 'Tis a rule that no wolf should cross onto Druid land. Marrock's domain stops just east of theirs, which is Lochalsh. If they felt that you were a threat, I couldnae have stopped them." They walked back to the fire where Alexina had awakened and looked up at them curiously. Weylyn smiled slightly at her letting her know that all was well. Lying back down beside her husband, she fell asleep again.

"They also gave us permission to use Moon Flower found on their lands. That is something that would no' normally happen. They guard Moon Flower fiercely and it is strongest if picked at night. Aedan, will you come with me?" She asked. "I must gather as much as I can for tomorrow we are faced with Wolf's Bane Field."

"Of course," Aedan answered. "Weylyn, will you be—"

"I will be fine," Weylyn answered. "Just be quick about it."

"We will be," Isla promised and they both disappeared over the rise of the hill.

"Liam," Cathbad whispered to him as he passed the darkened alcove of their keep. Liam looked down the hallway to be sure their women did not overhear. "Have you spoken with Maelogan?" Cathbad went on when Liam stepped closer.

"Nay, no' yet," Liam replied. "He will contact us when he is able."

"How do we ken what the druid priestess said was true? How do we ken Marrock is dead?" Cathbad pressed.

"Because I read it in the half-breed's eyes," Liam said. "Marrock is dead. Maelogan will contact us when he can. His plan has begun." Cathbad let out a harsh sigh. "I ken you want revenge for what they did to your cousin, Cathbad, but you must have patience," Liam said.

"Aye you are right, Liam," Cathbad replied. "I want the one named Weylyn. He is mine to kill."

"Aye and you may yet get your chance," Liam said. "But until we hear from Maelogan you must stay your hand."

"What he did to my cousin was no' right," Cathbad answered shaking with anger.

"Brietta was a kind soul who did nae deserve the kind of death he inflicted," Liam said. "I promise you, Cathbad you will get your revenge. Until then keep your wits about you."

"When Maelogan told me that Weylyn had torn her body to shreds after ravishing her I swear…" Cathbad started.

Liam placed a hand on his friend's shoulder.

"All things in time, hmm?" Liam asked. Cathbad finally nodded. "Now get some sleep."

Cathbad bowed to his priest and stepped around him. Walking down the hall, he entered his room and shut the door. Liam watched him go and the moment he disappeared into his room, Liam's eyes flared yellow and a grin spread across his lips.

"He believes us, Maelogan," he whispered. "Everything is going as planned."

Chapter Fifteen

Weylyn gently shook his son's shoulder that next morning. Aedan woke, peeled away from his wife and looked up at his father.

"We need to leave," Weylyn said, his eyes trailing to Tristan. Aedan's gaze followed and saw that the wolf's bane had nearly reached Tristan's shoulder.

Aedan nodded and gently rocked Isla awake as Weylyn went to Alexina and woke her quietly. Once the camp had stirred, Weylyn began covering the fire when Isla stood.

"I will take care of it," she said smiling through a yawn. Weylyn nodded and stepped back allowing her to stand over the fire. She spoke the same words Alexina had heard her say over the fire in Brietta's cottage when they left. As before, the campfire went out immediately. Crouching down, Weylyn touched the embers.

"Cold," he said confused. "As if the fire has been out for a day."

"Useful when eluding an enemy, do you no' think?" Isla

winked at him. He smirked.

"Very," he answered standing. "Maybe those powers of yours have purpose after all."

"Why, Weylyn, are you actually complimenting my druid ability?" She asked teasing.

"Never," he winked. "Merely stating a fact."

She laughed and shook her head. Aedan smiled hearing the teasing exchange between his father and wife.

"There is enough venison from last night," Isla said. "We should eat."

"I am fine," Weylyn replied. "As you ken wolves can go a several days without food."

"Is that why I am no' hungry?" Aedan asked. "I normally starve to break my fast."

"Aye, things became different when you phased for the first time," Weylyn explained.

"I believe our women should eat," Aedan said.

"Aye," Weylyn answered. "But I donnae want to wake Tristan. The more he can sleep the less pain he will be in. Alexina, Isla, come take something to break your fast."

The moment Weylyn unwrapped the meat in Aedan's plaid, the smell assaulted Isla's nose; her stomach heaved and she rushed to the edge of the woods just in time to cover retching the contents of her stomach. Aedan raced after her and held her tightly as she shuddered, pulling her hair out of the way.

"Isla?" Aedan questioned when she finally slumped against him. "Are you all right, my love?"

"I am no' certain," she replied. "The smell churned my stomach." Aedan helped her back to the camp, where she felt Weylyn's and Alexina's concerned looks. "I am sorry," she went on. "The smell twisted my senses the wrong way. I am all right now."

"Are you sure?" Alexina asked.

"Aye, thank you," she answered. "I donnae believe I could eat right now but perhaps I could find some mint. That should help with the retching."

"I will go with you," Aedan replied.

"We donnae have much time," Isla said. "But I saw some last evening."

"Take the time you need, lass," Weylyn answered. Isla nodded her thanks and clutched Aedan's hand to steady her as they walked back to the woods.

"Is she all right?" Alexina asked.

"I believe so," Weylyn replied. "Nothing a few months will no' help."

Alexina's eyes snapped to where they had disappeared into the woods.

"Och… of course," she breathed. "She does nae ken."

"Nay how could she?" Weylyn asked.

"'Tis true, I did nae ken when I carried Giorsal in the beginning," Alexina said.

"They will return presently," Weylyn replied. "Perhaps we couldnae mention our suppositions to either of them?"

"Aye, 'tis something they should find out together," she smiled. "I must feed Giorsal."

Weylyn nodded once and finished packing their camp. Aedan and Isla arrived back to the camp within moments to see Alexina finishing eating and Weylyn sitting with a ladle of water to his lips.

"How are you feeling, lass?" Weylyn asked.

"Better, I thank you," she answered. "We should go," Isla

said.

Once Aedan was sure his wife was all right he went to his father and helped pick up Tristan's cot. Tristan woke with a start, his eyes yellowed.

"Who? Where?" He shouted.

"'Tis all right, my love," Alexina reached for him; Giorsal wrapped in her sling around her mother. "We are heading to Skye."

Tristan seemed to calm and he strived not to fall back asleep but his body craved rest.

"It will be a full day before we reach Wolf's Bane Field, Tristan," Isla called. "Rest. My spell will only work when you are asleep."

Nodding, he clutched Alexina's hand to his chest and fell back to sleep.

It was nearly dusk when Weylyn and Aedan stopped at the same time and groaned.

"Gods above," Aedan cried. "What is that god-awful stench?"

" *That* is wolf's bane," Weylyn grimaced.

"Nay, it cannae be. It has never affected me like this," Aedan replied. "I have always carried it and it has never smelled like that. It is worse than anything I have ever felt and it burns my nose and throat."

"'Tis because you never phased before, my love," Isla said. "You were unaffected by it until your first phase."

"That is the curse of the wolf," Weylyn said. "Many things about you changed that day. You are nae fully human, son."

Isla pulled out the masks she had soaked in moon flower the previous evening and wrung them out. After she gave one to

Weylyn and Aedan, she cautiously walked to Tristan, lying in the cot. "I ken you have no' reason to trust me, but this will protect you from the wolf's bane."

It was a moment before Tristan spoke but when he did, his voice was strong. "You were willing to sacrifice yourself for me and you have kept me alive. I have several reasons to trust you, Isla." It was the first time he had not called her *Druid* and it made her smile.

"Then, Alpha, wrap this around your mouth and nose. It will help with the smell," she said. He raised himself up with Alexina's help. Reaching for the kerchief, he tried to tie it, but his body was too weak. Alexina held him and nodded at Isla. Looking Tristan in the eyes to show she meant no harm, she reached around him and tied it for him. He nodded his thanks and his eyes turned down to his arm. The blackness in his veins had reached his shoulder again. "All will be well," she said. Turning to her husband and Weylyn, she saw they had wrapped theirs around their mouth and nose. "How is it?"

"'Tis still there, but 'tis tolerable," Weylyn said.

"Good. And you, Aedan?" She asked.

"No' as bad as it was," he replied. "It does nae hurt as much."

"Good," she put a hand on his arm and looked him in the eye. "Now you must tell me if or when the smell comes back. I have plenty here. I donnae ken how long it will last."

"Isla," Alexina called. "What about Giorsal?"

"She has no' phased," Isla explained. "She will be as unaffected as you or I." Alexina thanked her. "Are we ready?" Isla asked. Once in agreement, she turned to the field. "Then follow me." Stepping out of the woods, Isla took the first step into the field of purple flowers. Aedan and Weylyn picked up Tristan's cot and followed Isla, grimacing at the overpowering smell. Tristan writhed and moaned as the scent of the flowers wafted up and, like fingers, clawed at his open wounds.

"What is wrong with him?" Alexina demanded.

"The flower is very potent," Isla explained. "The smell is like a smoke. He is feeling it in every wound."

"Is there anything we can do?" Alexina asked as Giorsal began to cry.

"I can cover him with a blanket soaked in moon flower, but it would take all of the reserve we have," Isla said. "I will have none for Aedan and Weylyn."

"Nay," Tristan said through clenched teeth. "Weylyn and Aedan need it more than I. I rely on them to get you all to safety. I will be all right."

Weylyn's eyes scanned the field. It was a vast wide-open space and Weylyn did not see anything in it that remotely resembled a secret entrance. The field was covered in poison and the smell was intense making his eyes instinctively turn yellow.

"I wish to the gods we could burn this whole field," Weylyn's voice was still human.

"I was thinking the same thing," Tristan groaned.

"How can something so beautiful be so deadly?" Aedan asked looking around.

"Some say the wolves actually utilized this flower centuries ago as a healer," Isla started. "Then during the great battle, the highest ranking Druids, kenned as shape-shifters, put a curse on it so that the wolves' greatest ally turned into their deadliest foe. The last great battle between the wolves and druids took place on this field."

"Thousands of wolves died that day," Tristan started, his

voice sad. "They say the moon mourned so many of its loved ones; the wolves, that it turned red with their blood and did nae turn white again for many days. My great grandfather, Bannock, was the Alpha at the time. He lost his two youngest sons that day. We used to be all over this island and now only a handful of us remain. My father's pack is the last of them."

"His is no' the only pack left, Tristan," Weylyn said.

His Alpha looked up at him; eyes shadowed with pain but said nothing. They were quiet for a long time following Isla through the field when suddenly a howl ripped through the silence. Turning, they saw dozens of fully phased wolves coming out of the woods behind them. Seeing the wolf's bane surrounding them, the wolves howled again and tried to cross into the field but were forced to fall back as the smell burned their senses.

"They have found us," Alexina cried clutching Giorsal closer to her and gripping her husband's hand tighter.

"They cannae get any closer," Isla replied calmly. "They are just as affected as Weylyn and Aedan were."

"But let us keep moving. We have only to cross this field to get to the secret entrance to my land," Isla said.

"Where is it?" Weylyn asked.

"Close," she replied. "I swear to you, Weylyn, I would no' lead you astray."

"How far, Isla?" He demanded.

"Do you see that mound yonder?" She asked. His eyes scanned and he nodded. "There."

"Aye, well... Aedan," Weylyn looked back at his son who nodded and they both half-phased. "Stay here," he said to the women. Isla stopped them.

"My sisters willnae let you through without me," she

said. "We go together or not at all."

"Weylyn!" Alexina shrieked. He turned to observe what she had seen. Dozens of wolves that stalked on the outskirts of the field looking for a way in, were joined by nearly fifty more. All of Marrock's pack had been unleashed, even the wolves from the dungeon who were once human but were just as affected by the wolf's bane.

"Be at ease, Alexina, they cannae reach us," Weylyn explained.

"They would have to cross the entire field to get to the entrance," Isla confirmed. "'Tis in the center of the meadow."

Continuing at a much faster pace, the women ran to keep up. Wolves howled on the outskirts as they tried to cross the field but felt the burn of the poison.

"There," Isla called and pointed to a mound in the field. "Sisters, come to me!" She cried and then said something in Gaelic that no one else understood.

The mound sunk in and a door opened to two woman dressed similarly to the druids they had met the night before. Beckoning them to the entrance of what looked like a cave, Weylyn heard Alexina scream his name, this time, with a fear he had not heard. Turning, he saw Maelogan crossing the field at a horribly fast pace.

"Aedan, get them inside!" Weylyn ordered.

"I am staying with you," Aedan shouted.

"I said go!" Weylyn yelled. Aedan looked at him for a moment, then, nodding picked Tristan up and carried him over his shoulder. Weylyn saw them disappear and the part of the mound that had sunk in filled up again. They were safe. Weylyn turned to face the man running up to him.

"Coming for me, Maelogan?" Weylyn shouted.

"You will do," Maelogan answered still racing across the field.

"How can you cross Wolf's Bane Field?" Weylyn yelled.

"How could you no' smell me?" Maelogan smirked.

"You are nae wolf..." Weylyn said.

Maelogan smirked and slowed down.

"Och I am a wolf," Maelogan's eyes flared yellow. "But I am nae all wolf." His body shuttered and Weylyn watched in shock as Maelogan changed his form and became Brietta. Weylyn's brows drew together as he watched the woman he loved walked towards him.

"What are you?" He breathed standing frozen watching her.

"Donnae you ken me, love?" Brietta's voice came from the man, who not a moment ago, was a hated enemy. "Och, perhaps no'. Would you would rather someone else?" Brietta's voice asked as Maelogan changed form again and turned into Aedan.

Knowing he needed to defend himself, Weylyn tried to think but he was too dumbfounded. He could not believe his eyes. Maelogan was a shape shifter.

Weylyn's father's words came back to him; *the highest ranking Druids, absolutely dangerous, fierce warriors who could never be trusted* and they were supposedly extinct.

"Nay? To your own son?" Maelogan asked watching Weylyn's reaction.

"My son is safe," he said. "You are nothing but a parasite."

"Och, such harsh words, Weylyn," he said. "What would your father say?" With that, Maelogan changed form again and Weylyn came face to face with his own father; Kinnon.

"How?" Weylyn breathed. "How do you ken my father?"

"I am your father, Weylyn," Kinnon's voice brought back so many memories.

"Nay you are no'!" Weylyn shouted. "How do ye ken my father? He died."

"Hmm… well… I could tell you, but that would no' be any fun, would it?" Weylyn shuttered hearing his father's voice from such a vile man. "Nay again? Very well, how about this?" Maelogan changed form yet again and Weylyn stared into his own eyes as Maelogan reached him. Every instinct told Weylyn to defend himself, but his body would not respond.

"Why come after me?" Weylyn breathed.

"You donnae remember me, do you?" he asked.

Weylyn swallowed hard but he could not get the words out of his mouth. Maelogan looked at him and with a sick grin, changed into a form Weylyn had not seen for forty years. Marrock's former lieutenant. A man Weylyn never trusted, a man of the same name.

"You!" he breathed. Maelogan, the form he recognized as one of Marrock's lieutenants for years grinned at him.

"'Tis good to see you again, Weylyn," he said.

"I kenned! I wondered at the time if it could have been you! You… *sionnach ann an craiceann na caorach*!" Weylyn cried. Maelogan chuckled.

"Och, that is no' a very pleasant thing to say to an old friend," Maelogan said.

"You are no friend of mine!" Weylyn cried.

"Ha! When I followed you that night years ago and found you and your human whore mating in the woods, I always kept an eye on her to see if you fathered a child. When Aedan was born, I kenned from the beginning that that half-breed was yours. I made sure to befriend him in a form he would trust," Maelogan said.

"It was your doing that Marrock forced me to never see Brietta again! It was you who told him she was human!" Weylyn yelled.

"My only regret is that I wasnae given the right to punish you. I would have taken great joy in meting out Marrock's sentence," Maelogan sighed. "I do miss my old form, but I had foresight to ken never to use that form again after you figured out what I was. So your Maelogan died and I became a new one... I do so love the name though."

"How are you even possible?" Weylyn demanded. "My father told me that all shape-shifters are dead."

"Och nay, we are very much alive," he grinned. "But I am also wolf kind and I have an army of my kind ready to follow me. When Marrock bit me, instead of me turning into a complete wolf, my druid blood protected me and turned me into a man-wolf. I cannae fully phase, only half, but then no other wolf can change form like I do. So, I stayed hidden. Marrock's greatest asset as I am unaffected by wolf's bane and I can change my scent to whatever form I take."

"Who are you really?" He asked. "Who were you before Maelogan?"

"I am sure Isla has mentioned me?" He asked. "'Tis a pity if she never did... but then, she has no' been to Skye for several years."

"Who are you?" Weylyn demanded and watched as Maelogan transformed into an old man.

"I am Gabhran, High Priest of Alba and Druid of the Isle of Skye... oh and Isla's Druid father... no' by blood mind you, just as her priest. They called me Father," he chuckled. "I actually liked you, Weylyn," he mocked. "You were the first in a thousand years to... *venture* outside of the pack," he said. "How was she? Your human... was she worth it?"

"You wanted to stop me from being with Brietta? Why?" Weylyn demanded.

"Assuredly you ken of the prophesy... a half-breed will be the destruction of all shape-shifters, one conceived under the Hunter's Moon. As Aedan is the last... only *you* stand in my way. The choice is obvious. If I am to follow Marrock and take over the pack, I need to rid myself of the one man who can prevent me."

"You want to be Alpha," Weylyn said.

"Aye, who wouldnae?" He asked. "You ken, you are correct, The Hunter's Moon is important to both our people but mostly to mine. It is the forerunner to our death. 'Tis Aedan's destiny to kill me as the child of the Hunter's Moon. I ken he is the half-breed of the prophesy and if I can prevent the prophesy from ever coming true, then what is to stop me? Once you are out of my way, I will kill him."

"You cannae. I willnae let you," Weylyn said.

"I ken," Maelogan replied taking a step forward and placing a hand on Weylyn's shoulder. "And I want you to ken that I am sorry... 'Tis no' that I donnae like you, Weylyn, 'tis merely you are in my way." Weylyn gasped as he felt an arrow tip ram up his chest. His hand grasped Maelogan's shoulder as Maelogan twisted the arrowhead and pulled Weylyn closer to him thrusting the arrow in deeper. Weylyn gasped for air as the arrow pierced his lung.

"Shh, shh 'tis all right," Maelogan whispered in Weylyn's ear. "I want you to ken that I have the highest respect for you, Weylyn. But, you are standing in my way. Can you feel it? Can you feel the wolf's bane entering your body racing up to your heart? I made this one especially for you. Tell me, how does it feel?" Weylyn gasped but said nothing. "You have failed to protect those you love. Brietta. Tristan. Aedan."

"Aedan is safe," Weylyn panted. "He is protected."

"You think that just because Aedan is inside there he is safe?" Maelogan asked indicating the entrance. "You forget that I am the high priest of Skye. That is the entrance to *my* land," Maelogan lowered his voice to a silent whisper near Weylyn's ear. "I created the password..." Maelogan pulled back and looked into Weylyn's eyes.

"Your son will be first to feel the wolf's bane on my knife but it will be only enough to immobilize him. I will kill that human and her baby. I ken Isla will try to stop me, but I have something special planned for her. Then I will kill your Alpha. With Aedan immobilized, I will kill Isla right in front of him and will relish his screams as he watches her die. He will be the last to go, of course and it will nae be quick. You have failed, Weylyn. I am the last of the shape-shifters and I am the most powerful being on this earth. Nothing can stop me, especially no' you."

"You talk too much," Weylyn gasped out. Feeling the knife handle that Aedan slipped into his hand, he reached up and jammed it up under Maelogan's ribs. Gasping, Maelogan released the arrow and Weylyn fell to the ground.

Aedan, who had come out of the cave in time to see Maelogan stab Weylyn, had crouched down so no one could see him and placed one of his knives into Weylyn's hands. He stood, stepped around his father and straddled the writhing form on the ground. Slowly he sliced his knife across Maelogan's throat. The gurgling sound coming from Maelogan as he choked on his own blood satisfied the highlander in Aedan. "That was for my mother," Aedan said. As Maelogan stared at him wide-eyed, Aedan leaned on his knife and severed Maelogan's head from his body. Seeing no life left in his dull eyes, Aedan took a deep breath.

"Aedan," he heard from behind him.

Suddenly, Aedan turned back to Weylyn on the ground reaching for him. "Weylyn!" He cried racing for him. "'Tis all right," Aedan kept saying. "It will be all right. Help! Isla, help me! Donnae think about dying. Nay!" he shook him. "Stay with me. Please."

"Aedan," Weylyn gasped holding his son's tunic. "Aedan!"

"I am here," Aedan said cradling his father in his arms, his chest to Weylyn's back.

"I want to tell you..." Weylyn started, looking up into his son's eyes. He closed his eyes against the pain and his body writhed as the poison made its way to his heart. "Tell you... that I am... I am so proud of you..."

"I ken," Aedan said. "I ken already. Please..."

"I love you, son," Weylyn finally said.

"I love you too, Father," Aedan replied. Weylyn's entire body relaxed hearing that name. It was foreign to him and yet somehow familiar. His heart swelled hearing his son finally call him by the name he had longed to hear. "Please stay with me. Donnae leave me... Please!"

"I wanted to hear you say that, just once," Weylyn gasped out.

"Live and you will hear it every day," Aedan whispered.

"Aedan, forgive me, I donnae want to leave you," he replied.

"Then donnae! Please, Father, donnae leave me!"

Aedan's voice slowly slipped away as Weylyn closed his eyes.

Chapter Sixteen

"Can you do something?" Aedan's voice was panicked.

"Lay him out on the stone," an unfamiliar female voice said.

"The arrow was coated with wolf's bane," another female voice said.

"It has nearly reached his heart," Isla observed.

"You ken the only thing that can be done," a third woman's voice was soft.

"He would no' want that," Isla breathed.

"How do you ken?" Aedan demanded. "Do it!"

"Aedan, the only thing we can do is... the only way for him to survive is if we give him immortality," Isla said.

"Then do it!" He ordered.

"'Tis no' a blessing," the second voice said. "He will live forever, nothing will be able to kill him and since he is no' a Druid he will never be able to give it up to grow old. Everyone he loves will die and he will live on."

"After losing Brietta I ken he would no' want to live

forever without her," Isla said. "He would rather join her."

"You donnae ken that," Aedan's voice shook.

"Aedan, you must no' be selfish," Isla said. "He would want to die to be with her. He would no' want to live to watch you and I grow old and die and he would be alone again. 'Tis no' a life he would want. You have to let him go. Say goodbye, for both your sakes."

There was silence for a long moment.

"He is my father," Aedan's voice was soft but intense. "I will join him."

"Aedan," Isla gasped.

"You have nae given yours up yet. We can live forever, all of us together," Aedan said. The cave was quiet for a time. "I ken I am no' worthy, but I would strive to be," he said. "Please," his voice was a whispered plea.

"'Tis no' something to take lightly. It is a very dangerous thing to live through," Isla finally said. "You will re-live parts of your life that mean the most to you. Parts that you enjoy and parts that you would want to change. You cannae change them."

"But I will still have you and my father," he said. "Will I keep my memories?"

"Aye, but you will be given a choice to change the past or to just watch. That is the fire you must go through. If you survive this..."

"What do you mean, *if* I survive?" He asked.

"You will be given the opportunity to undo every mistake you ever made. You will be able to change your past, but if you do, you will die," Isla said. "That is why we are given this curse when we are young and have few experiences. But you, my love, you have a part of your life that I am sure you will want to change... you will go through losing your mother again and you cannae change it. If you do, you will die," she stressed.

Aedan swallowed.

"But he will survive," he said.

"There is no kenning," she answered. "But as he is no' fully conscious, there is a better opportunity that he will think 'tis only a dream and awaken. You will live through it all fully conscious, aware. It will be hell."

"But he will survive," he said again. "And we will all be together."

She nodded. Aedan looked back at where Alexina sat beside Tristan, unconscious beside her.

"Will Tristan be immortal as well?" Aedan asked.

"Aye," Isla replied. "When he wakes. It was his choice and our privilege to bestow it on him. You all are great men. As you have always fought for peace and justice in this world, we will do this if it is what you truly desire."

Aedan looked at his father and took a deep breath.

"Aye, 'tis," he said.

Isla looked at her sisters. They nodded and went to prepare the potion.

"Take your tunic off and lie down," Isla replied. Lying on another stone table near his father, Aedan calmed his rapid heartrate and focused on Isla stroking his hair.

"Remember you must no' try to change anything," she said. "You must be a bystander watching your life as a dream."

"What would I want to change?" He asked. "I have all I need right here."

She smiled and leaned down to kiss him.

"And soon, you will have something else to live for," she replied taking his hand and placing it on her stomach. He looked at her surprised. "So you ken why you have to survive... you are going to be a father, my love."

"When did this...?" He breathed.

"Just after your mother passed," she smiled slightly.

He grinned and leaned up to kiss her. When he pulled back, he held her face in his hands and rested his forehead against hers.

"That is why you were sick this morning," he said.

"Aye," she smiled at his look of pure joy and amazement. "You have to come back to me, Aedan. I cannae do this alone," she whispered.

"I promise you, I will. How long will I be unconscious?" He asked.

"You will die, my love, that is what happens and you will be reborn into an immortal," Isla explained. He took a deep breath and nodded. "You will have to find your way back to me. There is no kenning how long you will be unconscious. But I will be right here until you wake."

"I will see you in a little while then," he gently rubbed his hand against her stomach. "I will come back for both of you... Take care of my father. If he wakes before me, tell him I will be all right."

She nodded as tears ran down her cheeks. He wiped them away with his thumb.

"Isla," one of the voices said. "'Tis ready. I will give it to Weylyn myself."

"Thank you, Eithne," Isla said.

"Donnae worry, Aedan," Eithne said looking at him. "I will watch over your father while he sleeps. I will do what I can to guide him back to you."

Aedan thanked the beautiful young woman. Her deep auburn hair reminded him of Isla's but unlike his wife's light brown eyes, Eithne's eyes rivaled the green of the pine trees. He watched as Eithne worked around Weylyn, cutting his tunic away from his body revealing the gash of Maelogan's arrow and the blackness of the wolf's bane in his veins. It had almost reached his heart. Eithne soothed Weylyn's hair from his face. Looking up, she handed Isla an odd looking stone and bowl.

Isla took what Eithne offered her and looked down at Aedan. Climbing onto the stone, she straddled him. Out of the corner of his eye he saw Eithne do the same to Weylyn. Isla leaned down and kissed him but when she pulled back she took the stone in both hands.

"This will hurt, my love," she said. He nodded and watched as she raised the sharpened stone in her hands over him. Locking eyes with her, he nodded. "I love you," Isla said as her tears streamed down her cheeks and she rammed the stone into his chest. He cried out when he felt the stone pierce through his ribs and into his heart then something hot poured into his chest and the pain radiated down to his fingertips. Opening his eyes for a moment, he saw his wife crying over him but her image blurred and slowly blackness overcame him.

"Aaaeeedaaaan," A sweet voice called to him through the darkness. "Aaaeeeedaaaan," it called again. Slowly opening his eyes Aedan looked up at the sky. On his back in the middle of a courtyard, the sun's dusky rays shining down through the clouds, he recognized where he was; his mother's cottage. Rolling to his side as he tried to stand, he groaned as his body protested. Finally, on his feet he looked towards the thatched cottage. His mother opened the door and emerged from the cottage wiping her hands on her outer dress. She was young, no older than early twenties and had such a beautiful smile on her face. "Aedan, where are you, love?" She called sweetly.

"Mother?" Aedan breathed as he watched her. Reaching out as she passed him, his hand went through her as if she were a specter.

Hearing a squeal, he turned and watched himself as a young boy, no more than five summers come running out of the woods. She swept him up into a big hug. A smile crossed his lips when he remembered what it felt like. "Where were you, my darling boy?" Brietta asked.

"I was in the woods!" his five-year-old self said.

"In the woods?" She asked excitedly, kissing his cheek. "What were you doing there?"

"I was looking for a wolf," he grinned.

"A wolf, huh?" she asked smiling back at him.

Aedan suddenly remembered that moment; it had been lost as he grew older. Gowan came out of the house and Brietta passed Aedan over to his father. The smell that clung to his father's clothes; peat fire smoke, mixed with fur pelt and pine, the feel of his ticklish full red beard against his soft, young face was a memory Aedan had not had for a very long time.

"A wolf, eh lad?" Gowan asked; his voice making Aedan smile. "And why would you be wanting to look for a wolf?"

"I wanted to ken if they are real," Aedan's five-year-old voice replied.

"Och, they are real," his father replied glancing at his mother. "They are just hiding. You are getting to be such a big lad that they donnae want to be scared of you."

"Papa," Aedan stated. "That is no' true. They are huge! They are nae afraid of anything! When I grow up I want to be just as big!"

"You concentrate on growing, son," his father began.

"Then when you are a grown man, you can be whatever you want to be."

Brietta lovingly stroked Gowan's shoulder as she turned back inside; his father smiled at her and they all three headed into the cottage. Aedan felt a tear slide down his cheek as he watched his father; the pain of his passing still strong.

He heard Isla's laugh before he saw her. She ran right past him and he followed as a younger man. Grabbing her hand, his younger self gently pushed her against the side of the cottage, his hands rested on the cottage wall, framing her face on either side of her head. He leaned down to her.

"Isla," he whispered against her lips. "Say you will, love."

"I will… what?" she teased.

"Marry me, you daft woman," he replied.

"Hmm," she thought a moment then kissed him quickly. "Ask me again tomorrow." She pushed out of his hold and ran back towards the village.

"That is what you said yesterday," Aedan called after her. She laughed and disappeared down the hill.

Smiling at the memory of their courtship, Aedan watched as he touched his lips grinning at the feeling of her kiss. Aedan's eyes were drawn to the cottage just as Gowan walked out.

"Please, donnae do this," Brietta was saying.

"Brietta, if they get any closer and we donnae have any wolf's bane around the house, what is to stop them from killing us?" He asked.

"You ken why we cannae," she said her eyes drifting towards the barn that was Aedan's bedroom.

"Aye, I ken," Gowan sighed. "And I think I have accepted this far better than any other man would have." Brietta gasped and tears rimmed her eyes. "Och, love, I am sorry," he said stepping towards her and reaching out. After a moment, she stepped into his embrace. "I am merely trying to protect my family."

"As am I," Brietta mumbled into his chest.

"The wolf that was seen is no' him," Gowan said. She stepped out of his hold and looked up at him. "From what ye told me he is brown, this wolf was black. I will nae harm Weylyn. I ken what he means to ye, woman. I will make sure, before I strike... But, if it is him," he paused before continuing. "Do ye want me to tell him anything?"

"Just..." she started. "Just ask him why."

"You donnae want me to tell him about Aedan?" Gowan asked.

"Nay," she gasped. "Nay," she said softer. "Just ask him why he wasnae there that night."

"Gods, I love you, you daft woman, and I donnae want to lose you or Aedan. If Weylyn is alive, and this is him, he will be fine," he promised kissing her hair.

She closed her eyes as he walked into the woods.

"'Tis no' him I am worried for," she said softly.

"Father," Aedan called to him. "Donnae do this, please!" He saw Gowan stop a moment as if he heard Aedan's plea. Everything stilled around him and he heard Isla's voice *remember you must no' try to change anything. You must be a bystander watching your life as a dream.*

When he said no more, the scene before him continued and he watched his father go into the woods. Closing his eyes not wanting to see what happened next; Aedan heard his father's screams as he was attacked. Then all went silent. Aedan watched as he stepped out of the barn, knives at the ready and raced to the woods.

"Gods, nay, I beg of you," Aedan begged remembering what happened next. "I donnae wish to see this again. Please donnae make me!"

But, it was too late. When he opened his eyes, he was walking alongside himself unable to control his own body. Aedan came across his father and remembered the yell he let out as he fell to his knees next to the mangled corpse. He watched as he mourned over him and felt the tears afresh. Lifting Gowan, not understanding or caring how he was able to do so, he carried his father's lifeless body back to the cottage. Brietta had run outside when she heard him yell and, seeing her son carrying her husband, she let out a shrill scream and ran to him.

Like a dream, Aedan blinked and another scene unfolded before him. Weylyn, Aedan and Maelogan stood outside together after the battle. Blood dripped from Aedan's wound as he ordered Maelogan into the house.

"I meant no offence. Merely that any father would be proud to call you his son," Weylyn answered. "There is no need to be angry with me."

"Is there no'?" Aedan asked. "Because of you I am to lose my humanity tomorrow. To never again see my wife or even ken who I was. None of this would have happened if you had just left when we arrived."

"You are wrong," Weylyn said. "If we had left, the wolves would have been here still and killed your mother and that I couldnae allow. I am truly sorry for it."

"Sorry?" Aedan asked.

"Aye, trust me if I kenned how to reverse the process I would," Weylyn replied.

"Or would you let me die? I ken your kind. You have no love of humans. All you have ever wanted is Mother. You. Cannae. Have. Her."

"That is no' true," Weylyn said. "'Tis true I love your mother but I would never sacrifice her only son just to be with her! What can I do to convince you?"

"Get out and take that half-breed with you!" Aedan cried.

Weylyn's hand swiped across Aedan's face in a hard slap. Aedan looked back at him stunned.

"That is my Alpha's wife and child you speak of," Weylyn snapped. "I ken you are angry but I donnae think you are in any danger."

"What do you mean?" Aedan questioned.

"There is no sign of the poison," Weylyn explained. "Wolf saliva carries with it a poison to humans but only when we bite. It discolors the skin leaving it red and the veins that carry the poison to the heart turn red as well. You have no sign of discoloration."

"Maybe I wasnae bitten then," Aedan said, his voice suddenly lighter.

"The teeth marks are clearly visible," Weylyn replied observing the wound. Touching Aedan's arm, Weylyn felt the heat radiating off it. "Are you feeling all right?" He asked touching Aedan's forehead. He was far too warm especially standing in the snow without a tunic. He burned with fever.

"I am fine. I have never been better actually," Aedan said not pulling away from him.

"You are very warm," Weylyn replied concerned.

Aedan pulled his arm free and took a step back. "Am I infected or no'?"

"I donnae ken," Weylyn said.

"Then I would like to go see my wife now," he said turning away from Weylyn and heading into the house.

"Och, nay, no' this too, I beg of you!" Aedan shouted. "I cannae see Mother die again!"

Just as he said that, he was at the window and saw the whole scene before him. He watched as his mother was shot and told him that Weylyn was his father. He felt the pain of mourning once again.

"Nay!" He cried out. "Isla, I cannae do this anymore!" Falling to his knees, Aedan wept.

Epilogue

Isle of Skye, Scotland - September 2013

A young boy and his father walked out of one of the castles on the Isle of Skye. The boy, no more than eight, was pulling his father's hand.

"Come on, Daddy!" He cried.

"Slow down, Lucas," his father called. "It's been there for nearly seventy years it'll still be there, in a moment or two."

"Come on!" the boy pressed, pulling his father to a statue just outside the castle gardens. "Wow," he breathed gazing up at the bronze statue of six figures, three men whose faces were split half-human, half-wolf, and three women, one of whom had a baby in her arms.

"Luc," his dad scolded him. "Don't cut in front of the man. Sorry," he said to the guy standing in front of the statue. The man smiled, his dark eyes dancing.

"Dinnae fash yourself," the man answered, his voice heavily accented from the highland region. "I've got one meself about his age."

"Oh, I am so sorry," the father laughed. The man smiled, his floppy dark hair blowing in the wind.

"Isn't it cool?" Lucas said. " '*Tristan, Weylyn, and his son Aedan, the last of the wolf-men. After the great battle on the fields of Wolf's Bane. The three and their human mates fought to prevent the wolves from overtaking the Isle of Skye. 650 A.D.*' " The boy read the plaque. "There's an inscription but I can't read it, Daddy," Lucas looked over at his father.

"Probably Scots Gaelic," his father said.

"Do you know what it says?" he asked.

"Luc, you know I don't know Gaelic," his father chuckled.

"But you're smart!" Lucas replied.

"Not that smart, I'm afraid," the father answered.

Lucas looked dejected then peered up at the man standing beside them.

"Can you read it, mister?" he asked.

The man smiled warmly at the boy and crouched low beside Lucas.

"Let's be seeing what they have written," the man said. "'*Cuideachd gu bràth*,'" the man quoted. "It means 'together forever'."

"Cool!" Luc cried. "We had a section on Scottish history last year and our teacher told us the story of the wolf-men!"

"And it's just that, son, a story," his father stressed as the stranger stood.

"No, Dad, they found a manuscript! It's so old they had a hard time reading it, but it tells the story of the three wolf-men and their human loves," the boy insisted. "It's said that Weylyn, who is Aedan's father, fell in love with a human woman and they had Aedan. She died, though. And Aedan and Tristan had human wives. Weylyn was injured during the battle but he fell in love with one of the women who nursed him. Legend has it that after nearly twenty years as nothing more than friends, they finally married and all of them joined together as the last wolf-pack in Scotland! The men were able to change into huge wolves! And my favorite, they could half-phase, teacher says, their eyes turned yellow!"

"Son, it's a story, a fairy tale," his father replied.

"No, Dad, it's a *legend* and Ms. Russell says all legends have true origins," he said.

"Do you know what that means?" His dad asked him.

"No, but it sounded cool when Ms. Russell said it," Lucas said.

The father and the man standing in front of the statue laughed.

"How else do you explain that there are no more wolves in Scotland?" Lucas went on. "They are the last of their kind."

"Son, like all animals, wolves have a natural habitat and when humans disturb their homes they move on. It's not because of some great battle. It's the circle of life," his father explained.

"Nope," Lucas said. "It's because they fought them all."

The father sighed and looked down at his phone as it rang, rolling his eyes at his son's innocence.

"I have to take this, son, it's Andrew," he stepped away from him for a moment and answered the phone.

"Do you believe in them, Mister?" Lucas asked the man standing near them.

"I have little choice I'm afraid," the man's eyes flared yellow as he looked at the boy. Lucas' jaw dropped when he saw him.

Reaching for his father and pulling on his jacket, his voice was small when he spoke, "Daddy." When his father didn't answer him, he turned to look up at him. "Dad!"

"Hold on a minute, Andrew," his father said into the phone. "What is it, Lucas? I'm on the phone."

The boy turned and pointed at the man beside him but he looked at Lucas questioningly, his eyes back to dark brown.

"But your eyes were—" the boy started.

"Stop bothering the man, Lucas," his father said and went back to his phone call.

The man bent down to be eye level with the small boy.

"You know, you're right," he said. "Every legend has its own origins and they're all true. Especially this one," his eyes flared yellow once more then went back to brown.

"Aedan," they heard. The man turned and smiled. The boy's eyes bulged as he recognized the name. Aedan winked at him and went towards the man who had called his name. "What was that about?" The man asked, handing him two bags so he could have a free hand.

"Just thought I'd take a look at our statue, Da'," Aedan said grinning.

"And you decided to flash your yellow eyes at the boy?" Weylyn asked smirking. "He could be scarred for life."

"Dinnae think so," Aedan answered. "As usual, the so called, battle after we woke up from our *transition* has been misinterpreted."

Weylyn chuckled.

"The most epic battle in the history of Scotland?" Weylyn asked as if proclaiming a title.

"Pretty much," Aedan replied chuckling.

"Well, it did bring about the end of Marrock's pack and

the extinction of wolves," Weylyn said.

"Och, only because they were stupid enough to try and charge us as soon as we set Maelogan's body and the field afire," Aedan said. "The smoke was a poison to them."

"Trust me, I dinnae need to be reminded just how much that stuff burned," Weylyn said. "I cannae say how happy I am to have been unaffected by it for over a thousand years."

"I am somewhat sorry that we are the only wolves left in Scotland," Aedan replied. "They've all died out."

"It's a fact of life, son - normal life - that everythin' has its end," Weylyn answered.

"I'm no' complainin'," Aedan said. "I'm verra happy to be with you."

"As I am with you," Weylyn smiled.

"All right, you two," Isla came up beside Aedan and slipped her arms around his waist. "Where are we off to?"

"I'm famished," Tristan walked up and took the other bags from Weylyn.

"Me too," Alexina said. "How about lunch?"

Tristan wrapped his arms around his wife.

"Lunch sounds amazing," Eithne walked up to Weylyn and he draped his arm around her shoulders. Grinning, she leaned into him as his lips came down on hers in a gentle, all too short, kiss.

Oblivious to their moment of intimacy, the rest of the group was talking about the castle on the hill. They had finished their tour of the ancient building and had just left the gift shop.

"I could nae believe they made us buy a ticket to that place," Tristan teased. "Do they ken who helped build that?"

"If you told them it was us, we would all be put into straitjackets almost immediately," Aedan smiled. "Besides," he turned up to look at the view. "It's still a fascinating sight."

"Aye, 'tis," Alexina said. "I just cannae believe they hae roped off me old bedroom and willnae let me back inside. It's no' like it'll crumble at my touch and even if it does, I do ken the men to call and fix it." She grinned turning into her husband.

"I'm sure you will find a way to get back in, Alex," Isla replied. "The one I want to see again is Edinburgh Castle. That was a glorious sight."

"We just saw that last month," Aedan grinned. "Or hae you forgotten our boy Alan?"

"Nae, I have nae forgotten," she smiled. "We should hae spent more time with him."

"He'll come to the gathering," Tristan replied. "At least he now knows he cannae be talkin' about his kin to strangers even if it is under the guise of 'lore'."

"Aye," Weylyn said. "I gave him an ear full," he winked at his son. "Keep yer pups in line, Aedan."

Aedan laughed.

"I would if they listened ta me," he said. "He's how many generations removed now?"

"Too many," Isla teased. "I am surprised ye still accepted him, Tristan."

"He's one of us," he said. "I accept all of me kin."

"Aye, I ken it and am grateful," Aedan replied.

"So, Edinburgh for a time then?" Weylyn asked.

"Aye, I do miss Princes' Street," Aedan answered.

"Maybe we can move down to Edinburgh for the next few hundred years," Weylyn winked.

"I'll miss the statue," Aedan laughed.

"Is that what you be looking at just now?" Tristan asked.

He nodded gesturing back. Lucas stood wide-eyed

staring at the group.

"Did they at least get me prince's profile correct this time?" Tristan teased.

"I personally think it looks nothin' like us," Weylyn laughed. "Now about lunch."

"You got the last one," Aedan replied. "This is on me."

"I'm nae arguing," Weylyn said. "Lunch, then the distillery?"

"So touristy," Eithne grinned.

"Darlin', you ken how much I love me whisky," Weylyn teased.

"Aye, I do," she answered and leaned up to kiss him. "It makes shopping for you for Yule that much easier."

Weylyn barked his laughter and kissed her hair.

"Let's get a move on, I'm starving," Tristan said.

As everyone walked together toward the village for lunch, Lucas watched.

"Now," he heard his father say as he hung up his phone. "Let's go find your mother, and get back to the hotel... What is it, Lucas? Are you all right?"

The boy nodded and turned back to the statue again.

"It's all right, son, they're fiction. They're not real," his father said. "There's nothing to be scared of. Come on, let's go."

Lucas took his father's hand but, taking one last look at the statue, bounced up and down.

"They're real," he whispered. "I knew they were real!"

An Deireadh

Keep an eye out for the next book in the Wolf's Bane Saga:
Midnight Sky coming 2017.

Acknowledgments

In 2013, my family and I took a vacation to Scotland and Ireland. While we were in Scotland our tour guides, Danny and Alan told us a story. Wolves are extinct in Scotland and have been for about six hundred years. Geologists and Zoologists have studied the reason behind their sudden and overnight disappearance. There has not been any answers as of yet. One popular theory is that the farmers went out and killed all of them overnight...

When I flew back home, I had a very vivid dream of a man carrying a woman though a forest. The man stopped at an old oak tree, sat down and leaned against it, cradling the woman. Her grip on his knees increased and then decreased. I knew she was in labor. Walking forward, I stepped on a twig and the snap made the man look over. His eyes were yellow, his hair was in his face (dripping wet) and his body was muscular to the extreme. I woke up and immediately wrote everything down. Those notes turned into The Wolf's Bane Saga and I could not be more excited or proud to share this story with all of you.

A big thank you to my editor, Ashton, my beta readers Kate and Amanda, and my Mama and Dad for staying up on Thursday night – Reading Night! You guys are amazing! Thank you so much for all your comments and suggestions!

And to Derek Dammann, the amazing artist of the foundation photo of the cover-*Lupines in the Fog*! Check out all of the amazing photos on his website ddphotos.com.

I hope you all enjoyed this story and do not miss the next installment in the Saga!

The Wolf's Bane Saga

Midnight Sky

Prologue

Weylyn looked up from his manuscript as Tristan entered the hut. Smiling a greeting to his student, Weylyn took a deep quiet breath. A foreign scent clung to Tristan's clothing.

"Where were you?" Weylyn asked as if in passing.

"Out for a walk," Tristan answered, shuffling to his cot.

"In the village?" Weylyn asked taking a sip of mead.

"In the woods," Tristan replied pulling off his cloak causing Weylyn to smell the same scent but much stronger.

"Alone?" he asked.

"Aye," Tristan replied.

Weylyn chuckled silently. All beings gave a very pungent odor when they lied, but none more so than wolves and Tristan had clearly lied to him.

"Are you certain of that?" Weylyn asked.

"Aye," Tristan answered.

Weylyn said no more and went back to his manuscript until Tristan moved to the fireplace to stoke the flames.

"Human," Weylyn finally stated.

"What?" Tristan whirled around, but still crouching low, he fell on his back looking up at his mentor.

"She is human, is she no'?" Weylyn asked not lifting his eyes from the story he read. After a moment of silence, he finally looked up. Tristan's eyes were petrified as he stared at him. Setting aside the manuscript, Weylyn leaned forward. "Talk to me, lad. I am here."

"My father..." he started then swallowed as if his mouth had gone dry.

"Is no' here," Weylyn said softly. "But I am."

Tristan eventually stood, went over to Weylyn's chair, knelt on the floor and finally spoke.

"I met a lass," he admitted. "Her name is Alexina."

Chapter One

Wolf's Bane Field, Scotland – 652 A.D.

Alexina held Tristan's hand as he lay unconscious on the blanket before the fire. His transition into immortality was excruciatingly slow and knowing that without it, her husband would surely be dead did not help her. Three days had passed since the druid sisters had rammed the stone into Tristan's chest and poured the potion into his heart.

With an aching back and a weary mind, Alexina gave into her need for sleep and lay beside her husband, moving his arm to rest in the crook of his shoulder. Facing away from him and toward their infant daughter, Giorsal, Alexina watched Isla standing over Aedan's still form and another, younger druid woman beside Weylyn. Tears formed in her eyes as all three men she had grown to love, fought for life. Clutching Tristan's hand to her chest, she whispered softly.

"Come back to me, my love. I need you."

Giorsal moved in her sleep and Alexina reached out a hand to her makeshift bed soothing her child. Before she fell asleep, her eyes drifted once more to Isla as she stroked Aedan's hair and then placed her hand on her stomach. Alexina smiled slightly. Life was growing before her eyes even as the three men fought for theirs.

Isla stroked Aedan's dark brown hair as he lay unconscious. Soothing him as his body shuddered once, she immediately whispered a reminder to him not to change anything in his past no matter how difficult it would be. If he did, he would surely die.

When another shudder overtook him, she gazed up pleadingly with her elder sister, Labhaoise who came up beside her.

"Any change?" Labhaoise asked.

"Nay, apart from his shudders. I fear for him greatly," Isla replied. "He is no' a man to stand by and wait."

"He will be strong for you and the child's sake," she answered. "I will sit with him, if you would like. You should rest."

"I cannae rest until he awakens," Isla replied.

"For your child's sake you must," she argued.

"If it were Bowdyn lying here, would you allow me to take over for you, Labhaoise?" Isla asked.

Labhaoise looked down and shook her head. "Nay, I would no'. But my husband has gone through the transition before and I recall how it felt to watch him," she replied. "Allow me to at least give you something to eat."

When Isla nodded and Labhaoise left to get some stew, Eithne, the youngest sister, though she was over one hundred years old, looked up from Weylyn and locked eyes with her. Isla watched as she wiped tears from her cheeks and looked back to the wolf-man she was protecting.

"Eithne?" Isla gently called to her. Eithne looked up; her big light brown eyes anxious. "Are you well, love?"

"Who is he, Isla?" Eithne asked.

"Weylyn?" Isla questioned. At Eithne's nod she continued. "He is a great and courageous man. He is my husband's father."

"I feel... drawn to him," Eithne's voice trailed off. Isla watched her sister as she stroked Weylyn's dark brown hair. "He will be all right, aye?" Eithne asked.

Isla stood from kneeling beside Aedan, wincing when her back protested the movement and went over to the table. Pulling the furs down to reveal his chest, she saw that the arrow wound Maelogan had inflicted was still black with wolf's bane and the veins in Weylyn's chest showed that the poison had not retracted fully from his body. Isla felt Eithne's eyes on her as she studied Weylyn and she forced a smile.

"He is still breathing," she answered. "That is something." Eithne held a hand under Weylyn's nose and sagged in relief. "There now, allow Geileis to take over for you, hmm?" Isla offered. "You need your rest."

"Nay," Eithne replied vehemently. "I will nae leave him."

Isla's eyes narrowed slightly watching her sister's uncharacteristic behavior. Fortunately, Labhaoise came back with a bowl of stew and a plate of bread for both Isla and Eithne to eat. Isla did not have the heart to tell Eithne that Weylyn lacked the will to live. Without Brietta, he would not wish to survive, even for Aedan's sake. And that thought made Isla's heart ache, not for Eithne but for herself. Despite their rocky start, she had grown rather fond of Aedan's father and hoped he would live to see his grandchildren.

Chapter Two

Just as the sun was rising on the fourth day, Tristan groaned. Alexina woke from beside him and gripped her husband's hand. Labhaoise strode over to her and placed a hand on her shoulder, easing Alexina's fears. Both women watched Tristan take a deep breath and release it. For a moment, they held their breath, waiting for him to breathe again.

"His transition is almost complete," Labhaoise whispered. "He has died and will now be reborn into an immortal."

Alexina stared at her husband willing him to breathe again. At long last, Tristan gulped in a large breath and Labhaoise reached for his hand to check that life pulsed strong and steady through him. The wolf's bane poison that had affected him was gone. His tortured body was healed and he looked healthy for the first time since they rescued him from his father's clutches. His breathing steadied and grew stronger and eventually he opened his eyes.

"Alex," he breathed seeing his wife beside him. She let out a small cry and threw her arms around him.

Nearly half a day later as Isla stood and headed to the

kitchen to see about boiling some tea to calm her stomach, she heard Aedan scream her name. Rushing over to him, Geileis moved out of her way as he sat up from the stone table. She stroked his hair and wiped the sweat from his brow.

"'Tis all right, my love," she soothed.

"Isla," he panted, looking over at her. "Isla?"

"I am here," she answered.

"What happened?" He asked.

"You made it back," she replied.

"Back? Where?" He questioned.

"Here, with me, in Wolf's Bane Field," she explained.

"My father?" He asked. Her eyes trailed over to Weylyn lying unconscious on the other stone table, with Eithne beside him. Aedan's eyes followed.

"He is still in transition," Isla explained.

"How long has it been?"

"Four days."

"It only felt like moments," he said. "Are you well?"

"Me? Aye, my love, I am. Are you?"

"Aye I think so," he answered and pulled her closer to him.

His eyes searched hers and, without another word, he clutched her to him and kissed her, his hand exploring her body and resting on her stomach. Pulling away from kissing her, he looked down as he felt the small knot in her abdomen. His face lit with an indescribable joy as his eyes fixed on the spot. "Hello," he whispered. "I am your father." Leaning forward he kissed the tiny swell and looked up at his wife. "I love ye."

"I love you, Aedan," she answered tears in her eyes. "I am so thankful you returned to me."

"Exactly where I want to be," he replied.

"Do you think you can stand?" she asked.

"That was no' exactly what I wanted to hear from you," he winked. Isla laughed and patted his cheek.

"Later," she whispered. His boyish smirk lit her heart. Staring into his dark brown eyes she saw them turn questioning. "There was a time where I thought I would never see your smile again."

"That will never happen, my love," he said.

"As long as you swear it."

"I do."

"Good. You must need some fresh air," she replied.

"Tristan?" He finally asked after his alpha.

"He woke earlier today," she explained. "He is outside with Alexina."

"Outside?" Aedan asked. "But there is wolf's bane out there."

"Aye," she answered. "But there is some here too." She indicated the flower over the doorway and Aedan flinched away. "'Twill nae affect you."

"Why?" He asked.

"Because you are immortal, my love," she replied. "Nothing will ever harm you again." When he did not speak for a moment, she took his hand and whispered, "come with me."

Aedan squinted as the midday sunlight hit his eyes. Blinking away the shadows and flares, he saw two shapes standing before him.

"Aedan," he heard Tristan's voice and felt a hand on his shoulder. As his eyes adjusted to the light, he recognized his alpha standing in front of him. "'Tis glad I am you are awake."

"Tristan," Aedan smiled. "'Tis good to see you well."

"Indeed, I feel better than I ever have," he answered. Before Aedan could reply they heard the wolves howling and turned towards the woods surrounding them. "My father's pack," he went on. "Still trying to find a way in. 'Tis refreshing no' to have the sickening smell of wolf's bane lingering in my nose but I do wish there was a way around my kin."

"Is there no'?" Aedan asked.

"Even though we have granted Alexina the gift of immortality to stay with her husband as I am to stay with you," Isla began. "She is still of human blood and would nae be allowed to travel through our druid portal to Skye. We are stranded here until we can safely find a way for us all to leave."

Aedan turned to Alexina. "I did nae realize you were to endure the transition," he said.

“’Tis to happen as soon as I am ready,” Alexina answered. “I was stealing a few moments with my mate before I am led to my fate.”

“All will be well, my love,” Tristan answered. “And I will watch over you and our lass.”

Leaning into him, her bravado weakening for a moment, she continued. “Aye, I ken that well, Tristan. I have nae fears of that.”

“From the short time I have kenned you, Alexina,” Aedan began. “I have found you to be a strong lass as strong if not stronger than any man. You will be just fine.”

“I thank you for that, Aedan,” she answered. “I do worry for Weylyn.”

“Has there been any change?” Tristan asked.

“Nay,” Isla replied. “But Eithne will look after him. He is in nae danger with her. But she may be in danger from him.”

“Why is that?” Aedan asked.

“I do believe she is smitten with him,” she confided.

“Truly?” Tristan asked.

“I must confess I have seen evidence of that as well,” Alexina replied. “But she is a sweet lass and fiery from what I ken of her.”

“Da’ will nae ken how to handle that,” Aedan chuckled.

“Donnae underestimate your father, Aedan,” Tristan laughed. “He just may surprise us all.”

Made in the USA
Columbia, SC
26 October 2017